Praise for *A Dictionary of Mutual Understanding*

"I loved this book. I don't often say that much anymore, but this one had me rapt. I read it on an airplane, and when I looked up weeping from the last several pages, my husband, alarmed, said, 'What's the matter?' And I said, 'This book is so beautiful.' And it is. This is a mesmerizing, heart-wrenching story of love and regret, but ultimately, and most assuredly, the healing generosity of hope; I couldn't put it down. Lovely . . . An exceptional tale of a family in crisis whose lives are shattered by the bombing of Nagasaki. At once intimate and sweeping, profoundly subtle and yet remarkably affecting, the story reminds the reader that public catastrophe interrupts myriad smaller, but no less devastating, private troubles, magnifying their consequences and obstructing their resolution."

—Robin Oliveira, *New York Times* bestselling author of *My Name Is Mary Sutter*

"Extraordinary . . . Like *Snow Falling on Cedars* and *The Reader*, here is one of those rare life opportunities to look again at ourselves, and forgive our shameful past, achieved with striking style, an unflinching eye, and through a clever narrative. Brava Jackie Copleton. I cannot wait to read your next novel."

—Mary-Rose MacColl, author of *In Falling Snow*

"Iojima, Nagasaki—names of places known from war. Jackie Copleton's debut novel delivers an impassioned story of family, loyalty, and love that allows us, as she writes, 'to appreciate the human foundations' of these historic locations. It is through such intimate stories of people who have lived through war do we begin to understand the vulnerability of survival and the real meaning of peace. Following the surprising turns revealed in one woman's remembrances—a memory made selective by loss and frailty—this story took me on an unexpected journey through Japan in a rarely examined era, and I closed its cover satisfied to learn it had led me to an elevated mutual understanding of our difficult global history."

—Eugenia Kim, author of *The Calligrapher's Daughter*

"A fully drawn portrait of a city and a life, this novel will hold appeal for history buffs, lovers of literary fiction, and readers of high-drama romance." —*Kirkus Reviews*

"Astonishingly accomplished . . . A gripping love story and family dynamic is woven seamlessly with graphic descriptions of the aftermath of the bomb and the historical and cultural changes sweeping Japan. . . . While this is an often heartbreaking portrait of a mother's love told through diaries, letters, and flashbacks, it is also a meticulously researched history of Japan. The graceful style and clarity of [Copleton's] writing makes this an addictive read. With the seventieth anniversaries of Hiroshima and Nagasaki approaching, this novel is a must." —*Scottish Daily Mail* (UK)

"Full of delicate imagery drawing on Japanese nature and culture, this is a rich, romantic story, brimming with restrained emotion—with a twist that will take your breath away. Superb." —*Daily Mirror* (UK)

PENGUIN BOOKS

A DICTIONARY OF
MUTUAL UNDERSTANDING

Jackie Copleton graduated from Cambridge University with a degree in English before she moved to Japan to teach in English language schools in Nagasaki and Sapporo. She has worked as a journalist in the UK and the Middle East and holds an MLitt (Distinction) in creative writing from Glasgow University, where she was the joint winner of the 2011 Curtis Brown prize for best fiction writing. She lives in Glasgow, Scotland, with her husband, though they hope to one day live by the sea. *A Dictionary of Mutual Understanding* is her debut novel.

A Dictionary
of
Mutual
Understanding

A NOVEL

JACKIE COPLETON

PENGUIN BOOKS

PENGUIN BOOKS

An imprint of Penguin Random House LLC
375 Hudson Street
New York, New York 10014
penguin.com

First published in Great Britain by Hutchinson,
a division of The Random House Group Ltd 2015
Published in Penguin Books 2015

Published by arrangement with Hutchinson.
Hutchinson is one of the Penguin Random House group companies.

LIBRARY OF CONGRESS CATALOGING-IN-PUBLICATION DATA
Copleton, Jackie.
A dictionary of mutual understanding / Jackie Copleton.
pages cm
ISBN 978-0-14-312825-0
1. Families—Japan—Fiction.   2. Hiroshima-shi (Japan)—
History—Bombardment, 1945—Fiction.   I. Title.
PR6103.O694D53 2015
823'.92—dc23
2015006931

Printed in the United States of America
1   3   5   7   9   10   8   6   4   2

Set in Weiss

To Robert Brooks and William Copleton

I was very thirsty, so I was looking for some water.
I found some oil on the surface of the water.
I really wanted something to drink.
After all, I drank that water.

— Nine-year-old girl injured during
the A-bomb attack on Nagasaki on
August 9, 1945

The voice of the waves
That rise before me
Is not so loud
As my weeping,
That I am left behind.

— Thousand-year-old Japanese poem

A Dictionary
of
Mutual
Understanding

Endurance

Yasegaman: The combination of yaseru (to become skinny) and gaman-suru (to endure) literally means to endure until one becomes emaciated, or endurance for the sake of pride. Anthropologist Ruth Benedict once said that Japanese culture is based on shame while American culture is based on a sense of sin or guilt. In a shame-oriented society, for persons to lose face is to have their ego destroyed. For example, in olden days, samurai warriors were proud people. When they were too poor to eat, they held a toothpick in their mouth to pretend they had just eaten a meal.

Even the kindness of the half-light could not hide his disfigurement. The man stood on my doorstep hunched against the chill of a winter morning. Despite the scarring, I could tell he was Japanese, in his forties or fifties. I had seen such burns before, blacker versions, in another life. He wore a suit, no coat, and held a briefcase in fingers fused together. He bowed his bald head low, cleared his throat and apologised for the intrusion. Years had passed since I last heard it but the southern Kyushu dialect was unmistakable. He asked if my name was Amaterasu Takahashi and, despite my apprehension, I nodded. The muscles in his face twitched, perhaps in a smile. 'Then I bring you good news.'

Few visitors came to my door except for passing men with their preacher pamphlets or health insurance policies.

I had use for neither. The stranger before me looked like no salesman, despite the briefcase, which he placed by his feet. He glanced at the ground, breathed in as if drawing up courage. The silver sun broke through the clouds and I saw the full force of his injuries. His expression was impossible to read, lost among the ruined flesh, but he sounded happy. 'I have long dreamt of this day. It really is extraordinary when you think of it.' He seemed almost to laugh. 'Miraculous, even . . . but also a shock.' He bowed once more, and then stood tall, arms stiff by his side. 'Please don't be alarmed. My name is Hideo Watanabe.'

Who knows how long I stood there before I realised he was asking me whether I needed to sit down. I looked again at what passed for his face. Hideo is seven years old, dressed in his school uniform, his hair brushed forward on his forehead. He holds my hand as we walk down the garden path. We spot a praying mantis on the bird table. He asks if he can keep the insect as a pet. I tell him no. We walk to school and he waves to me from the gates. That is Hideo Watanabe. That was how I chose to remember him. The man standing in front of me was an aberration. I had mourned Hideo for too many years to believe him resurrected.

'Hideo is dead. You can't be him. I'm sorry.'

'This must be hard to take in. You might need some time.'

'Please leave. I want you to go.'

The man nodded, put his hand in his suit pocket and pulled out a business card. He said he was staying at the Penn's View Hotel. His flight home was in a few days.

He offered me the card but I did not take it. He reached again into his pocket and this time produced a letter, crumpled by age or the journey undertaken. 'This will help explain why I'm here today, why it's taken me so long to find you.' I did not move and the envelope and card trembled in his grip. 'Please, you will find the contents difficult, but helpful.'

Seconds passed before I took both from him. I looked at my name printed on the top left corner of the letter. He picked up his briefcase and as he moved to go I asked, 'If you are Hideo Watanabe, you will know what we saw in the garden that last morning?'

His words when they came were as delicate as a spider's web caught by a summer breeze. 'I ask that you read the letter. That will get us started. It is good to see you, Grandmother. It really is.'

He raised that claw hand in farewell and began to walk away. I confess, when he spoke, I recognised some echo from the past. For one moment I imagined my daughter, Yuko, was talking to me in that careful staccato beat of hers, but I did not call him back to my door.

Human Feelings

Ninjo: Japanese people believe that love, affection, compassion and sympathy are the most important feelings that all human beings should nurture. This assumption emanates from the fact that one of the virtues that Japanese society emphasises is cooperation among people. In daily life, Japanese people are bound by the code of ninjo in their attitudes toward others. Suppose that you are sent many apples by your relative. Then you will want to give some to your neighbours. This 'give and take' attitude is based on the belief in the wisdom of mutual reliance.

I try to imagine how Yuko would look if she were alive today but instead I see her thin from the privations and worry of war, head bowed by the weight of the burden she carries. She sits on a pew with her back to me. Light from the west illuminates her hair which is cut short to her shoulders. I want to call out, warn her to go home. She needs to go far from Urakami and she must leave now. But the words do not come and instead I see her slowly turn around until I must close my eyes before they meet her gaze. Dear Daughter, the life I sought for you was not a bad one, was it? Could you understand why I acted the way I did? Could you see I had no choice? Only child, did you forgive me in those final moments? Did you forgive yourself?

I want to believe she was at peace when the clouds

parted over Nagasaki and that B-29 dropped its load. I cannot bear to think of those last moments as a torment for her. I need her to have died if not content then maybe reconciled to the decisions she made as she prayed to her god. My husband and I would tell each other when pikadon fell over the north of the city her body would have evaporated: bones, organs, even the ash of her, gone in an instant. We were adamant she had felt nothing and this gave us a kind of solace. The absence of a body to bury or cremate helped us sustain this version of her death: she had not suffered on August 9, 1945, at 11.02 a.m.

No, I am not haunted by how she died but why. If I am to be the only remaining teller of this tale, what and how much can I admit to myself and to others? Should I begin with this acknowledgement: my daughter might be here today if it had not been for me. I tell myself I acted out of love and a mother's selflessness but how important is the motivation when you consider the consequence? The darker truth is this: she wouldn't have been in the cathedral unless I had insisted that she meet me there. I have carried that knowledge with me through these long years. Not even Kenzo knew. What an impossible admission to tell a husband and a father. I taught myself to carry this guilt lightly so that no one could see the monster in their midst; but sometimes, when my guard was down, I would tell Kenzo I wished it had been me that the bomb had claimed. He would hold me in his arms and say he too would swap places with Yuko and Hideo if he could. He would reassure me there was nothing that could change what had happened; forces

5

beyond our control had taken them. We were all victims, only he and I had lived, that was all. He did not understand what I meant: death's greatest cruelty is to claim the wrong people. Sometimes the weakest live.

I convinced myself an edited version of my past was necessary for a bearable life. I told myself I must not think too long on the mistakes I had made that led Yuko to the city's death zone. How else could I get up in the morning and face another day? How else could I endure the years as they trickled by, one too slowly following the other? Me, the last one left, or so I had believed until that winter's morning. I had thought leaving Japan would keep Kenzo and me safe from the past. When people asked me about my life before America I changed details I didn't like, underplayed or erased entire years depending on my mood or audience. Sometimes my inquisitors made the connection between my age, Nagasaki and the war. Too curious perhaps to retreat from their question, they would ask in the embarrassed tone of the victor, 'Were you there that day?' I could not lie about this one fact but at least my poor English helped. It allowed me to reduce my account to a few nouns, weak adjectives, a verb in the wrong tense. *Grandson and daughter kill, gone. Too sad. Big problem for me.* In response, they grasped for the best words to use, so as not to confuse my limited language: how terrible, just horrible, simply awful, you are very brave. I hated that word, brave. It implied choice. Others hid behind my poor understanding of English to tell me what they really thought, and I guessed at what they said. Those bombs ended the war; think of the thousands of lives saved by your daughter's death; at least you and your husband have each other. Such casual dismissal of the loss. This was the survivor's sorrow: people expected you to be grateful. I didn't edit my past for sympathy, or persuasion; I did it to ease the guilt just enough to function. These lies or omissions gave me the strength to look in the mirror and be able to stand the woman I saw. And yet, if called upon to turn the magnifying glass on my past, how to cleave fact from fiction? My memory had intertwined the two like wild nasturtium to some rotting trellis, inextricable, the one dependent on the other. This man who had stood at my door would want to know the truth. What a request to ask. To look back would bring neither forgiveness nor release.

I took the letter he had given me into the kitchen and sat at the table by the window. The red Formica shone with bleach, the plastic jars by the cooker stood neat in line and only the hum of the refrigerator broke the silence. We had bought it not long before Kenzo fell ill. He insisted on buying an American brand, Frigidaire, which came with an ice dispenser. He loved to press against the lever with a plastic tumbler and watch the chunks of ice clatter down. 'America,' he declared that first time, shaking his head in wonder. 'What will you think of next?' I had planned to feed him good meat and fresh vegetables but in those last weeks he wanted nothing more than processed food in tins. Macaroni and cheese, SpaghettiOs and corned beef delighted him the most. His last meal before he went into hospital had been vanilla ice cream and chocolate syrup. He watched me from the kitchen table as I squirted Reddi-wip into the bowl and brought him his dessert. We sat across from each other and held hands while he ate a few shaky spoonfuls. A drop of cream rested on his unshaven chin. 'Good?' I asked. 'Good,' he replied. I could not help myself, I leaned forward and wiped the white blob away with my thumb. 'Let me give you a shave, you look like a wild man.' He shook his head. 'My skin hurts.'

'I bring you good news.' Those were the words the man had used. I looked at the white envelope in front of me, the thick paper, *Amaterasu Takahashi* printed in neat black ink. The last time I had seen my name written in kanji was eight years after we left Japan, in a letter sent by my former maid, Misaki Goto. Her daughter was getting married, we were invited, she would be so happy if we could make the journey from America to Nagasaki. I was delighted for her but sent my sincere apologies. I hope she understood why I could not go back. Instead I shipped off a painting of the Rocky Mountains, even though Kenzo and I had never visited. We moved from California to Pennsylvania not long after receiving the invitation and Misaki and I lost touch. I had kept in contact with no one else, which forced me to ask the question: who could be writing to me?

I glanced up to a picture framed in black wood on the wall. The sun had bleached the figures but you could still see Hideo dressed in his school uniform, standing between his parents, Yuko and Shige. On August 9, every year, Kenzo would bring out his best malt, imported from Scotland, in preparation for the day. We would work our way through the bottle, the peat flavour smoky on our tongues, and my husband would create new stories for our dead grandson. Some years he was a sailor, in others a lawyer, or sometimes a poet who lived in the mountains. He was handsome and kind and witty. He had a brood of solid children or a mistress from France. His life was joyful and exotic and full of adventure. The man at my door did not fit this movie-house picture. This was not the ending I wanted for any of us. Here was another monster raised from the rubble of Nagasaki. I did not believe him. This envelope could not contain good news and yet still I walked to the cutlery drawer, retrieved a small knife and returned to my chair. The blade slid too easily through the paper. I took out the note, laid it flat on the table and read the signature. Two words rocketed toward me, only two words, but what words: Natsu Sato. The doctor's wife. Sweat prickled across my body. I walked to the window, and even though the street was empty, I drew down the blinds. I could have thrown Natsu's letter in the garbage; I could have turned on the TV too loud and drowned out the possibilities of its contents, but instead I sat back in the kitchen chair and began to read.

To Amaterasu Takahashi,

Firstly, I must apologise for the shock of this revelation. The man that you have no doubt just met is your grandson, Hideo Watanabe. I can confirm this. You may have little reason to believe me, but I do not lie. Hideo didn't die that day, he survived. Is that not marvellous to know? But as you will have seen, he was severely wounded during pikadon. So injured in fact that the authorities could not identify him. He was sent away from the city a year after the end of the war to an orphanage for child victims. This is where my husband found him and where we later discovered who he was. You would have already left for America by this time. It took many years for us to find you. As luck would have it, a former employee of yours, Mrs Goto, read an article about our peace organisation that mentioned Hideo's birth name. She contacted me and provided an address for you and your husband — an old one, as it turns out. We are trying to locate your whereabouts as I write. I apologise for this delay. I can only imagine the confusion this must be causing you.

My husband and I decided to adopt Hideo. We brought him back to Nagasaki and he grew into an accomplished man. But I will let him tell you his own story. We are proud of him as I know you will be. Hideo has a package for you. This will help you understand what happened all those years ago, should you wish to know. I have not shown Hideo this package. Whether you do or do not I will leave to your discretion, but I ask that you read the contents first. I'm sure when you have, you will know how best to proceed. I return your grandson to you today not only because I can but also because I want to. This final act is the least I can do after so many years of forced separation. I hope he will bring you as much joy as he has brought happiness to our small family.

Yours in sincerity,
Natsu Sato

There was no date, a message caught in the vacuum of time. I folded the letter up and walked out of the kitchen, down the windowless hall to our bedroom. Kenzo had first taken me to see our home in Chestnut Hill in 1956. 'I've found the perfect spot for us. It's a commute for me, but it is beautiful, very traditional.' The Victorian house was painted green with a white wooden porch and set back from a quiet street lined by beeches. As a realtor showed us around, I whispered to my husband that it felt gloomy. He was prepared for my objection. 'We'll paint it with strong colours, pale wood, bring the light inside.' Ever the engineer, he saw brighter possibilities among the shadows.

He hired carpenters to replace the oak wardrobes in the bedroom with maple. 'Reminds me of cherrywood,' Kenzo said, running his hand down a panel. Decorators painted the walls yellow. In Japan this had been the colour of lost love; here it meant the sunshine. I bought a rose-print duvet, pictures of purple mountains for the walls and lilac cotton curtains so flimsy you could see your hands through them. When we were done, we stood in the doorway and appraised our rendition of an American life. Kenzo asked, 'You like it? It's much brighter, yes?' I nodded. He never realised: he was my only sunlight after the war.

We'd lived in that home together for sixteen years. When Kenzo died in 1972 I'd considered moving, but where? At least here I had a routine of sorts, the territory was known, the boredom familiar. I filled the silence with the noise of wildlife documentaries, rolling news, soaps. Without him, mornings could go by with me just sitting on the couch. At night, I began to drink neat whiskey in growing amounts, the curtains drawn. You live with loneliness long enough and it becomes a kind of company. Besides, those solid walls and polished floorboards contained all I had left of my family. I still saw Kenzo sitting on the couch reading the newspaper, filling in forms or shouting answers at a quiz show, proud of having mastered this foreign language enough to make it almost his own. My resistance to learning English had provoked arguments, but what could he do – force me to read textbooks, march me to classes? 'Contrary, stubborn, wilfully ignorant,' he would say in those early years before Chestnut Hill, when we lived north of San Francisco, near Mare Island and close to the shipyard. He'd speak in Japanese and then translate the words into his adopted tongue. 'Ugly words, ugly language,' I would reply in English, trying to mimic the accent to prove my point. Kenzo would shake his head and go back to his crossword, which I noted, with cruel satisfaction, he could not do.

One Christmas a year or so into our American life he gave me a book wrapped in gold tissue. The paper cover was the colour of a red autumn poppy with the texture of frost on a windowpane. The kanji was translated as: *An English Dictionary of Japanese Culture.* Kenzo smiled at me. 'I thought this could be a compromise. See, the Japanese is here, and the English is on the other side.' I flicked through the pages, some decorated with crude black-and-white sketches. I read one of the entries: *'Wabi: A simple and austere type of beauty. The word is derived from the verb wabu (to lose strength) and the adjective wabishi (lonely). Originally, it meant the misery of living alone away from society. Later, it gained a positive aesthetic meaning: the enjoyment of a quiet, leisurely and carefree life.'* I wrapped the gift back in the sheath of delicate gold and asked him where he had found the book. He reached for another parcel. 'You can get anything in the USA. You just need to know who to ask.' I flashed him a sceptical look. 'Honestly, Ama, sushi, teppanyaki, even shabu-shabu, they're all here. America is the world.' He never understood my reasons for not learning the language. This country was shelter from pikadon but it was not home, the people were not my own, I did not want to be close to them.

In the bedroom, I went to Kenzo's side of the wardrobe, opened the door and eased myself to my knees. We were forty-four and fifty-one years old when we left Japan in 1946, too old for a new life but too broken to remain in the one we had known. We took two trunks stuffed with pictures, documents and the rags we called clothes, most dyed khaki, the National Defence Colour. Smuggled inside those cases were other mementoes that I stored away without Kenzo's knowledge. When he died, I moved these few small items to my husband's side of the cupboard, so he could share them at last. Beneath his clothes, ties and sweaters, I reached into the recesses and pulled out a shoebox, placed Natsu's letter inside and slid the box to the back wall. I picked up another container, slowly rose to my feet and sat on the edge of the bed. The weight of the contents was heavy on my lap. I ran my hands over the lid, sticky with age, and removed the top. One thought hammered in my mind: why should I trust the wife of Jomei Sato, the man I also blamed for my daughter's death?

A Relation

En: The term is derived from the Buddhist belief that there is a cause to all things. The medium through which a cause brings about an effect is en. Any social relationship starts with and changes with en. It is en that realises the relationship between man and woman, and that between neighbours or business partners. Thus, en creates opportunities and occasions for forming relationships. It very often enables people to carry things on smoothly.

Nagasaki still feels more real to me than this old Victorian house. The nights spent alone in my bed take me back to our home on the hill with its view of the city growing inland from the narrow entrance of the harbour. Our house stood in a garden of chinaberry, purple maple and blue beech. Two floors of black wood rose up to a triangular roof topped with slate tiles. A carved trim ran down the eaves, and each beam was decorated with metalwork of dragons and ships coated in verdigris. The god of war straddled a wild boar over the main entrance. Inside, the family room was first on the left, lined with tatami mats, the woven rice straw bordered in green and gold silk. Black lacquer chests ran along one side of the room and a square table and four cushions sat in the middle. Scrolls of calligraphy hung on the walls and to the left was the long window overlooking the garden and to the right the alcove that contained the family shrine: a small Buddha, a candlestick, an incense burner, a bell and a mallet. Typical, yes, but ours.

When I think of our home, I see Yuko sitting in this room, bathed in the glow of rape myrtles, oleanders and canna. She seems a trick of the light, a chimera created by a weak sun on wood panels. I see her pick up a cream tea bowl with her right hand. She turns the bowl clockwise in her outstretched palm. Next she pours hot water from the teapot over the green powdered tea and picks up the bamboo whisk. She stirs until the liquid froths and bubbles like spittlebug foam on grass and then she passes the bowl to me. She is dressed in a kimono the shade of young winter cherries, or camellia, but always red, the colour of happiness, of life, of the womb.

All I had left of her had been reduced to the contents of a few shoeboxes. As I sat on the bed, the damp of the cardboard nipped my nostrils. I held her notebook in my hand. The green leather binding had disintegrated, and crumbs of paper dust glittered on my fingers. On the inside cover she had written her name in careful script. *Yuko Takahashi*. Later her surname would be replaced with *Watanabe*. My daughter's diaries. I saw her sitting at her desk, writing. I saw the indent of the pen against her middle finger, the delicate kanji of hers on the page. Kenzo had wept with defeat when he found a shopping list she had left on her kitchen table after we went to her home in the days following the bomb. *Flour, needle, soap*. Three words. Imagine thousands of them. I closed the diary, held the solidity of it to my chest for a moment, and then put it back in the box. Neither of us was ready for the intrusion.

Next, I opened a folded square of paper. The lines of

charcoal were faded but clear enough. The perspective was fine but there was something awkward in the composition, as if the artist had been trying to cram too much detail into the space. On the bottom right of the sketch, Yuko had written the place and date: *Iōjima, August 22, 1936.*

The summer had been a fierce one. The humidity stained everyone's clothes as if it was rain and the air burnt deep into lungs. I could feel that heat as I looked at the contours of the face before me, the high cheekbones, the neat moustache, that mole. I could see the charcoal smudged between Yuko's fingertips; I could picture the sheen of sweat as she worked; I could feel her longing. His expression was as unfathomable as it had always been. I placed the sketch face down. I did not want to think of Jomei Sato. I did not want to remember him, or that brutal summer, or that last morning all those years later.

New unanswered fears gripped me. How had Hideo survived? Kenzo and I looked for him; we were sure pikadon took him. How to face the possibility that he might have been alive all those years since? And if that were true, how had the doctor and his wife managed to adopt him? This could be no coincidence. Perhaps the man on my doorstep was another victim of the doctor's, or an accomplice. How pathetic of Sato to wait this long to take revenge. No punishment could match all the years lived since that summer, that morning, that minute.

Treasure of Children

Kodakara: As an eighth-century Japanese poet says, there is no treasure more precious than children. According to Japanese folk beliefs, children are Heaven's gifts, and those under seven years of age deserve special attention. These beliefs have had a deep influence on child-rearing, resulting in a close contact between mother and child.

That last morning the mist hung low over the two valleys and a spur of mountain poked through the clouds. Kenzo had collected Hideo from school the previous afternoon and brought him to our house so that Yuko could work an early shift at the hospital. She had agreed to meet me at Urakami Cathedral during her break. I knew this meant she had reached her decision, and I worried about what I might have to do to ensure it was the right one.

I went to the bedroom where she had slept as a child. Hideo was lying beneath the yellow butterflies Yuko had drawn on the wall when she was not much older than him. They flew from the ground up to the window. His mouth was open, his arms wide, as if crucified. He seemed so at peace, all the worries of an absent father, air raids, hunger and the closeness of the war kept at bay in that moment before waking. A bamboo box was open by the side of his mattress. He had filled it with his identity tag, address and blood type, a knife, a magnifying glass and

17

cotton bandages. I knelt by his futon and stroked his hair the way I had done when Yuko was a child until he woke up, an anxious smile on his face. I kissed him on the forehead as a wave of pure love washed over me for this boy, so small, so precious, so vulnerable. Awake he carried that shy, self-conscious bearing of Shige's. I watched him get dressed in his school uniform, frayed and faded. Yuko had insisted on keeping her clothing rations for an emergency. I made his breakfast of rice and tea, recycled from dried leaves, and we left the house. Cicadas throbbed through the undergrowth in the garden. Next to a chinaberry sapling, plump figs were beginning to darken and the air carried their summer scent. As we neared the gate Hideo spotted a green praying mantis on a bird table and we watched it eat a white moth, which was trapped in its spiked legs. Hideo glanced at me. 'Is the moth in pain? Can we save it?' I told him this was nature's way. There were hunters and prey but we were top of the food chain and he should not worry. I remembered something I had been told. 'Do you know that the female praying mantis sometimes eats the male after they have mated?'

He looked confused. 'What does mated mean?'

I blushed. 'Never mind, we should get going. We don't want to be late for school.'

Hideo smiled, hopeful. 'Can we keep her? As a pet.'

'She's better out here, free, don't you think?'

He considered this and then took my hand in his own.

Our journey was no different to the others we had made during those days of 'wartime emergency'. We passed the soba store as the owner laid out his meagre daily supply on bamboo racks. The tempura shop next door had been turned into a collection point for any remaining metal we could forage from our homes. Kenzo had long ago sold what gold we had to the government and donated gardening tools, ceremonial swords, copper pots, buttons from our clothes, even the grate of our hearth. Outside the shop the women's association had left a box of cloth strips, which would be sent to our soldiers abroad. Each one had the word 'strength' printed on them one thousand times. Kenzo would watch me at night as I worked on my own contributions and shake his head. 'Trust me, those will do no good.' He would never admit so outside our home, but he believed the war was lost. Still he went to work, still I made my senninriki, still I believed somehow our family would be fine.

Hideo and I waited for a street car and then pushed our way onto the crammed carriage next to young women dressed in their loose-fitting monpe trousers and white shirts. They would be heading to the locomotive depots, the railroad stations, shipping companies and the munitions factories. Kenzo had admired their hard work but when students in the last year of elementary school were recruited to help at similar labour units, he asked in despair, 'When will this stop?'

My grandson's palm was clasped in mine and his school shirt was damp with sweat. The day would be another hot, humid one. I pointed at the window. We watched members of the Nagasaki Fortress Defence Unit march alongside the tram tracks in uniforms that hung from them. Many no longer drilled with guns but bamboo poles. Their weapons had been sent to those on the front lines. A couple of nights earlier my women's association had organised a national defence evening where similar spears were handed out. We wrapped sashes across our chests and tied hachimaki to our heads. Then we picked up our weapons and ran toward life-size effigies of Roosevelt and Churchill as we shouted, 'Annihilate America! Annihilate England!' The sight was ludicrous, but I could not speak such treachery. We had to be seen to be loyal among those who still were. Days earlier, as I sat in the cinema, I watched police arrest a man in the theatre for not taking his hat off when the Emperor appeared on the screen. Better to be obedient and wary.

We got off the tram and walked toward Yamazato school. Down by the river, some boys older than Hideo crouched in the shallows and searched for eels. They prised stones from the riverbed and looked for their catch. A few yards farther on, where the river was deeper, another boy, stripped to the waist, threw a rock tied with string into the water. Two of his friends dived down. They came up gasping and one of them held the rock aloft in his hand. We arrived at the school gates and I handed Hideo his lunch box of buckwheat and okra which I had managed to grow in the garden. He loved to bite into the green vegetables to the white hollows of flesh inside, hold them up and declare, 'Look, a star.' He reached up and pressed hot fingers against my cheek. I told him, 'Work hard, Hideo-chan.' I put my hand over his and we smiled at one another and leaned forward until our fore-heads touched. 'I promise, Grandmother.' Our morning ritual. 'I'll collect you later. Dried cod for dinner tonight.' He made a sour face. 'Or whale ham if I can find some.' He smiled at this. I watched him walk through the school gates. I did not say goodbye, I did not say I loved him, but I hope he knew how loved he was, how loved he has always been. This is Hideo Watanabe. This is my grandson.

I was nearing the tram stop when the air-raid sirens began. The city had been spared the air raids experienced in Tokyo, the incendiary bombing so dense even the rivers were ablaze, but the week before fifty bombers had targeted the Mitsubishi shipyard, steelworks and the medical college hospital. Thankfully Yuko had not been working there at the time and Kenzo had laughed off the danger at his workplace. A woman, with her baby strapped to her back, glanced up at the sky. I did the same but could see no planes. She asked, 'What do you think?' I thought just for a moment that I should go back to get Hideo but I reasoned the teachers would take the children to a shelter if the sirens continued. 'We'll be safe,' I told her and she nodded her agreement. As I took a tram back up the hill the all-clear rang out across the rooftops. I was due to help collect empty charcoal bags, which would then be delivered to City Hall for recycling. I calculated if I worked for two hours, I would have plenty of time to get a street car back down to Urakami to meet Yuko.

Two incidents made me late for her. I wonder now if I meant to be? I was terrified by what she might say and how I would respond. These thoughts distracted me as I worked with a young widow, Tukiko. She pulled a wooden cart while I knocked on doors calling out for the bags. We had designed the route so we would finish close to my home. Tukiko would then head on to our neighbour-hood association to make her delivery. When we were done I noticed my hands and shirt were stained with soot so at 10.30 a.m. I ran back to my house to change my clothes and wash off the dirt. By the time I closed our garden gate, it was probably 10.45 a.m. As I turned on to the main road, I saw the tram about fifty yards in front of me coming to a standstill. By the time I reached the stop, the street car was halfway down the hill. I checked my watch. It was 10.50 a.m. Yuko may already have been inside the cathedral. She had come to follow Shige's Catholic faith and would often go there on her work break. The next tram would be along in fifteen minutes. I knew I would be late but also that she would wait for me. I remember I turned and saw a sign advertising tinned fruit in the window of the grocery store behind me. I wanted to buy some for Hideo and checked my ration book before heading into the shop. And so I was paying for a tin of mandarin oranges when a new light flooded our world. Those who dare to ask me how I survived pikadon are rewarded with the same answer: a sweet tooth. My humour unnerves them. The truth is less glib. Nagasaki saved me; its geography contained the power of the explosion to a third of the city, mostly the Urakami district and part of downtown. The harbour, the historic area and the centre were shielded by the higher ground around the river. While those beautiful hills, thick with green trees, nesting kites and outlying villages narrowed the bomb's range, they also intensified its force. Although I was too high up, too far away, too sheltered within that dark grocery store, I was close enough to know what the end of existence sounds like.

I had never heard such a noise before. It felt as if the world's heart had exploded. Some would later describe it as a bang, but this was more than a door slamming on its hinges, or an oil truck thudding into a car. There can be no word for what we heard that day. There must never be. To give this sound a name might mean it could happen again. What word can capture the roar of every thunderstorm you might have heard, every avalanche and volcano and tsunami that you might have seen tear across the land, every city consumed by flames and waves and winds? Never find the language for such an agony of noise and the silence that followed.

I was thrown backwards into a pile of wooden crates, a small window above the door shattered and sprayed shards across the shop, cracks ripped across the wall as if it were ice tapped by a hammer. The shopkeeper emerged from behind his counter, blood running from a gash above his eye. We stared at one another, too scared for some seconds to leave the sanctuary of the store. He held out his hand and I reached for him. We picked our way through the upended shelves and crates and those tins of fruit. We emerged into a cloud of red haze and heat, blinking in the dust that filled the air. This was pikadon: flash and bang. A new word for the new world that greeted us. The sky seemed to be on fire. A group of people had gathered at a clearing next to the laundryman's shop. We joined them and looked down to what we could see of the city below, too confused to speak in those first moments. We must have known it to be a bomb, or bombs, but how could man alone do this? How could that be possible? A black fog

23

clung to the ground but through breaks in its cover we saw an unimaginable sight. Urakami to the east of the river looked as if some god had stamped down on it, over and over again, kicked the debris away into the air and then moved on.

What survivors saw differs in the telling. To some, the explosion was like a giant pulsating chrysanthemum, a thousand boiling clouds of purple and cream and pink, or it was a giant tree ablaze, shooting high into the sky, or yes, it was shaped like a mushroom, collapsing into itself and then rising away. I can't tell you what I saw. I was looking to where the cathedral should have been. I could see the terraced hills behind where farmers had sliced into the land, but nothing else. When did I decide Yuko was dead? In that moment. At 11.03 or 11.04 a.m. I looked to Hideo's school, about a mile away from the cathedral, and tried to make out the U-shape of the building. I turned to the shopkeeper and said, 'My daughter and grandson are down there.' His silence felt like an executioner's blade wet from the kill. Eventually he said, 'You should go home, wait for them.' How could I go home? How could I wait for them not to return? I was a mile away from the edge of the bomb's reach. 'If I walk, I can get to the school in under an hour.' The shopkeeper looked at me, suspicious. 'There's nothing you can do. Don't go.' I shook my head, refusing to accept his judgement. Instead I ran down the hill toward Urakami. At first the world seemed normal; the buildings, the banks, the street stalls, they were familiar. But then I entered a landscape so alien my nightmares could not have dreamed such terror.

Should I speak of the horrors that I saw? They still seem so unreal to me. The tombs of the city's cemeteries had been blown open and the dead walked among us. Shards of glass carpeted the ground and barefoot children ran over these splinters, their feet shredded and bleeding. Some had strange patterns etched on their exposed skin. There was a man with a broken jaw held in a silent scream. I passed a woman who was sitting on the ground trying to breastfeed her baby. The woman held the bloody rags covering her child up to me. 'Help my son, he won't feed.' All hope was lost for the child. Rain started to fall, gritty and black. Much later I would learn this was what made my gums bleed and clumps of hair fall out in the days that followed. An old man stumbled out of a house and held a broom aloft. 'Crush the enemy,' he shouted over and over again. The nearer I drew to the school the less human the creatures left alive became. Their flesh was black or red raw, like the skin of a ripe pomegranate, their feet were bare. Shoes had melted into the asphalt, still hot underfoot. A woman ran past, naked to the waist, her skin dragging behind her like a cape. Faces were swollen horribly by burns. The smell of burnt flesh and charcoal choked my nostrils. Other wounded people lay where they had fallen. One girl, about five years old, sat in the dirt, her left foot gone. 'Water,' she called out, but to my shame I did not stop.

Everything seemed to be burning or burnt. The hemp trees were alight and a charred body hung from one of the electricity poles. The heat from some of the fires was so fierce, I had to find other routes, doubling back, trying to find a way through the flames. What to say of the baked street car, the tram tracks twisted up into the sky, the charcoal statues inside? The carcass of a horse lay on the ground, as delicate as a burnt log. Yet more bodies were floating on the surface of the river. They must have run there to cool their scorched skin. I felt as if the world had been turned inside out. This had to be hell. Finally, I reached the gates of the school.

A blast had punched holes through the main building and fire had taken hold of what was left. Little of the smashed outhouses remained. The playground was littered with children who must have fallen as they played. I looked upon these blackened forms and thought Hideo surely to be dead then. Other people, parents presumably, searched with me. None of the bodies seemed alive, but perhaps I made a mistake? I don't remember a boy with a burnt face; I'm sure I don't. I shouted Hideo's name and I thought maybe he had run to one of the shelters the teachers had been building. I walked beside the rice fields and came across another charred lump and beside those remains was a magnifying glass, warped by heat, and then what looked like a necklace dipped in fire. Identity tags. I rubbed clear the black grime with my fingers. His name. Hideo Watanabe. My grandson. This happened. This I did not imagine. Deranged with hope I thought just for a moment he too had survived. I screamed into air-raid shelters already full of those who had crawled there to die, but no one answered to his name. I ran back to the schoolyard and knew I could not leave. To go would mean he was gone. A boy dressed in the uniform of the Student Patriotic Corps asked if I needed help. What can a grandmother do when she knows her grandchild to be dead? She does what she must do: she believes that he is still alive.

'I can't find my grandson.'

He pulled out a notepad. 'What's his name? I'll put him on the list. We're looking for survivors.'

'Hideo Watanabe. He's seven.' I watched the boy write on paper smeared with dust and blood. How could this one young boy find my lost one? When would Hideo be looked for? Where could he have gone? Desperation made me hope that Yuko had decided not to meet me but had stayed at work. 'The medical college hospital?' 'Gone,' he said. 'Try Michinoo train station. They're taking the injured there.' I started to head off. 'Mitsubishi?' He didn't know. Some of the factories had tunnels and if Kenzo had made it to them, he might be safe. I knew if he had survived, he would also be looking.

On the ruined streets that led to the station more wounded, so many, were making their way along the tracks to the station office. Some had wrapped crude bandages around their cuts and burns and broken limbs. The more seriously injured were carried in sheets, or on planks or carts. Despite the numbers, after the roar of the bomb and the screams of its victims, all was quiet. Footsteps, cartwheels, babies made no sound. The sky turned an impossible colour, a morning light or the shadows of dusk, I could not tell. I looked for the birds that soar above the city but there were none. Where had they gone? And then I understood the sky must have swallowed them. Later I saw a black kite alive on the ground, its feathers burned away, scalded wings flapping as it tried to take flight.

At the station, noise returned. People begged the defence corps troops or medics who passed them, 'Take my son, help my wife, save me.' They grabbed at the too few doctors as they tried to tend the wounded. Nurses tore strips of cloth and smeared castor oil on exposed burns. One young woman, her uniform wet with blood, stood up, turned away and fainted. I wished death on some of the people I saw to end their suffering. I could not tell if they were man or woman; I could not make out eyes from ears or mouths; so many cried out for water until their moans of pain became whimpers followed by nothing. At some point, there was a screech of iron and a train arrived, its carriage doors flung open. The doctors began to point to people to load up first, presumably the ones more likely to survive. I don't know how long I searched, but when I could no longer stand the sight of all those bodies I made my way back through the streets, past those too injured to move from the spreading fires, until I reached home. I sat in our kitchen and waited, hoping someone, anyone, would walk through the door.

Darkness had fallen when I heard the crunch of gravel on our garden path. I waited, my blood racing, and a ghost walked into the room. Kenzo was white from head to foot. His hair and suit were covered in plaster dust, his eyes bruised, his fingernails were bleeding as if he had been scraping away at the walls. I ran to him. 'It's you?' He nodded and held me in his arms. He checked me over. 'You're safe? Are you hurt?' I told him I was unharmed. He glanced to the shadows of the rest of our house. 'Are they asleep?' I could not speak, I could not say the words. He slumped against the sink, his back to me, his hands grasping the stone rim.

I touched his shoulder, felt the warmth of him. 'Did you go to the school?' He said nothing. 'Yuko was at the cathedral. I was on my way to meet her.' He gripped the sink tighter. 'What do we do now?'

He closed his eyes, defeated by the question. 'We need to rest. We'll look again when it's light.'

'I'm sorry, Kenzo.'

He turned his head to look at me. 'Why?'

'I should have gone back for him.' I shook my head. 'The air-raid warning, I thought it was a false alarm, I decided he would be safe with his teachers.'

He pulled me toward him. 'This isn't your fault, Ama.'

I tried to stop them but the tears came then. My heart felt crushed by the kindness of his words. 'Tell me he's somewhere safe, Kenzo. Tell me he's not scared, tell me he's still alive.'

Kenzo held my face in his hands, made me look in his eyes. 'He's alive until we know he's dead. They both are. Yes?' How could I tell him otherwise? He took my silence as agreement. 'We'll check in the morning. I'll go to the medical college again, visit the shelters. It's too late tonight. The fires are still burning. But I promise you, Amaterasu, I won't give up until I find them. I promise you that.' He took my hand and led me through to the living area. We sat on the floor and listened to the radio in the dark. A newscaster spoke of the Russian invasion of Manchuria. The USSR had struck only hours before the bomb fell. Japan was at war with another enemy.

'Turn it off,' I said and the voice crackled away to nothing. 'Why Urakami? The schools and houses?'

'The factories.' Kenzo began to pull off his jacket. 'The ordnance works are gone, the steelworks and arms plant are badly damaged.'

'But you survived?' One sharp nod and then he put his head in his hands, ashamed by his tears. We embraced, my body too small to soak up the sobs that made his shudder. The shipbuilder and his wife saved, the city's children and their mothers gone.

We woke before dawn, ate sour millet, looked for photographs of Hideo and Yuko to take with us to Urakami Dai-Ichi Hospital. We thought survivors might have been taken there. I tied bedsheets to my back and we made our way through roads scattered with bricks, metal beams and chunks of plaster. Shards of buildings smouldered across the flattened landscape; skeletal girders and the odd chimney stack twisted up into the sky. People were picking through rubble, some on their hands and knees, and when an elderly woman picked up a blackened skull, I realised they were searching for bones. The cremations had begun for the bodies not yet consumed by flames. Volunteers loaded corpses onto carts or piles of wood. A woman near them was gathering ashes in her hands and placing them into an empty can of powdered baby milk.

When we arrived at the hospital only its exterior red-brick wall remained but doctors had set up a ward outside in the yard. Some canvas shelters had been raised to protect patients from the sun but others lay on soiled blankets or the bare ground as the morning heat took hold. We handed over the bedsheets to a nurse too pale with lack of sleep and asked if we might search for our missing among the patients. She took my hand, her voice gentle. 'Some of them are very badly hurt, do you understand?' I nodded and she turned to Kenzo. 'I'm afraid we're having to dispose of the bodies as quickly as possible.' She patted the sheets in her arms. 'This is most kind.' We checked as best we could and then wrote Hideo and Yuko's names on a list that had been pinned to the entrance sign of the hospital. Others had left their own messages: *'Have you seen my parents, Aito and Nana Narita? Last seen in Urakami'*, *'If Goro Saito sees this, please go to your uncle's home in Shimabara'* and *'Lost: two children aged eight and six, called Yoshi and Akatsuki Yamada. Please contact Shinzo Yamada at Omura Naval Hospital.'*

We left the hospital and walked toward the stump of the cathedral. Kenzo squeezed my fingers. 'Should we check?' The stone entrance and some of the circular windows on the facade had survived the blast but the rest was rubble. I turned away. 'There's no point.' Instead we walked for hours past more attempts at first-aid stations, more pockets of fires, until late in the afternoon when Kenzo stopped beside a child's body, a girl maybe, covered his eyes with his hands and began to weep. I stood on tiptoes to place my cheek against his own. 'Let's go home, we're tired. We should eat.' He shook his head. 'I need to go to the factory. You rest. I'll keep looking.'

And he did. We both did. We went to the makeshift hospitals, stood in never-ending queues to register our missing, checked the piles of bodies stacked as if sandbags for cremation. Who knows how long we hunted for them?

Hours, days, weeks? Time was as broken as the land. Every body we passed, every burnt or bleeding patient we saw, we hoped that it might be Yuko or Hideo, but we never saw their faces again.

Fighting Spirit

Konjo: This is a key word in understanding Japanese stoicism, which has been practised by the male population since feudal times. A man who possesses konjo is highly praised for he would stop at nothing in the course of duty, willingly subjecting himself to unbearable circumstances in the process. Thus konjo is a symbol of masculine spirit.

Days before pikadon, I arrived unannounced at Yuko's home. She was writing in a book with such intensity that she could not have heard me come through the door. I called out to her and she snapped the cover shut before she looked up to greet me. I saw in her face an expression of guilt and frustration at the interruption. 'I was just sending Shige some news.' Maybe I believed her, but during those first nights after August 9, I lingered over the memory of her sitting at her desk. What had she written and why? Had she confessed secrets to Shige that no longer needed to be revealed? Maybe she had not sent the letter, maybe it could be retrieved and erased if the contents proved harmful? I could allow my daughter and my son-in-law this kindness.

Two nights after the bomb, while Kenzo continued the search, I stood in her garden. The blossom on the azalea bush looked too orange, the ash tree too large, the blood grass too alive for this shattered city. I opened the unlocked main door and stepped into the house. Laughter, tantrums and tears had once filled these rooms now so empty and silent. How quickly a home can become a mausoleum. A burnt incense stick lay on the table in the living room. In the kitchen, there was a vase of wilting red carnations. Hideo's shirt hung on a peg near the range. Upstairs in Yuko's bedroom I lifted back the drape of the mosquito net and lay on the unmade futon. I closed my eyes and smelled the sweetness of her on the sheets, a hint of lavender and the mustier odour of the summer damp that invaded their home. I sat up and looked around the room to the walnut cupboards and matching chest, the trunk beneath the window and the cabinet next to the door. Where would Yuko conceal a secret? I began to open drawers. I lifted up the folded cotton tops, thin sweaters and grey silks. I looked inside the cupboard and ran my hands over one of her nurse's uniforms. I lifted the lid of the trunk and felt beneath winter blankets until my fingers touched something hard. A book. A diary. *Yuko Watanabe*. Beneath this one were several more, all the way back to *Yuko Takahashi*. I had expected to find a letter and instead uncovered a life. I collected them up, took them home and found a new hiding place.

I guessed why Yuko kept a journal. She was like a photographer trying to capture the sunset before the last rays disappeared. We all need proof that certain things happened as we imagined they did, but those books were a dangerous indulgence. Leave no proof of transgressions, store them only in your mind. I had learned that lesson young. Some stories are best taken to the grave. Yuko had not written that diary for public record but for private comfort. No one would read my daughter's confessions. Not me, not Kenzo, and not, as I feared then, Shige when he returned. We had no way of contacting him. We thought he was stationed somewhere in the Pacific, Saipan maybe, or Burma, perhaps New Guinea. But even if we had an address, we would not have told him about Hideo and Yuko. We believed such news should be heard not read.

Kenzo was sure Japan couldn't last out much longer, not with the Russians razing our troops in Manchuria, not with the Americans in Okinawa, not with young boys barely old enough to have girlfriends trying to steer planes into enemy ships. In the aftermath of pikadon, my own anger coursed through me but I could not say out loud the dark thoughts that I had carried. Kenzo had helped build those ships to carry our men away. Those factories by the harbour had brought the bomb to our city. Yes, he had done his duty, we all had, but look at the cost. The nation had two options: surrender or suicide, Kenzo said. The war was lost but its end was meaningless to me.

Six days after pikadon, Misaki was taking tea with me in the living room after I had spent the morning in Urakami. I found myself drawn back to that blasted plain as if one day, I would just happen to see Yuko sitting by some ruin. I imagined her calling out to me, 'There you are, I've been waiting for you.' Misaki's family had been spared. Her daughter had been sent to work in a canning factory in a nearby village, her husband worked nights and had been asleep safe in their home, her son was stationed at a coal mine outside the city. I could feel her embarrassment that she had been so protected from the bomb when we had been so exposed. But I was glad for her. How could I not be? She was more a friend than a housekeeper, perhaps my only friend. Kenzo had employed her before we were married. More than twenty-five years had passed since we first met. Misaki was a little older than me, her hair was already shot through with grey, unruly in a bun. I looked at her hands resting in her lap, her chewed nails, the red, inflamed skin, the slight tremor in her fingers. I wanted to tell her that she need not feel such peculiar shame; I wanted to say that her companionship was succour to me, but instead I took hold of her hand, clammy in my own. Kenzo had phoned earlier to tell me to turn the radio on at noon when he said, his voice incredulous, Emperor Showa would address the nation. We listened to the announcer introduce the recorded message.

Misaki stared at me in amazement. 'I've never heard his voice.'

He spoke in classical Japanese as whines and crackles cut into his speech. We listened as one might to a god.

'To our good and loyal subjects, after pondering deeply the general trends of the world and the actual conditions obtaining in our empire today, we have decided to effect a settlement of the present situation . . .'

Misaki looked at me. 'I can't understand, what's he saying?' I gestured for her to be quiet.

'The enemy has begun to employ a new and most cruel bomb, the power of which to do damage is, indeed, incalculable, taking the toll of many innocent lives. Should we continue to fight, not only would it result in an ultimate collapse and obliteration of the

36

Japanese nation, but also it would lead to the total extinction of human civilisation . . .'

'Is he talking about us?'

I nodded, but I was not sure.

'Such being the case, how are we to save the millions of our subjects, or to atone ourselves before the hallowed spirits of our imperial ancestors? This is the reason why we have ordered the acceptance of the provisions of the Joint Declaration . . .'

He spoke of hardships and sufferings, of paving the way to a grand peace by enduring the unendurable. Misaki sighed. 'Why can't he speak plainly? Is the war over?'

'Beware most strictly of any outbursts of emotion . . . Unite your total strength . . . Cultivate the ways of rectitude, foster nobility of spirit, and work with resolution — so that you may enhance the innate glory of the imperial state and keep pace with the progress of the world.'

We waited for the announcer to tell us what we did not understand. Japan had surrendered. We did not hug each other with joy or relief, we did not weep, we were not sure how to greet this news. 'What will become of us?' Misaki asked. I thought immediately of Shige. He would come home now surely? What joy, what sadness, too. Later when Kenzo returned from the shipyard, he and I stood under our ginkyo tree. We looked at the stars as I took a sip of the sake we had kept to mark the end of the war. 'Why now? Why this day? Is our city the reason?'

He held his glass up to the moonlight. 'Don't ask that question, wife.'

'Were Yuko and Hideo taken for a reason, so that the war might end?' I insisted.

'They died because our enemy had bigger bombs, they

died because America wanted to teach the world a lesson, they died because they do not matter.'

'They mattered to us.'

He downed his drink, grimacing. 'We don't matter either, Amaterasu, don't you see?'

We waited a month to hold the memorial. We would have delayed the day longer but we had heard nothing from Shige. The news from overseas was one of chaos following Japan's surrender. But I clung to the belief he was still alive, somehow. He had to be. We couldn't lose all three of them.

His parents came to the city and we gathered at Oura Church, too numb to comprehend the size and depth of our grief. We were just one of thousands of families to mourn lost ones but these were our dead. Following the service, we invited guests to our home. What food we could find was served by a weeping Misaki. Some of our guests had lost relatives of their own. One of the wives told me that they were thinking of starting up a group for bereaved survivors so that they might draw support from one another. The thought of sitting in some cold hall or a stranger's home appalled me, and maybe my face for once betrayed my true feelings. The woman's husband took me to the side of our living room. He gripped my elbow as he spoke. 'This life is often beyond reasoning. We will never make sense of this but neither must we allow it to defeat us. We owe such fortitude to those no longer with us.' I tipped my head to the side as if I understood, but no kind words could heal the wounds inside me.

The day after the memorial Kenzo and I accompanied

Shige's parents to our children's home to start clearing away possessions. With so many people in need, we had decided to give clothes to the homeless and much of the furniture and kitchen utensils would go to shelters. Kenzo pretended to busy himself outside and Shige's father sat in the day room drinking what was left of the sake while his wife and I began to pack away belongings. Too quickly the proof of their lives would disappear. They would be reduced to photograph albums and token mementoes and tricks of our memory. Shige's mother and I started in Hideo's room, the black air-raid curtains drawn back, the sun hot on our faces. I was folding up what few clothes he had as I knelt beside his futon. Sonoko had opened a wooden chest under the window. Colouring books, bean-bags and a straw hat with a crease in the rim were piled next to her. She picked up a wooden cup attached by string to a ball. The toy was striped red and black, crude in its finish. She sat back and her mouth contorted in a way that made me realise she did not want to cry. Not here, not yet. 'I gave this to him, two summers ago, when he came to Iōjima. My neighbour, Toshi, made it. Hideo found it annoying, he could never get the ball in the cup.' She wrapped the string around the handle. 'Do you mind if I keep this?'

'Please. Take what you must.'

She thanked me and next she pulled out a piece of paper from the chest and smiled. 'Here, I think this is for you.' She handed me a drawing, which consisted of little more than circles for the bodies and heads and sticks for arms. Underneath, he had written 'Grandmother and Grandfather'.

I felt embarrassed. 'It could be either of us.'

She looked inside the chest. 'You were lucky to spend more time with him.'

The truth made me blush. 'We will keep looking for them.'

'They are gone, Amaterasu. I think we must accept this. I think we already have.'

I managed to look in her eyes. 'What will you do?'

She picked up one of the sweaters I had folded and held it to her face, breathing in the memory. 'Carry on, endure, live. What else can we do?' She ran her hands over the brown wool. 'And you?'

The words were even more hollow when repeated. 'Carry on, endure, live.'

And so I had, for nearly forty years, I carried on, I accepted Hideo was gone. Now the idea of him was back, not a boy, but a man, and every time I thought about him I saw pikadon and that empty home and that drawing. *Grandmother and Grandfather.* I returned to the bedroom and retrieved the sketch, the writing almost illegible, despite no sunlight to blanch the ink. In the kitchen I placed it next to Yuko's diary.

I had kept my promise. I had never read her journals. While I told myself I was doing a honourable deed by preserving her privacy, in reality, I was just a coward. I had turned away from what I could not face, but Yuko could sift the truth from the lies. She could bring Hideo truly back to life. Only my daughter would make me believe that this mutilated man was her son.

An Omen

Engi: In Buddhist philosophy, engi is the definite law that governs the mutation of the phenomenal world where all living things must die and nothing is permanent. In secular use, engi means an omen or luck. A dream about a snake is said to be a good omen and that about a fish a bad one. Good-luck charms are popular among shopkeepers who display them in their stores. Some charms are the exorcising arrows (hamaya), the decorated bamboo rake (kumade) and the figure of a beckoning cat (maneki-neko).

I opened the first of Yuko's diaries and ran my hands over the yellowed paper. The ink seemed almost too fresh, as if written weeks not years ago. This was not my daughter on the page, but these words were all I had. I started when the two of them began: July 29, 1936. They met in his office, a routine medical appointment, a young girl sent to a doctor by her father, a doctor who had been a family friend. The way she described the day, everything was heightened. The cicadas' song, the sun on the stone curves of Spectacles Bridge, the smell of seafood as she passed Shinchi in the taxi, the grey slab of the hospital and the stillness of Sato's office, all were bright and intense. She caught the details: the photograph of his dead brother in uniform, the cracks in the leather examination table and the Buddhist plaque on the wall, which said: 'We eat, excrete, sleep and get up. This is our world. All we have to do after that – is to die.'

If I close my eyes, I can see it all, locked inside her. Everything seemed to carry weight and portent. '*He introduced himself and asked after Father. He said they had known each other for more years than I had been alive. I thought it strange I had never heard of his name before. He seems younger than Father but maybe that's because he is taller, leaner, his hair thicker. His handsomeness made me shy. I felt self-conscious when he looked at me as if he could see a part of me I wanted to keep hidden. I'm blushing as I write this and it's been hours since we met.*'

He asked what was wrong and she said she could not sleep longer than a couple of hours a night. Her stomach was unsettled, she had lost her appetite. She said, 'I think my parents are being too anxious for me. It's summer, it's probably just the heat.' He told her to remove her kimono but she could keep her under-kimono on. She climbed onto his examination table. '*I could feel my face burn when he slipped the stethoscope between the cotton. The cold metal against my chest made me flinch. The room was so quiet I could hear birdsong from outside.*' Next he wanted her to lie back. '*His fingers prodded into my flesh, firm but gentle. I felt my veins and skin and muscle and bone; I was alive in the purest sense of that word.*' He wanted to know her age and she told him she was sixteen. He washed and dried his palms as she dressed. They sat opposite each other. 'What do you intend to do by way of a profession?' '*Mother had told me a girl of my class need only be a graceful and attentive wife but I did not tell him this. I said I did not know.*' He asked her what she liked to do and she told him that she drew. He said Japan had plenty of artists, and housewives; our new Japan needed scientists, teachers and nurses, not poets and printmakers. He said our personal aspirations had to match our country's ambitions. *'I told him he sounded like Father and he smiled. "So what would you say to him if he were here now?" I thought for a moment. "I'd say, don't scientists need some beauty in their lives?"'*

He laughed and walked to the door. 'Come on, there's something you should see.' They made their way down to the ground floor and walked along a corridor until they reached the children's ward. The doors were open and the white gauze curtains billowed in front of the windows. The air smelled of disinfectant. To their left, a boy was asleep, next to him lay an older boy, who was reading a book. Farther down the room, a nurse fed a girl water from a glass. He turned to her and said, 'I'm sure you draw well, Yuko, but your fingers may have other skills. You can play a role in this nation of ours, and not just by producing sons.' Her cheeks reddened at this and they walked back to the reception area of the hospital and out through the front doors. Sato lit up a cigarette and checked his watch. He told her he could find nothing wrong except mild exhaustion. Maybe this was a hard time for a girl her age, perhaps she had worries of some nature? School had been the biggest part of her life, the future was less certain, she might have some concerns about the months or years ahead? *'I listened to him talk. I liked his low voice, his steady speech. I liked the way the mole on his chin moved when he talked. I liked the way he shielded his eyes from the sun.'* He prescribed exercise, daily swims or bicycle rides, but she said she could not do the former and *'Mother did not allow the latter'*. He said, 'You don't swim? We are an island nation. The sea is everywhere.' Yuko told him that she had never had the need and this amused him. 'Why doesn't your mother let you ride?' She hesitated before she bent down and moved the layers of her kimono to reveal a white scar that ran the length of her shin. 'I was eight, my first bicycle, my last bicycle.' They smiled at each other. 'Well, swimming it must be.' He paused. 'I may have a solution.' He happened to know someone who was excellent in the water, a patient teacher. What did she think? Yuko asked who the person was. Another smile. 'Me.' That was how this all began: swimming lessons.

They arranged to meet the following week and as she left the hospital a tall, thin woman in an olive-green kimono passed her with a parasol in one hand and a small bamboo box in the other. Yuko wrote she had never seen such a face before. It were as if sunlight had burned the woman's features away to nothing more than clean lines of brow and cheek and chin, a perfect beauty. Yuko made her way to the main road and waited until she was on the edge of the path before she turned to watch the woman run her hand across Sato's chest and smooth the lapel of his jacket. The woman folded her parasol and he took it from her. As the sun slipped behind a cloud they headed into the dark, cool interior of the hospital. *As I made my way home, I realised right there, right then, that the world had changed irrevocably for me. I felt some new sensation, a spike of joy in my heart. This man, cold metal on my flesh, hands on my skin. What to say? He feels like a secret. The world has shrunk and yet expanded at the same time. I do not understand why but it exhilarates me. In my mind only he and I exist. I begin to count the hours until I see him again.*

A Charm

*Omamori: Many Japanese people still carry a religious amulet,
which they buy at a shrine or temple. It is made of a strip of
paper, plastic or wood, on which some blessing or prayer is
written. It is put in a small attractive cloth bag to be worn around
the neck, carried in a purse, attached to a wallet, or hung in a
car. People carry omamori, believing or expecting that it will
protect them from misfortune, or that it will bring forth divine help
in realising their wishes.*

Yuko and Sato had agreed to meet by the terminal office
at the pier. She said he was not hard to spot among the
fishermen and old women who were waiting for the boat
to dock. He stood with his back to her, dressed in a panama
hat, cream linen trousers and a white shirt, with the sleeves
rolled up. Before she could reach him, he turned round,
and the rawness of her reaction made her breathless. She
had seen romance at the cinema, in movies imported from
Hollywood, but she watched those actresses and saw
nothing of her own life. She was no Egyptian queen, or
Broadway star or wife of a tsarist. She was a girl but this
was her first experience of desire and it intoxicated her.
Sato handed her a ticket and revealed they were going
to Iōjima, a tiny island, thirty minutes from the city. They
walked onto the gangway of the berthed ferry. Midweek,
most of the seats on the lower deck were empty. They

took the stairs up to the open air of the upper level. The engine kicked into life and the boat pulled away from the land and growled its way out to sea. Sato disappeared down the flight of steps and Yuko turned to watch Nagasaki grow smaller and smaller. The factories that lined the harbour shrank and faded against the darkening hills and brightening sky. She had never seen her home from this perspective, slowly reduced to such insignificant proportions.

The doctor returned with two glasses. He offered her a glass of barley tea and she sipped the chilled liquid. *'He sat close enough for me to sense the sliver of air that separated us. He has that effect of magnifying everything around him: colours, noise, senses.'* She watched him put his glass down on the bench and light a cigarette. He leaned against the seat with his hat tipped back and his face to the sun. *'I dislike the smell of tobacco, but today the odour, mixed with the salt spray of the sea, gave me a heady pleasure. He closed his eyes against the rays and I studied his profile. I have never been alone with a man in this intimate way. My gaze fell from his parted lips, down his neck to the triangle of skin between the collar of his open shirt, down the crisp, white material to his waistband and down farther still. I took him all in. When I glanced up, I could see he was watching me with an unknowable look.'* Embarrassed, Yuko moved to the back of the boat, but Sato followed her. He placed his elbows on the rail. Beneath them, the propellers spewed out a trail of white foam.

They stayed that way for some time, silent but not awkwardly so. Then he raised himself tall before he asked her, 'I'm curious. Did you tell your parents you're here with me?' She considered whether to lie as she turned to face him. The wind whisked her hair against her mouth. He lifted his hand and moved the strands off her face and tucked them behind her ear. *'I felt the stirring then, an aching pleasure somewhere below my stomach. I told him no, I had told no one. He smiled and moved closer, lowered his face to the side of my cheek and whispered in my ear, "Our little secret." His mouth grazed the side of my face when he pulled away. I wish I could find the words to describe the feeling of that brief connection. Maybe no word exists for it but without the word how will I remember my reaction other than to repeat the spike of desire again and again until my body becomes its own dictionary?'*

Iōjima came into view; the island was little more than a couple of mounds carpeted in green trees. The ferry rumbled into the harbour and minutes later she walked down the gangway. She watched a fisherman in a rowboat at work with his black cormorant. The bird launched from its master's pole and dived beneath the surface. The bird seemed to swim beneath the water for a long time and Yuko stopped, worried that it might not return, but then it rose from the depths with a bream clutched in its beak and returned to the pole to drop the fish at its master's feet. *'I feel as if Sato is the fisherman and I am the bird.'*

They followed a path that disappeared around the southern side of the island. Concrete defences lined the track. The barricades had been deposited to keep the waves from devouring the land. Sea lice scuttled between the crevices and the sun was white above their heads, thickening the air until their nostrils burned. They passed a field where hundreds of dragonflies hovered. The hum of beating wings echoed across the brown earth and yellow grass. The place pulsed with heat in a way that Yuko said made the land seem one produced of a fevered imagination. A boy and girl crouched next to a heap of the dead insects. The boy stood up and threw two clam shells linked by cotton thread in the air. A dragonfly, caught under the makeshift trap, fell to the grass and twitched and jerked until it became still. The girl ran over and picked its limp body up and added it to the pile. They began to count their catch and looked up to study the doctor and Yuko.

Another path broke from this main one and they followed it past a small boat, bleached by the sun and perched high on a pebble beach strewn with fishing nets. A line of fish, flattened and salted, hung between poles next to the boat. They reached a wooden cottage, barely more than a shack. A man stood in the doorway. He picked up a bucket, walked toward them and Yuko looked down as they passed him. Sea urchins clung to the bucket's inside, their black spines interlocked. He would be taking them to market for the sushi restaurants of Nagasaki. Sato and Yuko turned one last corner and were met by a loop of white sand and grey rocks striated with pink and yellow quartz. A hundred yards from the shoreline, a wooden diving platform floated on the sea. Sato took off his shoes and socks and she followed him. Their feet sank into the burning sand until they reached a line of cycad trees. Sato pulled off his shirt and trousers until he wore only his swimming trunks. He ran down to the shore and crashed into the water, took strong strokes toward the bobbing platform.

Yuko peeled off her yukata and felt shy in the red

swimsuit she had bought for the occasion. The material was so tight around her thighs, so low at the back. She had seen pictures of those modern Japanese girls in a magazine, walking around the streets of Tokyo in their striped beach pyjamas and wide-brimmed hats. She envied their confidence and their daring. How could they be so defiant, so free? Sato stood on the edge of the platform. He held his hand aloft in a wave and then dived in, disappeared long enough for her to worry for him as she had for the cormorant, but then he appeared in a rush of spray and he made his way back to shore. She walked down the beach until the tide licked her toes. Beige baby flounder, their orange-dotted scales half buried in the sand, charged away with a ripple of their fins. Small waves lapped against her ankles and shins as she made her way deeper. Sato reached her and stood up on the sea floor. Rivulets dropped down his hairless chest as he wiped his face.

'You've never swum at all?' He said they would start slowly and he told her to lean back and float. 'Trust me. I'll catch you, don't worry.' She lowered herself down, kicked her feet off the seabed and lay flat. Sato's two hands held her back and the top of her legs. 'That's my kappa. We'll make a water spirit of you yet.' She looked up and the sun shone over Sato's shoulder so that he was little more than a black cloud of a man. She floated and listened to the crackle of unseen coral reefs and the blood pumping in her ears. *Jomei moved his hands and cupped them against the side of my chest and thighs, pulled me closer to him until my torso was pressed against his stomach. Somewhere on the island, I knew there was life other than the doctor: there was a fisherman and a bucket of sea urchins, a boy and girl and a pile of dead dragonflies, but in that moment, there was only me and Jomei, the sea and a diving platform, and his skin against mine.'*

Later they sat on the rocks and stared at the water. 'You did well today, you'll make a fine swimmer.' She thanked him and searched for something to say. 'It's kind of you to give up your time.' He said he was glad of the excuse to come back to the island. He had come here often as a student. Yuko stood up and went to look in a pool, lifting up stones as she searched for signs of life among the seaweed. She glanced up and saw that Sato was studying her. *'It felt as if he was appraising me. I wonder what he sees. A child? I must seem so half-formed to him.'* He joined her, hunched down, rested his arms on his knees. 'So what do we have here?' They peered into the shallows at a crab scuttling sideways, yellow-and-black periwinkles, red anemones shiny as eyeballs, shrimp and even a tiny blue starfish. 'It's like staring into childhood,' he said. Yuko wanted to tease him. 'I thought Japan didn't need poets?' He smiled and she saw him look at the scar on her leg. 'It's ugly, yes?' He disagreed. 'Treat it like a map of your life. You know, you should ride a bicycle. One accident shouldn't stop you. Your mother was always so careful.' This surprised her. 'You knew Mother?'

'Not well,' he answered. Curiosity led Yuko to the next question. *'I asked why my parents had never mentioned him before Father arranged my appointment at the hospital. He said Mother didn't like him. I asked why. She thought he had been a bad influence on Father when they were younger. Was he? He nodded his head in agreement but he did not laugh as I had expected. Next he had a question for me. Why had I not told my parents about the swimming lessons? I ran my hand down the scar and told him the truth. I didn't want them to say no.'*

When they met the following week at the ferry terminal, he was waiting with two bicycles. She held her hand to her mouth to stifle the laughter. 'I can't ride.' He shook his head. 'I don't believe you. Here, take this one, we'll try when we reach Iōjima.' Her first attempts made her squeal in terror and delight but soon enough she could stand on the pedals, her arms straight, hot air on her face, the sun on her hair. They kept the bicycles on the island, discarded under a tree at the beach, or chained to the post at the pier. She took her sketchbook on several visits but she drew him just once, on August 22, and only then because he was too tired to complain. Surgery had kept him up most of the night, meningitis, the child saved but limbs lost. He was dozing when she pulled the pad and pencil from her bag. She watched his chest rise and fall as she drew the outline of him and then filled in the detail. *'The heat shimmered just beyond him and his skin glowed honey gold in the sun. The nectar of him.'*

When he woke up he gave her sketch pad a rueful look. She showed her effort to him, shy with the longing those lines of charcoal revealed. He nodded and handed it back to her. 'You don't like it?' He told her he looked old. She found this funny and felt that need again to tease him, as if poking him with a soft stick of bamboo. 'How old are you?' He raised his eyebrows and sat up. 'Well, how old is your father?' She thought for a moment. 'So old, older than the oldest turtle in the world.' He hung his head in defeat. 'In that case, I'm two months

51

older than that.' Yuko let her curiosity bubble to the surface. She dared ask her next question. 'So have you been married as long as him? I saw your wife, I think, at the hospital, the day we met. She's beautiful.' He nodded.

'I saw him assessing me again, the way he had that day by the rock pool. "She is beautiful, yes. She is the envy of women and I am the envy of men." I didn't like him talking this way. His words made me feel jealous and seem foolish. A stupid girl with some silly infatuation, but I was too thirsty for more information. "How did you meet?" He told the story of them. Her name is Natsu, she is five years younger than him, the daughter of a colleague. She was impossible to resist for many reasons, he said. "We were young, she seemed perfect, as youth does to youth. Then we grew up." He paused as if reaching for the right words. "My wife is like my sister, do you understand?" I did not and he saw this. "Maybe it's good that you don't."'

He looked to the sea. 'I think you're ready now.' She did not know what he meant. 'Today you're going to go all the way to the diving platform.' The square of wood rolled gently in the tide. 'It's too far. I can't.' He chided, 'Of course you can. I'll be right behind you. Don't tell me you're scared?' This annoyed her. She said nothing and ran into the water. The tide was with her and she was determined to prove herself, however awkward her strokes were or however much water she swallowed. Just a few feet from the platform he swam past her, a neat crawl, showing off, but she did not care, she had made it. She grabbed the rusting metal and hauled herself up, breathless, the panic of the swim dying away. He was sitting with his back to her. She joined him, as the tide slapped at the wood and shadows of fish darted below. *'We watched the water, silent but content in the stillness of Iōjima.'*

When they did talk, he spoke of his childhood in Kumamoto, the war games he and his brother Tenri played in the field by their home, the day Tenri left to join the army in 1917, the night the telegram came of his death three years later in Shanghai, the morning his belongings were returned in a square box, letters written by Sato bound by a shoelace placed inside the wisteria wood. *He kept staring at the water and I wanted to offer some solace. I told him, "But he died a hero then, fighting for his country." He took his time to answer. "He died in a fight, yes, not on a battlefield, in some opium den, down a street called Blood Alley, where a child was included in the price of a beer." His revelation frightened me. I realised I knew nothing of life. My parents have kept me so cocooned. I am hungry for more knowledge, not of opium dens, but of other experiences life can offer up. Jomei lay back on the salt-stained wood and I wondered how it felt to live with the loss of someone so close to you. "You keep a photograph of him on your desk. You must be proud of him." He turned to look at me. "It doesn't matter how he died, he was still my brother. We'll always be two young boys playing in the mud, not the men we grew up to be." I wanted to reach for him then. Hold his hand. Rest my head on his chest. Know the right words to say. Instead I felt the creep of fear at how precious our time together was, how finite. These days with Jomei are rubies of joy. I can swim well enough. I no longer need lessons. I asked him how long our trips to the island would last. He raised himself up on his elbows. "The visits will end when the crickets start to sing." I smiled at this and so did he. "It seems I really am a poet, Yuko." We both laughed. No, I cannot imagine my life without Iōjima, without him. Did I dare tell him this? I could not. Instead I told him, "I'll miss this island. I'm happy here." Maybe this embarrassed him. He rose to his feet, reached for my hand and pulled me up. "Come on, race you to the* beach." He jumped into the sea and I shouted, "Not fair, cheat, wait." By the time I made it back to the shore, he was standing beside our bags, clapping as I dragged myself from the surf. I remember laughing as my lungs burned, the taste of salt on my lips, and my exhilaration made me careless. I was too close to the rocks, too distracted by Jomei as I watched him reach for a towel. I took one step and a searing heat shot up through my foot. The pain made me cry out his name and as I fell to my knees he came running toward me.'

The Chirping of Crickets

Mushi-no-ne: In autumn suzumushi (bell ring insect), matsumushi (a kind of cricket) and korogi (common cricket) start singing. This singing of the insects strikes the right chord in the heart of Japanese people. They find something sad and lonely in these chirpings, realising the end of the hot summer, the coming of the severe winter, the short lives of the insects, and by association the mutation of life.

He ran to her as she sat on the shoreline. 'I think it's a jellyfish,' she said, holding her foot. He knelt down and looked at her sole. 'Sea urchin. We'll have to get the spines out. Don't worry, you'll be fine I promise. Can you walk?' She could not. He told her to put her arms around his neck and he scooped her up. 'I'm too heavy.' He smiled. 'No, you're not. Hold on.' Her foot throbbed as the venom went to work. 'Jomei, it hurts.' He reassured her he would get rid of the pain as they made their way to the front door of the nearest cottage. He shouted out and a woman, dressed in trousers and a smock, appeared in the entrance. 'Can we have some vinegar, boiling water and a razor, if you have one?' She beckoned them inside and Sato placed Yuko on the floor, lifted her foot and began to pull black needles from her flesh. He sterilised the razor and then dragged it over the inflamed patch of skin. Next he rubbed the vinegar over her foot. When the treatment was finished the woman offered them tea. Sato thanked her but said they should get back to the mainland. He helped Yuko dress while the woman took one of the bicycles to a lean-to. '*I hopped to the entrance of the cottage and climbed onto the saddle of the other bike and held on to Jomei's waist as he began to pedal away. I turned to wave at the woman in thanks but she had already disappeared inside her home. His muscles must have ached with the effort but he did not stop until we reached the pier. As we took the boat home, he created a footrest with our bags, checked the swelling, reassured me I'd recover. I thought of the moment he picked me up in his arms, the concern on his face, the kindness of his voice. I understand so little of life but his actions hinted at the hope I carried: Jomei did care for me.*

'*Back at the ferry terminal in the city, we stood by the water reluctant to leave the afternoon behind. Those hours had changed us, created an intimacy that was different from the one we had shared on the sand and the diving platform. We were different in each other's company, exposed in a new light, a new way of being with one another. He asked whether I wanted to go home. I told him no. I wanted to stay with him longer. He considered this. "Won't your parents expect you home?" Not for a few hours. We looked into one another's eyes. No words were exchanged but they did not need to be. He knew a place where we could go. Did I want to go there with him? I felt as if electricity was coursing through my blood. I did not think of his wife, my age, our families. I could see only him. "Yes," I replied. "I want to be with you."*'

I stopped reading and stood up from the kitchen table. I did not want to go on. I knew what was coming, the inevitability of what she would next reveal. I walked around the kitchen, prodding canisters of rice and tea bags and coffee into alignment, replacing a dried cup on the mug tree. I stared back at the journal and saw once more Yuko bent over its pages, writing because she must. I made myself return to the page.

Their taxi followed a maze of streets down to Chinatown. They passed through a red gate lined with a row of paper lanterns and arrived at an apartment block with a black, crumbling facade. Laundry hung on the balconies above their heads, street hawkers were selling vegetables on blankets on the cobbles and children dressed in little more than rags ran past them. While Sato paid the driver, an old woman emerged from the building. She smiled a toothless grimace and shouted, 'Good to see you, sir. You've been missed.' The woman wore a mustard kimono too small for her frame. 'A nice new friend to visit.' She nodded at Yuko and bared her pink gums in another smile. 'What a pretty thing you are, aren't you?'

Yuko watched Sato deposit a bundle of money in the woman's leathery hand and mutter his thanks. *'Perhaps only then, as the woman with the whites of saliva around her mouth stared at me, did I truly understand what was about to happen.'* Sato held the curtain aside in the doorway. Yuko peered into the dark corridor and then looked at him and he raised his eyebrows. 'Do you want to go inside?' *'I had come this far, despite my nerves, I could not go back now.'* She ducked beneath his arm into a hall grey with age and damp. 'Hot today, eh?' the woman said as they took the stairs to the top floor. Sato led her to the end room on the left. He pulled a key from his trouser pocket, opened the door and indicated for her to enter. Inside was a kitchen with a table and a square bath behind a wooden screen. To the

57

left, someone had opened the paper sliding doors that led to the only other room. A faint smell of lily-of-the-valley hung in the air.

'Jomei pulled out a chair and I sat down. He knelt and asked to check my injury. I did not want him to be a doctor here. "My foot is fine, Jomei." He looked up, a frown on his face, not of anger but perhaps trepidation. I could not stop myself. I touched his face with my fingers, traced a path down his cheek. Still he held back, but I did not. My mouth was upon his and the sweetness of the connection stunned me. He dipped his head away. "Are you sure?" I looked around the room, at the patches of mould and a broken cobweb eddying in some unseen breeze, and then at him. He asked, "Is this what you want?" "Yes, Jomei. Yes, I want you." With those words, he carried me past a stone sink through to the other room. Rays of sunlight slipped through the tears in the drawn blind. A futon lay flat under the closed window and a dresser, with a jug and bowl on the top, stood in one corner next to a long mirror, frosted with age. He called me Cio-Cio-san, his butterfly. I smiled at this. My poet, I said. He laughed gently. Your poet, he replied. Then he lay me down and started to undo my yukata.'

I did not need to read about what he showed her in that room. I knew how intoxicating the physical contract they made that day must have seemed to one so young. She ended her entry that day on August 22 with this question and answer: 'Is this love? It must be.'

Such an easy, sloppy word to use, love, especially when you are sixteen. I had known the sharpness of that feeling when I was young, and as I read her diary all those years later, I realised I envied Yuko this moment. How despicable to be jealous of my dead daughter. I hated myself for this but I despised Sato more for such a selfish deed.

58

His sense of entitlement and ownership of her infuriated me. He did not look beyond the present, at least not in those days. He thought only of his immediate pleasure. He would have given no consideration to the repercussions of that first afternoon in Chinatown. I was sure for him the discovery of Hideo was just another careless act of possession to satisfy his needs.

Shame

Haji: In her book The Chrysanthemum and the Sword, *Ruth Benedict says that the Japanese live in a typical shame culture, which demands external sanctions for an individual's good behaviour. Some people stress, however, that the Japanese have internal behavioural standards and a deep sense of conscience regarding personal conduct whether or not exposed to public scrutiny.*

I thought of the man's invitation to visit him at his hotel. What would be the point of going to see this stranger? What good could come of talking about pikadon? Who wanted to think back on what the city had been and what it had become in the aftermath? Those shacks filled with the silent homeless, the US soldiers handing out bubblegum to the children, the patch of wild ginger that appeared one day in a field of scorched earth. Truth be told, I'm not sure I even wanted a grandson returned from the dead. I had so little time left. All those lost years where a relationship might have been established were long gone. Now the thought of a reacquaintance, all the questions and expectations, exhausted me. How could we not fail to disappoint one another? If this man was Hideo he would be a living reminder of all I had tried to forget by moving to America, by finding solace in the numbing welcome of alcohol. My weakness for liquor had embarrassed Kenzo, even if we mostly managed to keep my habits hidden from the outside world. I would often not remember the 'bad episodes' as my husband called them. Waking up in bed, unsure how I had ended up there, I would wait for his too gentle remonstrance as he brought me tea. 'Why would you hurt yourself like this?' or a harder question to answer, 'Isn't my love good enough?' The spells had become worse over the years since his death, despite my promises to him when he was in hospital to 'keep healthy'. I went to the kitchen and poured myself a whiskey with a drop of water.

I walked through to the bedroom and slid open the cabinet drawer, retrieving two photograph albums. I took them to the kitchen and reached for the top one, the cream silk cover stained with brown circles of damp. Our life in pictures began on our wedding day. Kenzo looked impeccable in his dark ceremonial kimono, the black haori robe with the family crest, the undercoat belted with a white knot, the black-and-white-striped hakama that fell like trousers with seven stiff pleats, and finally his wooden zori on feet encased in white toe socks. My wedding kimono was made of white damask silk with peacocks woven on the fabric. The white represented my death as a daughter, my rebirth as a wife. I could be painted any colour my new family wanted. The long sleeves of the kimono would be the last I would wear as an unmarried woman. My hair was coiled in dark waves on either side of my face. A wide white hood covered my head to hide any horns of jealousy I might have before beginning this new life with openness and obedience. My face was thick with powder, my lips stained with safflower. In the black-and-white picture, Kenzo is distracted by something but my gaze is dead centre. The ceremony had been a small one, the guest list composed of his mother, his spinster sister, a couple of his colleagues and their wives and three university friends. The blessings when they came from the guests were effusive toward my new husband, politely reserved toward me. No one really understood where I had come from. As they ate trays of white and red rice cakes, I could hear the whispers, the glances. Kenzo had been reluctant to lie about my lack of celebrants but he agreed to tell the story of an old aunt who had raised me but was too ill to travel. One other face was missing. The groom's friends could not understand why Jomei Sato had not been invited.

As I turned the album's pages, passing through the years, I sipped from my glass. There were pictures of our home, secured by Kenzo's job at Mitsubishi; Yuko as a baby, then as a child, and later she stood in her own wedding dress. Extraordinary how similar we looked. Kenzo had called us his cherry blossoms, but Yuko's beauty was softer than mine. I rose up, already unsteady on my feet from the whiskey. I walked to the hallway and switched on a lamp next to the telephone. The mirror above the oval table reflected an old woman back to me, loose skin around my neck, a neat grey bob, lines where dimples had been.

When younger, my hair had been sleek and long, worn high in buns or knots. When I moved to America, the extravagant styles and heavy make-up, those kohl eyebrows, they all seemed an affectation of a life that no longer existed. In the streets people would stare at me when all I wanted to be was invisible. I began to strip myself of adornments: first jewellery; then the powder on my face; next I dressed in the plainest of Western clothes, until finally one morning while Kenzo was at work, I took a pair of scissors to my hair, hacking off chunks with an elation I did not understand. My poor husband had tried his best to hide his alarm when he returned home. 'What have you done?' I told him I was too old for such vanity, I needed a more practical style. I patted one side, spoke in English. 'You think I look ugly?' He walked up to me and gave me a hug. 'Never. It's just unexpected . . . but modern, very fashionable, I'm sure. You look like a proper American.' Not quite. Fewer people looked my way but I never managed to disappear into the crowd.

The second album was full of pictures of Hideo, some taken by us, but many rescued from his parents' home. My grandson in the park, at the beach in swimming trunks, dressed in a dragon costume, sitting on Yuko's lap as they shared some smile caught by the camera. I stopped at one image of him standing outside Yamazato school, his cheeks so chubby despite the scarcity of food, that mop of hair, the bento box held in one hand, and in his other, a kite. I removed the picture from the triangles that secured each corner and read the caption written by Yuko: *Hideo insists on taking his kite to school, April 11, 1945.* The rest of the album was empty. We had other pictures taken in America but they were kept in another book, gathering dust for a different reason. Kenzo and I smiled in these snapshots of holidays taken in New York, or Niagara Falls, or cabins by lakes, but the cheeriness seemed too forced. The canvas was too wide, the cast of characters too few.

Blue shadows crept across the room and I realised it was already late afternoon. I had not eaten all day, another promise to my husband that I was failing to keep. Kenzo had told me as he lay in his hospital bed, his arm bruised purple and swollen from an infection caught during his dialysis, 'Remember to eat. When I'm gone –'

I'd interrupted him, furious with his acknowledgement of what was coming. 'You're not going anywhere, you're here and soon you'll be back home.'

He watched me smooth down his bedcover. 'It's time to face up to the possibilities.' I begged him to stop talking this way and he took hold of my hand with his good arm. 'Just promise me, Amaterasu, you won't lock yourself away. I lie here at night and worry about you.' I frowned, reminded him he was the one we should be concerned about. 'Promise me, you'll try your best.' His eyes filled with tears. 'I don't want you sitting in that house, just staring at the walls.'

I looked down at the bed as he wiped his face. 'I promise you, Kenzo. I'll try to be a good neighbour.' I kissed his cheek, tissue soft but smooth despite the years, ran my hand through his still thick, if white, hair. 'I love you, husband.'

He closed his eyes, exhausted. 'I know you do.'

When he died, a line of women came to my door with kind words and meals in Tupperware. Kenzo had been popular, charming and involved. These women invited me on shopping trips and to keep-fit classes. I had tried to keep the promise. I went to bake sales with them and could only taste the Portuguese sponge cakes Hideo had loved in Nagasaki. I sat in saunas at the leisure centre and tried to follow their chatter but it only reminded me of the bathhouses I had loved in Japan. I knew how to fake contentment and so I managed to smile if people said hello and asked how I was doing. I held on to the word 'good' like an anchor and gave an impression of being busy. I was their project for a while, a curiosity, but when I declined an invitation, I saw the relief on their faces. I was a burden in their company and after enough months had passed we seemed to reach an unspoken, mutual agreement to stop the pretence of friendship. I felt disloyal to Kenzo, but I did not imagine him in some heaven shaking his head in frustration. In my world, there was no afterlife.

All those days since spent alone had heightened my senses, made me attuned to the slightest change in my environment, and so when the security light outside my house clicked on, I knew no cat or passing dog walker had triggered the switch. I waited and then the bell rang, two shrill bursts in the hallway.

Cultural Deviation

Kiza: Particular types of deviations from the prevalent norm of behaviour sometimes irritate certain kinds of people and are called kiza (mind-disturbing). It is especially so when an act of deviation is perceived as the outcome of an effort to imitate patterns of another culture that is seen as higher than that of the community. This evaluation seems to apply most conspicuously to persons who are perceived to be obsequiously following Western patterns of behaviour.

'I apologise again. Two visits in a day, I realise, is . . .' He shook his head. 'I didn't handle the situation well earlier. I'm not sure how you deliver news like that?' He shivered in the cold. 'I didn't realise how chilly it would be, stupid really, unprepared.' He blew into his hands. 'I promise I mean you no harm, but can I come in? Just for a moment.' The whiskey was sour on my breath. I wondered if he could smell the alcohol. Maybe he would think it natural that I would dull the shock with a tipple? I needed to be careful; although my courage was reinforced, my judgement would be impaired. He pointed at the briefcase by his feet. 'I have a parcel I promised to deliver to you. Then I'll go.' His voice sounded kind enough. There was a warmth to the intonation, despite the stiffness of its delivery.

'From Natsu Sato?' He nodded. 'She adopted you, she said in the letter.'

'She did. She was a good mother to me.'

I looked beyond his shoulder to the tarmac street peppered with orbs of yellow from lamp posts. I could see no waiting taxi or rental vehicle. Curiosity and loneliness are terrible accomplices. 'Please come in.' I prepared a small lie. 'I have plans later so I'm afraid we can't talk for long.' I took care to avoid slurring my words. He stepped into the hall, saw the light in the kitchen and moved toward the glow. In a panic I realised he would see the bottle I had left on the table. 'No, not that way, let's talk in the living room.' I closed the door and pointed to the black rectangle that marked its entrance. 'The switch is on the left. One minute.' I walked to the bedroom, my stiff joints giving me the wide-hipped gait of a gunslinger. I pulled open the bedside cabinet drawer, where I kept a comb and breath mints. I freshened up and returned down the hall. He stood illuminated in his dark suit below the frosted glass and brass fittings of the ceiling lamp. His back was to me as he studied the contents of twelve identical black frames divided into three rows on the opposite wall. Kenzo had spent hours measuring out the gaps between the pictures with a ruler, pencil and spirit level. Here were more images of Nagasaki, of the family we had been. The photographs were our only homage to Japan among the Western furniture. The man glanced back and seemed too big for our room of moss-green walls, cream curtains, beige couch and pine coffee table.

'These pictures are wonderful.'

I walked up to his side and pointed at one. 'The botanical gardens at Nomozaki.' He nodded as he looked at

Kenzo and me with Hideo and Yuko, all dressed in summer yukatas, standing by a pond rippled with feeding koi, a picnic laid out on the grass. 'And this is Shige, not long before he was shipped out.'

'He looks good in the uniform.'

I said nothing. Shige had been reticent about his war service but duty-bound to perform it.

'Please sit down.' I indicated for him to take the couch beneath the pictures. I switched on a lamp beside him and turned off the overhead bulb, which fell too harshly on those ridges of discoloured flesh and keloids. 'Can I get you anything? Tea, or something else?'

'Perhaps in a minute. I didn't know if this would be convenient? I should have called. I'm just so glad to be here. You must have so many questions?'

A beat before I replied, 'And you too?' He seemed to hunch into himself at this, his enthusiasm checked, and there was a stab to my gut, of what? Some half-remembered emotion I didn't care to identify. I confess the gesture reminded me of my Hideo, so self-conscious, but I would not be so easily swayed. My next words were difficult to say and so I spoke them softly. 'I think you should know, I went to my grandson's school that morning. I saw the bodies.'

He lowered his head, the way a shy person does, and this too was Hideo, perhaps, a hint of the man he might have become. 'I know the statistics.'

'We searched for so long. If we had thought for one minute Hideo had survived, we'd never have stopped looking.'

'I understand. I'm sure you did everything you could.

Your doubts are natural. Can I show you something?'
He reached into his inside jacket pocket and pulled out
his passport. I opened the document at the page with his
personal details. Here was Hideo Sato, a teacher, born
February 22, 1938. The birth date was correct but that
didn't make it right. I ran my finger over his photograph,
the scars exposed under the flash of the photo booth. He
wanted to know who he was. Maybe this man thought
his request an easy one.

I handed the passport back to him. 'Hideo is dead. I'm
sorry.'

He said nothing for a while and I could not tell if he
was angry. Then he reached down for his briefcase, placed
it on the couch cushion next to him and retrieved a brown
parcel. The A4 envelope had been handled with care, the
folds uncreased, the seal unbroken. He placed the package
on the coffee table.

'She asked that the parcel should be given only to you.
I've not seen what's inside. I'm intrigued, of course, but
the instructions were you should read the contents first.
I'm guessing it may be documents that Father collected,
adoption papers, but I don't know.'

'Father?'

'Jomei. Kenzo and Father were good friends, I understand?'

Is that what the doctor had told him? It wasn't so far
from the truth. 'When they were younger, yes.'

What had Sato been up to all these years, what false
memories had he created, how had he found this Hideo
in an orphanage? But what I most wanted to know was:
is that bastard still alive? Instead I offered my visitor a

69

drink. 'Would you like that tea now, or I have something stronger?'

'Actually, if you're offering, something stronger would be good.'

'Did you come all this way to America just to see me?' He said yes. 'How did you find me?'

'I used a private detective. You'd be surprised how many people go missing, there are agencies to help you find them.'

'I see. So when did you find me?'

'Last year.' He saw me take in this information.

'Why did you wait so long to come?'

He sat back heavy against the couch. 'To be honest, I was scared about what I would find, your reaction, my response. You build the day up in your head, knowing the reality can never be a match to the expectation, good or bad.'

'Am I what you expected?'

He replied with the smallest laugh. 'I don't think either of us are.'

This made me smile. 'So what made you finally get on the plane?'

'A coincidence. I belong to a peace organisation, we speak all over the world, at conferences, schools, summits for non-nuclear proliferation. We raise funds, awareness, lobby for victims. There's a conference here, my group was invited to send a representative, I volunteered.' He dipped his head to the side. 'Sometimes the universe sends you a sign you cannot ignore, wouldn't you say?'

'Would you have come otherwise?'

He exhaled. 'Eventually, I'm sure.'

His own reticence was a relief to me. We shared this mutual caution for a moment and then I levered myself upright. 'I'll bring us some whiskey, Kenzo's favourite. I'll let you think of our toast.'

'That's easy.' He looked back at the photographs behind him. 'To my family.'

Somehow we knew not to talk about Nagasaki, not yet. Instead he asked about America. Less concealment was needed about our flight to the West. I explained how Kenzo and I could not stay in the city and live with our loss. We needed to go somewhere so alien and so different that all our energy would be taken up by the strangeness of our new lives. Another part of Japan would not do. We needed unknown terrain, a challenging culture, a language that had not invented words such as pikadon. When the occupation began, some American naval officers came to Kenzo's workplace. He had been chosen to show them around because of his seniority and his basic English skills. During his degree he had spent some time in Scotland, at the Glasgow Nautical College. The accent had nearly defeated him but he remembered enough vocabulary to communicate. When we decided to leave Japan he had spoken with one of these men, who, grateful for Kenzo's help, had arranged through connections a job offer in California. We studied a map. Vallejo, where Mare Island Naval Shipyard was based, was twenty or thirty miles from San Francisco. There were other private shipyards in the state if the naval facility didn't work out, the American said. The paperwork might be tricky but Kenzo's skills were in demand. We held no goodbye parties, made no final pilgrimages, only Misaki was there to wave us off at the train station on July 19, 1946.

As soon as we docked at San Francisco I felt overwhelmed by the size of everything: the roads, the cars, the flat-roofed diners, the people, but I was glad of the unremitting assault on my senses. Horns beeped, newspaper vendors shouted, radios blared. Bosses at the shipyard had found us a home and sent us a picture of a white wooden house with two bedrooms, a patch of grass at the front. We hired a black Chevrolet and drove to Vallejo. We stopped to look around by the ferry terminal, its blue roof shaped like a circus top, and I knew we had made a terrible mistake. Even in this new continent, the past followed us. The yellow and blue houses built on the hills overlooking the water reminded me of those that had perched on the inclines of Nagasaki. I could not tell Kenzo this but as the days passed to weeks and then months, I couldn't hide my unhappiness. He thought my struggles were with the culture. Yes, even a simple trip to the shop was a trial. I would stare for minutes at shampoos or cans and wonder what they contained if no picture gave a clue. I'd count out coins in my purse while trying to understand what price the shop teller had said. I didn't mind these inconveniences or embarrassments. They filled my mind and my days. No, it was Vallejo itself. When I finally confessed the real reason, he shook his head, exasperated. 'The hills and the Pacific? That's what you object to? Have you any idea how big that ocean is?' What a burden I was, but I couldn't stand the connection. This town and Nagasaki were joined by that water. The Pacific might as well have been a puddle.

Kenzo began to look for another job and heard of one at the Philadelphia Naval Shipyard. His reputation and his talent outweighed any concern about his nationality. He brought out a new map, found Pennsylvania and traced with his finger the confluence of the Schuylkill and Delaware rivers. 'See, the Atlantic.' I smiled. 'Thank you. I like the look of this place.' He laughed, 'What, just from the map?' I nodded. 'This will be good for us.' But pikadon followed us wherever we went. Years later, I learned laboratories at the yard had been used to help develop the bomb. Thankfully Kenzo was dead and saved from this mocking fact – unless he had known and chose not to tell me. We found a small townhouse nearby and by December 1947 we had begun the next chapter in our American story. If you could overlook our country of birth, we were typical in the Buick car we drove, the electrical appliances we bought, the cocktail hours we indulged in. But for some of our neighbours we would always be the enemy, especially those whose sons or uncles or co-workers had not returned home from the Asian jungles, French villages, or our shared ocean. Kenzo ignored the muttered comments, the blatant racism. America had given us a second chance and he was grateful. 'This is a meritocracy,' he declared. 'Rewards come to those who work hard, we can live the life we deserve.'

I smiled at this memory and my guest.

'Did the culture shock get better with time?'

I filled my glass, the alcohol freeing my reserve. 'To be honest, we learned how to behave through the movies. We'd go every week, Saturday matinees, mostly. Kenzo loved those films, he'd watch anything: musicals, westerns, romances, Doris Day, Hitchcock, Bob Hope. He hoped my seeing them would improve my vocabulary.' I paused, just briefly, realising despite the circumstances how good it felt to speak Japanese again. 'One day we went to see *Invasion of the Body Snatchers*. Have you seen it?' He shook his head. 'It's ludicrous. There's a small town, where aliens grow from seeds into exact replicas of the residents. These impostors look like the townsfolk but they have no emotions, you see?' He laughed, said he liked the sound of the plot. 'Kenzo was so taken by this film. He felt that we should be like the aliens. All we needed to do was assimilate into our new world.' I laughed, self-conscious. 'Let's just say, we learned to act American even if our emotions were always a bit off.'

'I have not expressed my sorrow at your loss. I hope he didn't suffer.'

I looked up at the picture of Kenzo in the park. How to explain a death after the event? How to condense the months of suffering into a few minutes? He had been such an active man, always on the go. I think he might have hidden how unwell he felt for a long time but the symptoms were too severe to hide: back pain, vomiting, fever. His kidneys were failing him. He spent three months in hospital as doctors, initially confident of his recovery, began to talk of end-of-life options. In the last days, his body raged with thirst. He became confused and frightened, then delirious talking to me as if I was his mother and not his wife. The chatter quietened and he took the shallowest of breaths, his eyes closed, as if he was enjoying an afternoon nap. I thought he might just drift off, but at the end, he managed somehow to turn back to life, for one final glimpse. I felt his gaze upon me as I sat next to his bed. We looked at each other, but I don't know if he saw me. He said nothing and I recognised in the blackness of his pupils that some other presence or thought had caught his attention. It seemed he knew death was there, in the room, and he was helpless in its shadow. I shouted his name to let him know he was not alone. He took one last gasp, and then he was gone.

I looked at my guest. 'Did your private detective tell you the date of his death?'

He nodded. Three days before August 9. Life's cruel calendar. We sat in silence, the whiskey low in the bottle, until my visitor roused himself. 'You said you had plans? I should go.' He pointed at the package. 'I hope what you find is not too distressing.' He placed his glass on the table and rose to his feet. I did the same.

'I'm sorry for my doubt. You seem so sure.'

'I have no definitive proof, no, but this is what I've been told and what I believe: my name is Hideo Sato, birth name, Watanabe. I was born in Nagasaki. I am forty-six years old. I am your grandson. I can only hope the package confirms this.'

'And if it doesn't?'

'Then you never have to see or think of me again.'

Problem Solving

Haragei: The term is a compound of hara (belly) and gei (art). Literally, it means belly-art. Most dictionaries define it as the verbal or non-verbal act one utilises to influence others by drawing upon one's power of accumulated experience in an attempt to solve a mutual problem. Haragei will enable people to reach mutual understanding without confrontation.

My daughter had shown skills as an artist from a young age. Perhaps she inherited the technical flair from Kenzo and maybe the love of colour and shape from me. Who knows how talent forms? Maybe she was only good because she practised. When aged no more than five or six, she would sit with paper at our table and ask me to draw a picture that she would attempt to copy. My efforts were clumsy but I would try my best to re-create a horse or a crane or a carp. Rubbing her nose, or singing away, she would choose a crayon and trace the outline. Soon she did not need my crude attempts to inspire her. Under the shade of our camphor tree, I would make flowers of raw silk for my hair while Yuko drew on fresh sheets of mulberry paper. As the years progressed, she moved on to thick oils and fine inks bought from an art shop not far from our home. She worked with bright colours: greens and reds and yellows, which she transformed into scenes from Nagasaki, our home and me in my brightest kimonos. Not long after her fifteenth birthday, we passed a print shop displaying old etchings of foreign sailors unloading goods and geishas strolling next to them under parasols. Yuko said she wished she had that kind of talent and I assured her she did. Shy suddenly, she said Himura, her art teacher, had said she would benefit from formal training, an apprenticeship, perhaps. 'Would that be possible?' She looked hopeful, flushed at the thought. Kenzo and I had discussed the matter and resolved to wait a year, to see if her interest remained. Lately, she had not been drawing as much and so I presumed the apprenticeship had only been a passing fancy. I did not realise she was still sketching, only these were images she could not show me. I found out why on October 16, 1936.

The church bells had chimed seven times when Yuko ran into the house. She said she had been taking tea at her friend Miho's house and had lost track of the time. I watched her bound upstairs, saying she would change before dinner. I noticed she had left her bag by the front door, and poking out, just an inch or two, was her sketchbook. I was pleased and instinctively reached for it. She had always shown me her work, keen for approval or gentle critique, and so there was no reason for me to think I was invading her privacy. As I turned the pages, sand drifted from the creases and fell to the floor. I saw the sea and a diving platform, rocks by a coppice, a man holding a bucket as he made his way down a path by the beach, two children playing in a field, dragonflies, sketched in detail, and then I reached the picture of a man in swimming trunks, reclining on a towel, asleep. *Iōjima, August 22, 1936.*

I will never forget the agony of that discovery, the sickness in my stomach, the rage and the confusion. How did they know one another? How had they met? And as I stared at that face, that body, the anger turned to dread as one more ugly question formed in my mind: what had he done to my daughter? The thought of that moment in the hall still stops me dead in my tracks, whatever I am doing. Every cell in my body wanted to climb those stairs and confront Yuko. I wanted to hit the truth from her, beat Sato from our lives. Had he done this on purpose? Had he sought her out? Why? What was she to him? I could think of no reasonable explanation. Thoughts came at me like the wind in a typhoon, uncontrollable, rising up and then falling away. This was not her fault, I told myself. Whatever had happened, Sato would be to blame.

I could hear Yuko upstairs, singing some folk song. Why had I not been more curious about all those missing hours? Why had I not noticed the bored lethargy that overcame her in the morning followed by the rush of activity come the changing light of afternoon. So transparent in hindsight the reason for her red cheeks as she ran to the mirror to brush her hair, the show of vanity, a new and disconcerting trait, lips ready to impart the explanation for another sudden departure.

What could I do to keep my daughter safe? She had been led astray but she was a loyal daughter corrupted only by this outside force. Sato had to be stopped. He must be stripped of his power, of his control over her. I would wipe him from our lives. This was my duty as a mother. I still try to believe all that followed I did only for her and no other reason, but who knows? Perhaps it is too easy to paint vile actions with the gilded hue of noble intent. I tore the drawing from the sketchbook, and sat there, waiting in the dark for Kenzo to return. I had no hesitation about telling my husband. He needed to know. As I had done he would want to act immediately and I would have to persuade him of the need for patience.

I only had to wait twenty minutes before he walked into the room. He had been working long hours and was always tired. The navy had grown to a formidable size since the turn of the century. Vessels once built abroad were now assembled at domestic shipyards. Japan had become bold, ignoring naval restrictions, snubbing negotiations with the West, expanding its territories. The country's interest in mainland Asia had strained its relationship with other world powers and divided the military at home. Maybe Kenzo already knew what was on our nation's horizon, the blood coming in the dawn. He looked at me kneeling by the table, the sketch in front of me. 'Why are you sitting in the dark?' He clicked on a light. 'Amaterasu, what's wrong?' He sat down next to me, picked up the piece of paper. 'What is this? Did Yuko draw it?' I felt the rage return. 'Why do you have this? This is Sato.'

'I found it in Yuko's bag. I don't understand. How do they know one another?' His silence betrayed him. 'You? You introduced them? Why, Kenzo? Why would you do such a thing?'

He shook his head in disbelief. 'I met him in the street by chance. We had a drink. We talked. We had another drink, and another. It was good to see him. I had forgotten how much I enjoyed his company. So much time had passed, it seemed harmless.'

'What did you talk about?'

'Work, friends from university, I don't know, golf.'

'And Yuko?'

'She wasn't sleeping, remember. She wasn't eating. I mentioned we were worried about her. He told me to send her along for an examination.'

The question tore from me. 'Why? You know what he's like. You know his tastes.'

'The picture means nothing. There will be an explanation.'

'Kenzo, must you make me say it? Don't you see what this is?'

He shook his head. 'There will be a reason.'

'The reason is obvious.'

Kenzo pushed the drawing away and clasped his head in his hands. He looked up, as if remembering he should be angry at this offence. 'Where is she?'

'In her room.'

'This must stop now.' He growled the words and began to stand up.

I reached for his hand to stop him. 'Wait.'

'What? We must tell her we know this minute. Send her away. To my sister. Fukuoka.'

'And Sato?' He said nothing. 'You would let him go unpunished?'

'Of course not. I will speak to him.'

'Speak?'

He bristled. 'What would you have me do?'

'We must make her realise what he has done here. We need to make her look beyond the fantasy she is caught up in. She needs to see what this means to us, to Sato's wife, to our friends, your colleagues, the city gossips.

Otherwise we'll lose her. She'll blame us when we drive them apart. She'll crawl back to him somehow. He'll win. We'll be the enemy.' I thought of all the lies I had told people over the years, the ones I had needed to tell and the ones that had fallen easily from my lips; fictions Kenzo was content to facilitate if it meant I would be his. 'Sato must force their separation, not us.'

'But we cannot let him —'

'This will be over, soon. Trust me. The damage is done. We'll go to a matchmaker, find a husband, the way we had planned if she'd decided against the apprenticeship.'

He rubbed his forehead. 'I can't sit here and pretend I know nothing. I can't stand the thought of him touching her.'

I took his hand. 'We can do this. We must be patient.'

'How can we let it go on?'

'Kenzo, this is why. What if she thinks she loves him?' He could not answer and I folded the picture up. 'Have dinner somewhere else tonight. Try not to drink too much. We'll fix this. Trust me. Go now.'

When Yuko came down to dinner I said her father had been detained at work. I studied her as we ate. My quiet child had flowered since that summer without us, until that day, understanding why. She was winter blossom burst from the chilled bud, delicate and yet defiant. Why had I not seen this? I should have been more watchful, more careful. She smiled at me as we picked at our food, recounted some tale about a friend, which must have been a lie. She frowned when I did not respond. 'Are you well, Mother?'

I managed to smile. 'There have been so many lunches and charity meetings, I feel I've been neglecting you.'

'No, not at all. Don't feel bad. I've enjoyed this summer. I feel . . .'

'Yes?'

She blushed as she replied. 'Alive.'

Maybe Yuko, eventually, would have realised how Sato had used her for her youth, for her convenience, for her beauty. Maybe she would have learned she was not his first infidelity, perhaps not even his youngest. He would have thrown her away as he had so many others before her. But my regret is this: maybe if I hadn't tried to prise them apart so forcefully and suddenly then perhaps she would have had time to appreciate his weaknesses; she would have broken away from him naturally, and yes, just maybe, if that had happened, she would have lived.

Moral Indebtedness

On: People incur social and psychological indebtedness upon receiving a favour from those in superior positions. The concept of *on* derived from Chinese philosophy and Japanese feudal society. The samurai warrior fulfilled his obligations to his lord in battle, risking his life if necessary. Sons and daughters exercise acts of *ko* (filial piety) and take care of their ageing parents. Human relations are bound by a complicated network of mutual responsibilities and obligations.

Kenzo and I only had to wait two days before Yuko betrayed herself. She put on her sandals, an excuse light on her lips and said goodbye. The slim rectangle of her grey kimono dipped out of sight of the garden before I followed her down the hill. Under the canopy of a butcher's shop I watched her step inside a street car. I signalled for a taxi and told the driver I would pay him extra for an unusual errand. The city passed by in streaks of colour, dappled by sun, illuminated in shadow. Down through the centre, past Chinatown into a street of noise, trade and poverty; this is where Yuko went. She walked past stalls selling baked squid, buttered peanuts and fried wasabi peas and disappeared into a building between a noodle bar and a cycle-repair shop. That he would take her to this corner of Nagasaki where children ran naked and toothless women long since sent packing from the brothels of Maruyama sold trinkets or themselves. That he would treat her like one of the city's whores. I vowed Sato would pay for this.

The driver stopped outside the building and I asked him to wait. I called out and an old woman appeared. She seemed amused by my presence. 'Yeah? You lost?' I tried to peer into the gloom of the hall. 'I'm looking for a girl.' She laughed. 'Any particular kind?' She shouted behind her and a man appeared, bare-chested, a phoenix tattooed across his chest and arms. 'Makito, who's around at the moment?' I opened my purse, a drawstring silk bag. 'I'm not buying. I just need to know where the girl in the grey kimono goes.' She looked at the money in my hand. 'The room number, that's all I want.' She gestured and the man disappeared. 'You're not going to cause us any trouble, are you?' I told her no. I just needed information then I would go. She looked me over. 'The wives normally don't want to know. Apartment 15.'

I told the driver to take me to Mitsubishi, and the smells and calls of the traders collecting excrement for the hillside farmers gave way to the stench of metallic smoke that belched from the brick factories of Kenzo's workplace. The receptionist cast curious glances at me when I delivered my note to Kenzo. My husband and I made an odd pair to many. They did not see what I loved in him and they could never know what he saw in me. I wrote the directions to Yuko's location and under the address I added, 'Bring my daughter home.' I handed the girl the message and left.

When Kenzo returned with Yuko an hour or so later she ran to her room, eyes bloodied with tears. He went to the cabinet and poured a drink. He walked to the window, kept his back to me. His voice was flat, as if it came from a place where emotion had been drugged. He said he had done what I had told him to do. He hadn't knocked, he hadn't politely waited, he had entered the room unannounced, he had found them together as planned. He paused and took a drink. 'While I waited for Sato to dress, there was an empty bottle of sake on the windowsill. I thought when he came through from the bedroom I could break the glass, drive that bottle into his neck, hurt him. That's what a father should do for this affront, yes? But I couldn't. What kind of man does this make me?' I told him Sato was the moral coward, not us. Why should Kenzo punish himself when the doctor was the one in the wrong? He shook his head. 'We did a bad deed today, wife. How can Yuko and I be the same again? How can this family be the same again?'

I went to him and put my hand on his shoulder. 'All pain passes, eventually. We'll get through this moment. We'll be a proper family again. What we did, we needed to do. I'm sorry for the hurt it caused, but I'm not sorry for the outcome. Did he agree to our demands?'

Kenzo nodded yes, finished his drink and said he should get back to the office. I watched him leave and made my way to Yuko's room. She was sitting on a window seat, her body twisted away, statue-still. 'I don't want to talk, Mother.' I knelt down by her feet. 'I must tell you this then I'll go.' I told her the arrangement made between her father and Sato had been one of mutual understanding. I told her the doctor had been in agreement. He wanted to safeguard his marriage and reputation; Kenzo and I wanted to protect her from the scandal. There must be no more contact, none. He had promised to leave the city. She looked at me then, anger and hate in her eyes. This I could stand as long as she was safe. I continued speaking. The arrangement suited everyone. In time, she would see this. Any disgrace for the family had been contained. We did what we had to do. 'How did you find out?' I reached for her hand and she flinched. 'The drawing, Yuko.' She started to cry and begged me to leave her alone. So I did.

We all tried to erase that afternoon from our memories, but the humiliation burned longest for Yuko and her father, perhaps indelibly. I believed Yuko and Sato's abasement was necessary. I needed Kenzo to see what kind of man his former friend was. He needed to witness the depravity of the doctor, and what better way than to put the evidence in front of his eyes? Yuko must be ripped from Sato. How else could we drive him away if any one of us clung to some romantic notion of him? All these years later, I dared not face what Yuko had written about the day but this cowardice forced me back to the page.

'I cannot stand the thought of Father standing there in the doorway. He could not look at me, only Jomei. He stared at him with an expression of bewilderment and fury. I tell myself he saw only a brief sketch of us, just the outlines of our bodies. I tell myself he could not colour in the detail, the shadowed limbs, the tensed muscles, the texture and contrast of hair against skin. I tell myself he saw none of this. How else could I look at him again? Father said nothing. He just slid the doors behind him and waited in the other room. Jomei began to dress and told me not to be scared, we had done nothing wrong, but whatever happened, he would take the blame. His last words were: "Cio-Cio-san, I won't let you go."

'He went through to the kitchen to speak with Father while I picked up my clothes. By the time I found the courage to join them, Father was alone, sitting at the table. I sat down opposite him and slid my hand across the surface until my fingers were an inch from the tips of his own. He moved his hand onto his lap. I wanted to beg his forgiveness but I just sat there paralysed by my shame. He stood up and walked to the door. I could not move. "Father, I love him." He turned away from me and I realised he was crying. "Well then, you are a fool, and a child." I started to cry too. "I'm not a child. He loves me too." He wiped his tears from his eyes. "Oh, Yuko. No he doesn't. If he did, he'd still be here." He opened the door. "Let's go home. We shall speak no more of this." I wanted to run after Jomei, call him back, make him tell Father the truth. I looked for him outside in the street. Father had to be wrong. Jomei had to be there. But he was not. I will never recover from the loss of him. His death could not cause me more agony.'

The end of a first love is operatic in its drama, physical in its showing. I could stand her tears and silence, her withdrawal from us; I could bear watching my daughter too unwell to eat or sleep or talk. This had to be done. I was saving her from Sato. She could never know why. And this too I could stand. I believed she would heal well enough, given time. Perhaps if I had remembered the anguish of my own early years, perhaps if I had been gentler with her, the intoxication of Sato would not have lasted so long.

'I am trapped in a perpetual present, the past torn from me. If the hours pass, I do not feel them. If days surrender to nights, I do not see the changing colours of the sky. Time is a prison. Caged in the house, I slither around like a snake, soaking up no heat from a cold winter sun. Father cannot speak to me, Mother can only look on me as if I am something foul that has polluted the home. That plans are afoot, I am sure, given the whispered conversations behind doors, the accusatory looks, the family dinners eaten in silence. I retreat to my room and torture myself with the possibilities. Where is Jomei? Is he out there somewhere among the streets, or bars, or maybe he is home with Natsu or working late at the hospital? Such thoughts provoke a retching that shudders through my body. "I won't let you go," he said. But he has.'

All friends were banished from the house, all excursions forbidden. Only Misaki acknowledged Yuko's existence. She would leave cake outside her door or put fresh flowers in her room. 'Mrs Goto appeared in the hall today, took my hands in her own. "How are you?" I did not know what to say. She squeezed my fingers. "I remember you as a child, so inquisitive. You would stare at, I don't know, a leaf, an insect, a crack in the soil, for hours. I never knew what you saw, but you were so fascinated." She laid one of my hands on her breast. "Feel my heart beat. Feel it? Blood keeps the heart beating, not love. Do you understand? We make do, child. That is all we can do. We make do." But how am I to make do? I cannot, I will not. I must meet Jomei again. What is the point of living without him?'

An Arranged Marriage

Miai-kekkon: Until the end of the Second World War, most marriages were arranged. Nakodo (a go-between) helps with the exchanges of information between the two families. It is customary for the man to send gifts (usually an engagement ring and some money) to the woman, when his proposal is accepted. This engagement ceremony is called yuino.

My enquiries were discreet but I knew word would soon spread that we were looking for a husband for Yuko. Mrs Kogi was the most highly recommended of Nagasaki's matchmakers. Her network of contacts was extensive. She made good matches and fast. I studied her as she consulted her notebook. She wore a black kimono and her hair was drawn in a tight bun high on her head. Round tortoiseshell glasses sat low on her nose and the smell of mothballs lingered on her skin. She assumed the guise of a widow with little care for personal vanity. The only suggestion of frivolity was the eyebrows she shaved off and painted too high on her forehead. Yuko sat opposite me, next to the matchmaker. A teapot and three red pottery cups decorated the low table in front of us. A beam of sun from the window fell across the room to our incense holder. I wanted to light the sweet musk to mask the odour of this woman Sato had forced into our home. She listened to me with her head bent to the side, a picture of sincere concern.

'The matter is rather pressing, Mrs Kogi. My husband stresses that while we don't want to lower our expected standards, we are happy to look beyond what would be the more obvious candidates.'

'Of course, of course,' she said. 'I understand.' She whispered thank you when I offered her more tea. 'I do have one young man who might prove suitable.'

'From a Nagasaki family?

'One of the islands, Iōjima.'

I saw Yuko's face pale. 'I'm not sure whether –'

Mrs Kogi placed a fluttering hand on the locket that fell across her flat bust.

'Yuko, dearest, have I told you about my husband?' Yuko said nothing and Mrs Kogi giggled.

'My Manabu, so handsome in his youth, clever too, and strong. Here, take a look.' She opened the locket and showed a photograph of her husband, dead five years. A fierce man with a large brow and long chin stared back. 'Manabu was an island man. Our deputy mayor is an island man. The assistant police chief is an island man.'

I could only guess Mrs Kogi created the facts to suit the business at hand. 'I meant no disrespect.'

'I apologise, Mrs Takahashi, that indeed is not what I inferred. Only this young man is quite remarkable. These island men have nothing of the flightiness of the urban male. He's just finished his engineering degree and has secured a position at Mitsubishi Mining. A good, strong character. Quiet, not showy. Solid, like my Manabu.'

'And his name?'

'Shige Watanabe.'

'A picture?'

'I'm afraid Mr Watanabe is only a new acquaintance and he has yet to provide me with a photograph but I assure you he has a good, honest, solid face.'

That word again. Solid. I imagined a giant cabbage embellished with a pair of spectacles.

'And his father?'

Mrs Kogi stroked the locket. 'His mother is a member of the Kawano family, the printmakers down by Dejima.'

I knew the Kawano shop. We had prints in the home; Yuko had copied them as a child. 'Very good, and the father?'

'A fisherman.' She must have seen my concern. 'A love match, I understand, Mrs Takahashi. They found each other late in life. The mother had made something of a name for herself as an artist. I heard she had been more married to work than marriage itself, despite her apparent beauty. Then she met her husband. I'm told there is money to be made in the harvesting of uni.'

'They eloped?'

'They took a less conventional path to marriage, certainly.'

'And the Kawanos had no objection?'

'The matter was rather taken out of their hands.'

'This is rather shocking, Mrs Kogi. I'm not sure if the association with such scandal would be beneficial.' I saw a smile tickle the matchmaker's lips and I knew she had worked out the transaction at hand; we were looking for a quick sale.

'The matter happened long ago and this little city of ours has produced far more food for the gossips in the intervening years. I can reassure you that Shige Watanabe has none of the impetuousness that his parents might have displayed. He seeks my services, I imagine, to allay such fears. He is an impeccable man, truly.'

'And are there other options available?'

'Always, but I'm sure you'll find Watanabe to be a fine prospect. And given your hopes for a spring wedding . . .' Her voice trailed off and she smiled. 'Would you prefer I look elsewhere?'

'He is perhaps not what we had in mind but he does seem a possibility.'

Our conversation completed, I asked Yuko to see Mrs Kogi to a rickshaw. I waited for her return, braced for battle. She sat down opposite me.

'Mother, these arrangements aren't necessary.'

'Your father thinks they are.'

'I can't accept this.'

'You have forced this upon yourself.'

'I don't want to marry this Watanabe.'

'Don't be ridiculous. What? Do you think someone else is ready to stake a claim?'

'They're recruiting at the medical college for nurses.'

'Did he put this in your head, this married doctor? Why stop at a nurse if you are so determined to ruin this family? I hear the brothels of Maruyama are recruiting too.' She lowered her head. 'This man, this doctor of yours, needed a whore, nothing more, and he was too lazy, too arrogant to find one by more regular means. We should all be grateful if this Watanabe, this fisherman's son, agrees to take you.'

'I won't marry him.'

I leaned forward and grabbed her chin. 'You promised your father.' I looked in her eyes and stroked her soft cheek. 'Daughter, why did you let him touch you? If you care for me, your father, this family, you will forget Sato. Be grateful only that this engineer will consider you.'

'I love Jomei, Mother.'

'You think this love? This was not love. Women are not put here to love. The folly of romance. This doctor would have ruined your life. We saved you, Yuko. I ask only one request from my one daughter: consider the engineer. Not for our sakes, Yuko. For yours.'

My words must seem harsh. I wonder now what the alternatives could have been. I think back to the years before 1936 when Yuko talked about wanting to become a printmaker. What if she had become an apprentice immediately? What if we hadn't made her wait that year? How would her life have been? Would she too have run off with a fisherman to some island?

I believed Yuko did not need a profession because marriage would be sufficient and the role of a housewife was an important one. I wanted to save her from having to work because you had no choice, because not to do so meant going hungry. I did not appreciate the satisfaction and use and freedom of a job. I looked only to my own life: an engineer had brought me emotional and financial security. Why couldn't this Shige Watanabe do the same for my daughter? As I read her diary, I realised I had been so preoccupied with my own strategy that I didn't see Yuko had her own.

'I made a mistake telling Mother about the nursing positions. She is even more determined to marry me off, no doubt terrified I'll

somehow find Jomei again. She wants marriage to become my new prison after this one. She tells me again and again that Jomei has left Nagasaki but I do not believe her. Yes, maybe he could leave me, but his work, his life, this city? She wants to kill my hope of a reunion. But if Mother is right, if Jomei never loved me, I need to hear him say this, not her. In his absence, I will believe what he told me. He will come back for me.

'I write him letters but I am never allowed out on my own so I have no way of delivering them. I need an excuse to leave the house. Perhaps the only answer right now is to go along with Mother's plans? Today I told her I would meet this Shige Watanabe. She said they would invite him to the house for dinner but the thought was unbearable. I asked that the meeting happen outside our home. She insisted I take a chaperone. At least, in the city, free to walk the streets, I can believe in the possibility of seeing Jomei once more. There will be a reason he hasn't contacted me.'

Quiet Beauty

Yugen: Elegant simplicity is one of the traditional aesthetic concepts of Japanese poetry and often regarded as a term for ideal beauty pursued particularly by poets and novelists of the medieval times. Later it became a kind of critical term used for discussions of Japanese classical literature. It has now several shades of meaning: the subtle and profound, the simple and elegant, or the tasteful and graceful.

I crouched down on the wooden stool between a woman humpbacked with osteoporosis to my left and Yuko to my right. She had coiled her hair high on her head in a damp, loose knot but tendrils had worked their way free and snaked down her shoulders. Other women, naked and wet, sat in the communal baths as steam sizzled from floor to ceiling in the tiled room. Frosted-glass windows high above our heads depicted green dragons and white cranes flying over autumnal orange ginkyo trees. Mirrors reflected the light from outside onto clouds spewing from the boiler room. I filled a bucket with hot water from a tap in front of us. 'Let me clean your back.'

Yuko slouched forward and I slid the bar of soap along her shoulders and down her spine and began to rub with a rough cotton towel. 'Give me your arm.' Yuko lifted her hand and we intertwined fingers. She closed her eyes and surrendered to my touch. The heat made my head dizzy and my heart pound. 'This reminds me of when you were a baby. You hardly ever cried. It made me worry so much. Aren't babies supposed to cry?' I picked up her other arm and my words caught and rode through the ringing of blood in my ears. 'You were born so prematurely. We thought for weeks we might lose you. Maybe those early fears never left and made me too protective.' She glanced up at me. I had not realised how physically alike we were but our naked bodies differed only by the weight of years. This difference made me sharp with my own vanity. 'You were so reserved as a child. I thought you shy, but it's not shyness at all, is it?'

She replied neutrally, 'Shall I wash your back?'

I thought of those hands on Sato's body. 'No, thank you.' The old woman next to us was cleaning her feet, the only part of her that she could reach with any ease. 'Excuse me, would you like my daughter to help you?'

The woman twisted around. 'Thank you, most kind.' Yuko accepted her offering of a cloth and soap and placed the rag against those domed shoulders. 'No need to be gentle, dear. Scrub away.' I remember the way the old lady sat with her hands on her knees, braced, her toes curled around the edge of the gutter that took the dirty water away. She would probably have been younger than I am today, but she seemed ancient, shrunk by life. Is this what people see when they look at me, this costume of old age: the liver spots, the raised veins and watering eyes?

I washed my legs upwards from ankle to knee and then

thigh. Wisps of air curved around my feet, calves and up to my hip and across my breasts. I shivered against the caress.

Yuko studied me as I reached for more soap. 'You never talk about your childhood.'

Voices from the men bathing in their own section seeped over the gap at the top of the partition that separated us. 'Don't I?'

'No.' She tipped the water from her bucket and turned on the cold tap.

'That's because there is nothing to tell.'

'You never say where you grew up, you never talk about your family or how you and Father met.' Maybe she felt emboldened in this public setting.

I washed between my legs and then rinsed the rag out beside a metal drain, where clumps of hair had gathered. 'I'm getting fat.'

The old woman tutted. 'No, you're not.'

'Believe me, you should have seen me when I was young.' I whistled.

The old woman laughed. 'You should have seen me too. What a body.'

'You still have a good figure,' I said in a chiding tone.

The woman patted the air and giggled. 'Back then, the men, so many, all taking turns to knock at my father's door with gifts and proposals and poems, so many poems. Always some dreadful haiku. He had to beat them away with a broom. It's true.' We all laughed then. Even Yuko. She lifted the strands of the woman's grey hair and washed her neck.

I wondered how many more visits to the bathhouse

I would have with my daughter after we found her a husband. I had always cherished my hours spent at the sentos, especially when her age. I'd come two or three times a week with my friend Karin. We would listen to the women chatter about annoying husbands or disappointing lovers and emerge into the cool air with tingling skin, blanched and renewed. Those visits had done more than clean me. I turned to the old woman. 'My daughter wants me to reveal all the secrets of my youth. Should I tell her, Grandmother?'

She cackled and tried her best to stretch up. 'Secrets are best kept just that. The past is the past is the past. No good can come of raking over those used coals.'

I soaked a fresh cloth in the water from the running tap and squeezed it over my breasts.

'Listen to the wise woman, Yuko. You would do well to follow her advice.'

Yuko handed the soap and rag back to the woman. 'There we go.'

'Thank you, most kind.'

The old woman smiled. 'You forget, don't you?'

'What's that?'

'The comfort of the human hand.'

I placed my palm on the woman's shoulder. 'Celebrate with us, Grandmother. My daughter is meeting a man today.'

The old lady clapped her hands together. 'A husband?'

'Maybe, if my daughter so wishes.'

'Want some advice?'

Yuko bent down to the woman's level, ever polite. 'Of course.'

'If he comes bearing a haiku run all the way home. No poetry.' This time Yuko did not smile.

'Come, Daughter, we must get ready.'

The woman raised her cloth aloft, a white flag on a twisted pole of sinew and bone. 'Good luck, good luck.'

We entered the changing area where steam, carried from the hot pool, lingered below the ceiling. I was surprised Yuko had agreed so easily to the meeting with Watanabe and this surrender in turn had led to many smaller ones. Her diary revealed her quiet cunning.

'I could feel the thud of my heart and the flush of burning skin. I felt woozy, drugged into submission. Mother was using a cloth to wipe her damp skin and pat dry her hair. I looked at the eggplant-coloured kimono she had chosen for me to wear. No patterns adorned the material, nothing vulgar, or garish, a blank canvas to be sketched upon as this Watanabe desired. I have agreed to Mother's demands, but she does not know why. The arranged meetings with him will give me enough time and opportunity, I hope, to apply to nursing college. Money is an issue. I cannot afford rent or food yet, but when I work out a way, I will leave, and if I find the courage, look for Jomei. I need to find him, whatever he says. Until then, I will submit to Mother's wishes. She is easier to handle when she thinks she is getting her own way.'

Yuko was right, she had fooled me. As we dressed in the baths, I had no idea that such plans were afoot. I was too involved in the immediate task at hand. 'Be polite to the man.' I stepped into my slip and it clung to my damp thighs. 'Do not embarrass us.' I pulled my white under-kimono across my shoulders. 'If not Watanabe, we will find you someone else.' I tied a ribbon around my hips. *'With each instruction, she covered the old painting of me with these clean, new strokes.'* I bared my teeth. 'And remember to smile. If there is one talent that most women possess, it is the ability to hide our worries.' I dipped my head and arched my eyebrows, curled my mouth into the teasing smile of the concubine. 'See?'

Japanese Women

Yamato-nadeshiko: Though very few young Japanese today use the word, it used to be very often employed as a synonym for a Japanese woman. It was the case especially when emphasis was put on her traditional virtues of modesty, obedience, patience and, moreover, bravery and determinedness when she was faced with difficulties. Yamato is another term for Japan; nadeshiko is a plant well known for its lovely flower and slender yet rather strong stalk.

I did not go with Yuko to meet the engineer but sent the matchmaker in my place. The introduction would be awkward enough without my presence. My daughter's resentment of me would cloud her judgement of Watanabe. I left her outside the baths and watched her take careful steps in her wooden sandals along the flagstones. She wrote that she found Mrs Kogi waiting for her at the bottom of the Dutch Slope. Mist clung to the path and covered the old woman's kimono up to her knees. The matchmaker's hair was dotted with frost when they greeted one another. Five minutes or so passed until Mrs Kogi looked up the hill and waved as a man made his way toward them. Shige Watanabe grew larger and larger until he was standing next to them.

There he was, the engineer from Iōjima, dressed in a suit and overcoat. He is a foot taller than me, broad-shouldered with a square face made up of flat, wide planes. He bowed and his cheeks were flushed when he raised his head. He introduced himself and I replied, "Well, who else would you be?" Mrs Kogi giggled and blamed my impoliteness on nerves. Watanabe said my reaction was understandable given the unusual circumstances. Nonsense, the matchmaker replied, this was quite the norm for her. He glanced at me. "But perhaps not for Yuko? Certainly, this is my first meeting of this nature. I'm not used to such self-scrutiny. What to wear? What to say? What not to say? A minefield." Mrs Kogi's eyebrows moved up and down in confusion as he spoke. I tried not to laugh at the sight but I think he caught my amusement because he smiled too.'

They headed up the steep path of stone slabs and Shige tried his best to make small talk. He was concerned Yuko was cold; she told him she was fine. He hesitated before telling her in a rush of words, 'Your kimono is most becoming.' Embarrassed perhaps by his forwardness, he turned to look behind them. 'We appear to have lost Mrs Kogi.' Yuko glanced around. The matchmaker was one hundred feet behind, bent at the hips with her hands on her knees. Yuko's smile was mischievous, if cautious. 'I hope we haven't incapacitated her.'

'Watanabe laughed and said, "You're right. No one would marry in Nagasaki again." He must have noted my unease at those words. He looked annoyed, not at me, but himself. He tipped his head down, as if in confession. "You know what I told myself? This is just a walk with a friend you haven't seen for a long while. A school friend. We lost touch many years ago, perhaps?" I asked, "Wouldn't that make us still strangers?" He considered this. "OK. How about acquaintances in need of reacquaintance?" I felt relieved that he too felt the circumstances odd. "So, Mr Watanabe . . ." He held up his hand. I must call him Shige; we were old friends after

all. "So, Shige . . ." The intimacy of his name on my lips made me blush.'

Yuko enquired after his health and he in turn asked how she was. She could think of nothing to say other than 'Passably well' and this amused him as they stopped by one of the Western-style clapboard homes painted olive-green. He turned to her. 'We're so fortunate, don't you think, to live here in Nagasaki? We've come so far. Think of it, Japan shut off for more than two hundred years, and then in 1859 our port was one of those chosen to open to the world. Can you imagine? All those young men from Britain, France, America, coming here, trading our tea, silks and seaweed, making lots of money, yes, selling us weapons and ships, yes, playing fast and loose with our politics, maybe, but helping Japan become what it is today. The end of the shogunate, our navy, the railroads, the lighthouses, our heavy engineering, it's extraordinary, Yuko, but our city helped start all that. We are so lucky to be here.'

She couldn't help but smile at his enthusiasm. He asked if she was laughing at him. 'No, but you make it sound as if we couldn't have done it on our own.'

He shook his head. 'I didn't mean to suggest that. But can you imagine, Yuko, doing what they did? When you see all those ships down by the docks, could you imagine one day, leaving all you had known, going to a strange country, building something out of nothing?'

His exuberance after so many days of misery was intoxicating. Yuko gazed at the sea and beyond to the horizon. She could not imagine a life beyond Nagasaki. Hers had been contained to her island of Kyushu, to visits

103

to her aunt in Fukuoka north of Nagasaki, eating smoked eel and caramelised pork in Kagoshima to the south, day trips to fishing villages to the east and west, and Iōjima. The rest of the world remained a flat map on her father's study wall. Kenzo would point out the Japanese footprint on other lands: Korea, Taiwan, Port Arthur, Tsingtao in China, the Marshall, Caroline and Mariana Islands and Manchuria, but that was different. She understood the world was more than naval bases and the stamp of soldiers' boots on foreign soil. If she were to leave, she asked Shige, where would he suggest she go? He spoke of Asia and Europe and America. 'Think of all those Japanese already living in Hawaii or the west coast of America. The Wild Wild West? Would you come, Yuko?'

Mrs Kogi was upon them before she could respond. 'You young things, so much energy,' she wheezed. Shige smiled at both women. 'I have a suggestion. Why don't we walk up to Thomas Glover's house?' The Scottish trader's bungalow had been built above the waterfronts of Oura and Sagarimatsu. The house, with its wooden veranda, a roof shaped like a four-leaf clover and the demon heads on red tiles, had a fine view across the bay to the Mitsubishi shipyard. Yuko thought of climbing to that high spot, the brief freedom she might feel seeing an expanse of water to those unknown lands. 'I'd like that.' He nodded, pleased. 'I hear a performance of *Madama Butterfly* is coming here in summer.' He blushed, perhaps embarrassed his remark sounded like an invitation. A rumoured love affair between Glover and a Japanese woman was thought to be the inspiration behind the opera's story of the young pregnant girl

Cio-cio, abandoned by an American husband and later driven to suicide. The matchmaker lifted a fluttering hand to her gold locket. 'Poor Cio-cio, such tragedy.'

'The name caught me. I was back in Chinatown in the mildewed room, Jomei's hand on my shoulder, whispering the name in my ear. Surely, the name was a coincidence, or was Mother right? Had Jomei only seen me as some plaything to use for a while? What would have happened if Father had not come that day? Had I expected Jomei to leave his wife and marry me? What if, like Cio-Cio, I'd fallen pregnant? What would have happened to me, the child? The distraction that Shige might have been, if only for some moments, was broken. Mrs Kogi filled the void with her chirrup but after a while Shige must have realised my silence was more than a bout of shyness.'

He asked if Yuko was feeling unwell. She hated the weak lie but could think of no other: she had slept badly but she had enjoyed their day. 'I apologise, Mrs Kogi, I'll be unable to eat cake with you.'

The matchmaker forced a tight smile. 'I'm sorry you're feeling unwell, Yuko.' There was an awkward pause, while Shige seemed to assess what had happened.

'He glanced at me and asked, "Might we do this again?" I looked at him, this engineer. He was not as unpleasant as I had feared, handsome even. Still, the thought of marriage is preposterous. The fever of Jomei will never leave; I will carry him forever. This Shige can never compete. He is some distant satellite to Jomei's sun, but the doctor is gone, I have heard nothing from him. No word. The cruelty of such disregard. What remains? Mother says marriage is not about love but practicalities, and that true lasting love is built over time. Maybe she is right, and even if she is wrong, I need to be allowed more time. Maybe a life exists beyond Jomei, beyond this engineer,

a life just for me, bound by no others. So I told this Shige Watanabe that I would agree to see him again. He smiled and said another meeting would be passable for him too.'

Sharing an Umbrella

Ai-ai-gasa: In feudal times, men and women in intimate relations were not supposed to be close together in public, to say nothing of linking arms or holding hands. One of the rare occasions this was permissible was a rainy day when they could enjoy intimacy by sharing an umbrella. Therefore, if a man offered one to a woman, it was often interpreted as an implicit expression of his love for her. Since then a man and a woman in love have been described as sharing an umbrella.

That is how Shige and Yuko began, on the Dutch Slope. If Sato was Iōjima and Chinatown, Shige was Nagasaki. Yuko and he would meet at some landmark, find ways to distract Mrs Kogi with cake at a cafe and retreat to a sheltered spot. He would tell her the history of her own city and she would marvel at how little she knew, so ignorant of such a familiar place. *'I have walked the cobbles, and passed the buildings, and watched the ships arrive and know nothing.'* Shige brought the place to life. They passed shops selling lanterns, spectacles or parasols and he conjured up those foreigners drawn here by trade and industry and adventure. Christians from the West and Chinese from the East marked the city's architecture and their bones filled the ground. Yuko would listen to his stories and beneath the wood and metal and stone she began to appreciate the human foundations that lay among the physical structures. Shige spoke of the Portuguese traders in the sixteenth century, the rise and then suppression of Christianity, the Dutch and Chinese traders allowed entry to Nagasaki. They lived within designated areas to suppress smuggling, the spread of the Bible, the debasement of public morals. Little remained of the houses built for the Chinese in Juzenji-Go in 1689 save for a few stones, a ditch, some lattice doors. Yuko tried to understand what it must have been like to be one of those inhabitants kept in isolation. Shige read from a history book, 'Tenkohodo was built for the sea goddess, Maso.' He drew a circle with his arm. 'All the buildings were surrounded by three rings of containment: a six-foot fence, an empty moat and another bamboo fence.'

Yuko thought of those traders handing over rent to live like this, cut off from the world, and yet a conduit between countries as they sent and received goods. The fan-shaped man-made island of Dejima was built for the Dutch in 1636 and stretched two hundred feet from east to west and two hundred yards on the north and south side. To enter over the bridge a ticket was required. Shige skipped on to a list of the exports that poured through this place to Holland. Yuko imagined the ships as they sailed past the circular stone arc built into the sea. She saw the shine of copper, silver and gold; she felt the textures of the ceramics and lacquerware, the raw silk, shark skin and wood. She smelled the spices and tasted the strange new food: the sweet biscuits, the chocolate, beer, sour coffee, ham and vinegar.

The weeks passed but still she could not extricate

herself from the siege of Sato. Summer and autumn played on a constant loop in her head, a cinema reel of sand and sea and Chinatown and that last afternoon. No matter how much she raged against her weakness, she still thought of him. *'Stupid, stupid, forget, forget.'* She wrote prayers on paper and burned incense and visited the temples accompanied by Mrs Goto and her wishes were the same: exorcise this man from my body and mind. But he remained. *'My imagination is my enemy. Thoughts of where he is and who he is with torment me. I see other women, giving themselves to him as I have. I fill my head with Mother's words. He did not love me. He saw how weak I was and he left with no afterthought or regret. Mother says Jomei does not grieve for me. I was a distraction, some toy with which to play. Forget him.'*

On those afternoons with Shige, she looked for Sato in the faces of men in the street, in the bodies emerging from restaurants or bars, and she saw him everywhere and nowhere.

As she fought this contagion of Sato, Shige would tease her. 'The Children's Society of Jesus, let's see, well, the building used to be Maria-en.' He stopped reading. 'Daydreaming again?'

'Just thinking.'

'Of what?'

'What you were saying. All these people here in the city, all their stories, all their joy, all their pain.'

Did he see the longing for a man other than him? She worried that she was snaring Shige in some lie. She did not think of love, or its more reckless relative, passion; she thought only of Shige's kindness and attention and the way he said her name as if it were a pleasure on his lips. His company was a comfort and they had the common currency of Nagasaki. These were not nothing. She began to catch the details of him, the way he rubbed his right eyebrow when preoccupied, the slight bruising around his knuckles from the boxing he practised to keep fit, the strength of his hands, different from Sato's slim, surgical fingers.

One day as bloated clouds carried the weight of rain, they went to Kajiya-machi and walked around the Sofukuji temple, which had been built for Chinese residents. More than three hundred years later, two stone lions still guarded the red entrance. They stood beside a robed gold Buddha statue in the main hall when Shige turned to her, aware once more that Yuko seemed distracted. 'You seem not yourself?'

She felt a surge of irritation. 'How would you know? We do not know one another.'

Shige said nothing but instead walked up to an inscription written in gold on a blue wooden banner above their heads. 'If one should some merit make, do it then again, again. One should wish for it anew, for merit grows to joy.' He smiled. 'I like the sentiment. Happiness must be earned by good deeds.' Shige looped his umbrella on his arm and pulled out a brown package from his suit pocket. 'I have a present for you.'

He watched as she unwrapped the paper to reveal a tin of pencils and a sketch pad bound in cream calfskin. 'Your mother mentioned you like to draw. I thought you could sketch on our excursions.'

Yuko had not drawn since Iōjima but she thanked

110

him, touched if also saddened by the gift. She walked up to a tree covered with hundreds of prayers written on folded pieces of white paper. These handwritten blessings for love, or children, or prosperity were knotted onto branches, which hung low with the weight of all those desires. Early-morning rain had turned some of the hand-written notes to ink smudges, but those underneath the top layer were protected and dry. Yuko touched one of the prayers. 'Have you ever felt your life is out of your own control?'

He was gentle with her. 'Of course.'

'Really?'

'Of course, right now, for a start. I wouldn't wish for you to be here if it were against your will.'

'And if I were?'

'Are you?'

'Of course not.' They walked past red and yellow lanterns and stood next to a giant cauldron made to feed victims of famine hundreds of years ago.

'Marriage is —'

'Perhaps we should not speak of that yet?'

He nodded his agreement. 'Shall we go somewhere else? If you have time we could go to the cathedral? Maybe you could draw?'

Their footsteps were silent on the flagstones as they made their way from the red temple. Shige looked up and even though the rain was yet to fall he opened up his umbrella and Yuko walked beside him, the closest they had been in each other's company. '*He gave me enough space and only our elbows touched but he is drawing nearer, working up to the question. I know the moment is coming when*

I will have to choose between the kind, living man who stands in front of me, or the ghost of the doctor. As the first drops came I could think of only one question: does Shige represent the three rings of fence, moat and bamboo, or could he be the world beyond them?'

A Very Male Society

*Danson-johi: While Amaterasu-omikami, the chief deity in
Japanese mythology, is a goddess, Japan has been an androcentric
country throughout recorded history. The imported religions
justified male-dominated social institutions. Women were regarded
as inferior and their subjection to men was considered a matter of
course. As an old proverb implies, women could have no will
of their own, for they had to obey their parents in their childhood,
their husbands when married, and their sons in old age.*

Sato had agreed to our ultimatum; he had promised Kenzo,
but he would not go. The conditions were simple: never
see or speak to Yuko again, never talk of the affair and
leave Nagasaki. There was no confusion to be had with
these terms. We knew he would be resistant to the last
demand but what could he do? Were he not to leave, we
told him, we would tell his wife, the hospital, our mutual
companions. He would be ruined, if not personally, at
least professionally. We reiterated that this was no hyster-
ical threat. We were determined that the doctor could
no longer remain in the city. When I say we told him
this, I mean Kenzo. I dared not face Sato, fuelled as I
was by wild fantasies of the violence I might do to him.
I wanted to hurt him physically for the pain he had
inflicted on Yuko, and if that wasn't possible, I wanted to
be free of him for good.

As the weeks passed and the air began to carry the first fragrance of spring, I realised that I should not have left the matter to my husband. Kenzo must have faltered, or hesitated, or implied something that allowed the doctor to doubt our words. Our city was a small one, and the circles of the wealthy were claustrophobic. His continued presence was easy enough to establish. Nothing had changed for Sato except Yuko was no longer available to him. He had not been punished. I watched Yuko as she helped me plant amaryllis bulbs in the garden. Later she planned to meet Watanabe. We had expected more resistance to the engineer, and while we had not pressed her on marriage, we dared to be quietly hopeful. Her diary proved we had not been wrong, I read with relief.

'I met Shige for lunch today at an udon restaurant. We sat side by side on a bench. He had tickets for a concert next week and wondered if I might like to go. I found to my surprise, and pleasure, I did, and not just for the music. The waitress brought us two steaming bowls of soup and I asked about his workday. He said he was bored with office work; he wanted to be out in the field. He said he might be posted to one of the nearby islands. "But it would just be for a few months," he said quickly and then he blushed, as if he had betrayed himself by admitting he had thought about how his future might affect me. He slurped up a noodle and asked, "What about you, Yuko? What do you plan to do with your life? Do you want to work?" I felt a surge of gratitude at his question. I told him I used to want to be an artist, now I was thinking about nursing. Shige drank some water and nodded. "That seems a fine ambition to me." We smiled at one another, and for the first time in weeks, I realised I hadn't looked around the room for Jomei's face as soon as I walked into a new place. The relief of being free of him, if only for a moment. Will it last?'

When they left the restaurant, they stood next to a store selling incense, little trays of fragrant wood lined on a table as sandalwood smoke rose up from a burner. A leaflet fluttered by them and Shige stooped to pick it up, some workers' literature denouncing capitalism, corrupt politicians, the suppression of labour unions, the occupation of Manchuria. The country had boiled with violence for years. Prime ministers assassinated, public figures murdered, Marxists rounded up, the military police on patrol at home and in territories abroad. Nagasaki was far from Tokyo but the politics travelled across the growing network of roads, rail and ferry routes.

Shige crunched the paper into a ball. 'These ambitions abroad . . .' He shook the paper in his hand. 'They don't seem to be about assimilating other cultures but using the sword to brand them with our own. I hear about these sacrifices we must make to build this great empire of ours, but what about you, me, ordinary people? What about an individual's responsibility to himself, to his family? Aren't these more important than our blood debt to Japan?' She had not expected political debate. Yuko told him that her father said we were uplifting our brothers and sisters in Asia and that we must do all we could for Japan. A strong military builds a modern nation. He sighed. 'Maybe. Sometimes I fear there is a fine line between liberating a country and invading it. Where will it end? Could you imagine sending a son to war, Yuko?' Before she could answer Mrs Kogi appeared from the cake shop where they had left her and they began to walk. *I allowed myself to imagine a child with this man and I was surprised to find that while the thought did not frighten me, the future for that child did. I stopped* and turned to him. *"You make it sound as if war is inevitable."* He told me that he hoped not. *"I don't want a child born into that kind of world, Shige."* He nodded at this. *"Neither do I, Yuko."'*

I knew nothing of her endorsement of Watanabe. She tolerated me but any closeness we once shared had been destroyed after Chinatown. Not knowing that she had feelings for Shige, I still believed Sato had to be eliminated. He hovered round the edges of our lives, a menace too easily within reach. What if their paths crossed down the years? The city was not big enough to be lost in. Sato had given me enough ammunition over the years to make him go. All I needed to do was send him a note. *'Meet me at Kyogamine Cemetery, tomorrow at noon, Amaterasu.'*

I dressed carefully on the day. I chose a navy-blue kimono, embroidered with herons in flight, and held my hair high with a pearl clasp. To anchor myself to my life with Kenzo, I wore the gold oyster-shell pendant he'd given me not long after we married. Before I left our home, I checked in the bedroom mirror for the lines and shadows that had crept onto my face. I concealed what I could with powder. Then I took a taxi to the cemetery.

One of the advantages of the spot was its proximity to the hospital and its relative seclusion. Sato could meet me there unseen. The place felt abandoned, as if no one had visited or thought of it for years. To reach the graveyard, one passed through an iron gate, orange with rust, and followed a dried mud path under a black locust tree. A collapsed wall marked the boundary of the graveyard, and within, pomegranate trees lent shade to the sandstone crosses and marble headstones. The city gravediggers brought the Christians here, but no burials had taken place for a long time. The names of Portuguese and Dutch traders could still be read on the crumbling graves. The path continued through the trees to the base of the hill at the far corner of the cemetery and climbed up to tombs carved into the soil in higher and higher layers.

Kyogamine bled into Hiagashi Cemetery. Here, Christian bones gave way to the remains of Japanese merchants and nobles. At the summit, a slab of another fallen grave, warm under the sun's rays, was my seat and I sat upon its flat surface and looked down on Nagasaki, the city growing like a giant metal insect across the land. I knew the doctor had arrived when a turtle dove beat its wings and rose from a branch. My heart pounded as I turned around and watched him approach. We had not seen each other for nearly seventeen years. The passage of time had been good to him, age had settled well on his face. He had kept lean and walked with that same slow swagger. My desire was still there too. How ashamed I would be if he realised this. I clenched my fists and placed my hands on the grave to steady myself. I must be unreadable to him. He lowered himself next to me. We sat in silence and then he placed his palm over my fingers. He looked at me but said nothing. I pulled my hand away; he could not soften me that easily. I readied for the fight as he lit a cigarette. I knew how to purge Sato from our lives. We do terrible things because we can, and only sometimes because we must.

'When are you leaving Nagasaki, Jomei?'

He laughed at this. 'I'm not. I had a change of heart.'

I watched him smoke. 'Kenzo made our requirements clear.'

He stretched his back. 'A little extreme, wouldn't you say?'

'Why would you do this to us? I'm not talking about me. Why do this to Kenzo?'

He sighed. 'It wasn't planned.'

'She's a child.'

He stubbed the cigarette out on the grave. 'She's a woman. She knew what she was doing. Who she was had no relevance. It was unfortunate, the connection, that's all.'

'Unfortunate? Have you no idea what you've done? We'll tell Natsu.'

He leaned back, a portrait of calm. 'That's your choice.'

'You don't believe us?'

'I do, but I won't leave Nagasaki.'

'Must I repeat it? We will tell Natsu, your boss. How would either feel about you bedding a young patient? You do remember your wedding and professional vows?'

He laughed. 'If only you were as clever as you think you are. I admire you, Amaterasu, I do. You've worked so hard, left that past of yours behind, and look where you are now, an engineer's wife with wealth and a home and status among our city's rich. I'm happy for you. You got what you wanted. It's admirable, but I wonder what those wives would think if they knew how far you had come. Would they be as impressed as I am, do you think? I could ask them.'

I mimicked his insouciance. 'I didn't think you'd stoop to blackmail, Jomei.'

'Well, I could say the same. Let's not call it blackmail. Persuasion, perhaps.'

The sun was low, his profile merging with the light. 'I see. So why did you come today? What was the point?'

'Curiosity . . . and I wanted to apologise. Not about Yuko.' He cleared his throat and turned to face me. 'I wanted to tell you that I'm sorry for what happened. I never got the chance to say so at the time.'

I touched my necklace. 'That was long ago, Jomei. I hold no grudges, I promise you.'

'Amaterasu, has it occurred to you that Yuko and I are in love?'

I clenched my fists once more. 'Don't be ridiculous. How can you say such a thing?'

He stood up, put his hands in his trouser pockets. 'I am married to Natsu, yes. I know my responsibilities, but I will always be here for Yuko if she needs me. I want you to know that. Tell Natsu, if you must, and I will tell the coven of witches you call friends, if I must. So be it.'

How dare he think he could dictate what we would do. 'Jomei, Jomei.' I forced a smile, tipped my head, as if in pity. 'Don't you see what's happening here?' I kept my voice low but strong. 'I won't only tell Natsu about Yuko. I'll tell Yuko about what happened when I was not much older than she was. I'll tell her everything . . . *everything*.' I walked up to him. 'I wonder how she would react to that news?'

His face contorted in anger as he took his hands from his pockets. He grabbed me by the shoulders. 'You would do that to your own child?'

'Gladly.' He let go, as if contaminated. 'Now, when did you say you were leaving Nagasaki?'

I can still see him standing by that fallen grave, defeated

119

by his own cowardice. We had all been taken in, and let down, by him: Kenzo, Yuko, Natsu and, yes, even me. He and Kenzo had been the closest of friends, for many years. Remnants of that bond surely remained? Who would seduce a friend's daughter with no care or shame? Sato talked of love but he was a foolish man who had exploited Yuko. He was more than double her age; he had no right to sour her young life with all those extra years of experience, regret and cynicism. And lastly: I too felt betrayed. I sent the doctor away not just for Yuko, but for myself. This was the maggot that burrowed into my own rotten heart.

Conjecture

Sasshi: Loosely this can be translated as 'understanding', 'sensibility', 'consideration'. It is an important idea in interpersonal relationships in Japan. According to the concept of modesty and sincerity that Japanese people esteem, direct self-expression is frowned upon. People are expected to guess what others intend to say. If they are not perceptive enough and dare to ask for information left unsaid, then they are branded as rude.

The sky was still dark when I rose and wrapped one of Kenzo's brown woollen cardigans over my crumpled clothes. A mug of coffee steamed in the cold air as I went through to the living room. The lamp had been left on all night, a comfort in the dark. The world outside seemed blurred, coated in frost. These four walls, the twelve black frames, the brown package were all that mattered. When the man had left the night before I had stared at that envelope as I finished the bottle, but I knew even through the stew of alcohol that a clear head would be needed. My hands shook as I broke the seal. Inside someone had bundled letters together and secured them with elastic bands. I pulled one batch out and checked the seals. Each one had been marked with a red hanko: Jomei Sato. I sat back, sickened and confused. The doctor would not write to me. We had left no possibility for further communication.

I picked up the first envelope from the pile, the glue so old the seal came apart with the lightest of effort. A date, *August 9, 1946* and her name: *Yuko*. I cried out in that empty room. What was this? Why would Sato write to my daughter a year after her death? He knew she had been killed. I had told him. I opened more of the letters, my hands shaking. Every year on August 9 he had written her a letter. Why torment me with this fantasy correspondence? Why now when I no longer had the strength to fight him? And what was Natsu's involvement in this? I hated that he was in control again but what could I do other than pick up that first letter. The doctor's voice echoed through the years and the room filled with his low, assured delivery.

So you want to know what I did during the days after the bomb? Surely the answer is obvious. I looked for you, whenever I could, but there were so many injured people that needed what little help I could offer. I was posted to Fukuya; the department store had been turned into a makeshift hospital, its floor slippery with blood. The rooms filled up with creatures barely human, their skin black as charcoal, metal, glass and wood embedded so deep into flesh, the shards rattled in lungs. I felt more like a mortician than a doctor, administering morphine to the dying only when it could be spared. I could not bear to think you were among the wounded. I went to the relief centres: Urakami First Hospital, Shinkozen school and Ibinokuchi police station, hoping, like me, you were tending patients. Nothing. I went to the temporary town hall again and again to see if there had been reports of you, but always there was nothing. Photographs and addresses had been posted across walls and fences. I scoured them for information but you had vanished. I searched your home. I even spoke to your mother. That's how desperate I was. She said you and Hideo were dead. I told her I did not believe her. She said why should you be saved with so many others lost? The world did not owe you sanctuary. She said I had killed you; I had placed you in the path of pikadon. I refused to believe you were dead, even though the city was all the evidence anyone needed. So many places gone: the municipal office, the district court, the prison, the water building, the medical college hospital, but I could not let the possibility of you go. If I had survived, why not you? This made no sense to me.

As the contagion spread, we thought we were dealing with dysentery. We ran crude experiments on how to contain the sickness. Every day I checked the arrivals to see whether you were among them. I tried my best for them because I thought that one day you might be there. And so when I injected them with glucose or calcium chloride, or gave them vitamins or fresh blood, I did so for you. I watched them and learned the signs of coming death: the hair, the black spots, the bleeding gums, the convulsions, and I feared that somewhere this might be happening to you.

I haven't found you but I haven't given up on you either. Know that. I am always searching and hoping that you might return. Even now, when I catch sight of a certain woman in the street, I find myself following her, waiting until she turns around so that I can see your

123

face again. No human bones to find, no tombstone to visit, nothing to prove you are dead but the constancy of your absence and my love.

I thought I could smell jasmine. I lifted the letter to my nose but the scent was just a vapour of memory. There had been a vase of flowers in my room the day Sato came to our home. Kenzo was out looking for Hideo and Yuko. I was too unwell to go with him. My husband called me his miracle. So many taken, not by the executioners' flames, but by the sickness carried in the air. I must have caught something of the poison but not enough. Misaki had pulled my soiled nightdress off me to wash my body. I was too sickly to be embarrassed by my nakedness. She was running a wet, cool compress down my arm when she stopped, alerted by some noise. She stood up and called out, 'Mr Takahashi?' but there was no reply. She pulled up a bedsheet so that I was covered. 'Who's there?' Footsteps came fast up the stairs and along the hall landing and by the time she reached the open doorway, Sato was pushing past her. She clung onto his arm. 'Out, how dare you, out.' He was still wearing his doctor's coat. He looked at me, eyes pleading. His voice caught when he said, 'Please tell me she is alive.' Misaki turned to me. 'I'll go and get help.' I looked at his face, pale and unshaven, with dark shadows carved below his eyes, and I told her I was fine. 'Sato, I'll tell you what I know but will you give me a minute before we talk?' He seemed paralysed for a few seconds but then left the room. Misaki helped me pull on a fresh nightdress before disappearing downstairs. I watched him enter the room, dazed with fever and his presence. I hated that he would see me this weak. How dare he bring his grief to our house uninvited. Who was he to mourn her here? Given our last words spoken before pikadon, he must have been wretched to seek me out.

He sat on the window seat and rested his head in his hands. 'Tell me she's alive and then I'll go.' Maybe I felt a tremor of sympathy for him then. To soothe his pain would ease my own, but he had asked the impossible, the one confirmation I could not give him. I told him the small nails of facts I held, hammered each one into a coffin we would never need and she would never be contained by. Yuko had gone to the cathedral where we had planned to meet. I had been delayed. She never returned home. Neither did Hideo. What more was there to tell him? The doctor had seen the city, the air so thick with the dead you could taste the dust of them. But Sato rejected what he could not bear to be true. He said Yuko couldn't be gone; she would be helping survivors, or maybe she was sick in some medical centre, or maybe she had been taken out of the city. He offered so many possibilities. I had thought of them all. How could I tell him I knew she was dead because I felt the void of her, a vacuum inside me where a mother carries the soul of her offspring? Sometimes I would feel her, like a ghost limb that causes pain despite its amputation, but I knew this was a trick of the mind. She was dead, and so was her son.

August 9, 1947. In the next letter Sato wrote that the December before he had taken up a position at the Holy Mother of Immaculate Conception Order Convalescent

Centre for Children of the A-bomb on Fukue Island, sixty miles from Nagasaki. The home was opened six months after pikadon and filled with eighty orphans and children who could not be reunited with their families. Church collections mostly paid for its upkeep, along with a generous donation from the women of the Church of First Friendship Institutional Baptists in Sioux Falls, South Dakota. The centre was overseen by the Knights of the Holy Mother and Sato had taken the job for at least a year. He planned to visit the orphanage for extended visits while continuing research work in Nagasaki.

He wrote that his first approach to the house would have appealed to Yuko's artistic eye with *'its bare trees coated in hoarfrost, tips tinged orange by the winter sun'*. A gravel walkway led past a fountain of leaping carp frozen in white marble and the path then cut the lawn into halves, which were bordered with frost-ravaged rose bushes, their brown flowers rotten on the stem. Built in the European tradition, the building had three floors, topped with a slate roof. Someone had begun to repaint the timber frame, which was covered in peeling, grey paint save for this square of white underneath one of the ground-floor windows. A veranda ran the length of the front and a trellis of ivy covered most of the right-hand side of the house.

The inside of the home was all dark halls and low lamps that led to eight bedrooms, several living rooms and serving quarters. The nuns lived on the upper floor, with the older children. The second floor was for the younger charges, and the two teachers resided in the summer house next to a pond, suffocated with red algal bloom. Many of the children had been injured by the bomb and their needs were such that the scullery in the basement functioned as a medical ward. That was where Sato could be found. He arrived at lunchtime and the Mother Superior took him to the refectory. The children sat in silent rows, eating overcooked udon from chipped bowls. One boy in particular had caught his attention, or rather, his burns had.

I have seen severe injuries before, but his are not for the faint of heart. The nuns call him Ko. An optimistic name for the boy: how can he represent happiness, light and peace? He has not spoken since his arrival. His muteness is not a physical impediment, I am sure. Pikadon has left its mark, not just in broken limbs and burnt flesh, but hidden in bones and muscles and fibres and young minds. I suspect I have a lifetime's work of observations and medical studies to undertake. And you, Yuko, are the one who drives me on. I still cannot believe you are gone. If I had seen your body or held you one last time, or I could say here is where my Yuko is buried, would that have helped? The love remains; it never dies. It still grows until some nights I wonder if I can stand the pain. So many questions that can never be reconciled but this is the one that plagues me most: why would your god take you and leave me in this world?

I folded the letter up and placed it back in its envelope. Sato was doing what so many of us had done; he was mourning a loss that could never be regained, but his was a more dangerous kind of grief; he was trying to keep

Yuko alive, somehow, in these letters. Wishful thinking alone cannot resurrect the dead. Neither can medicine. Flesh decays or burns in an instant; either way, we are no more. Why would Yuko be the exception?

His years after the war were marked by study and experiments, analysis and conjecture. The Sato I had known had not been so dedicated to his profession. He had worn the uniform of a doctor lightly when we first met. Pikadon had sharpened his focus, honed the skills he had acquired too easily in his youth. Twenty-four of the children required ongoing medical care, mostly for burns and compression wounds that had not healed satisfactorily. In 1948, he wrote:

> The job is lonely. I imagine us working together. I imagine you sitting beside me, annotating notes or differentiating between contact and flame burns. I see us mapping out the fissures of damaged skin to explain the topography of the bomb. I have pinned a map of Nagasaki on the wall of my sleeping quarters. My information is crude and unconfirmed, half-guessed statistics, but I record them on paper and add them to my lists.

Estimates of the casualty numbers had been logged somewhere but Sato had no access to them. The closest he came was a visit from a group of American doctors, engineers and scientists who came to the hospital where he worked that first September. They shook his hand, walked around the beds of those yet to die, took notes and photographs, asked to see medical records while interpreters translated what they read. When Sato asked if these experts from the West had a cure for the sickness they had unleashed, they said nothing. The precious cargo of information they took with them was censored by the American authorities, sent to government departments and stored away in files. Sato had written to the Atomic Bomb Casualty Commission for help accessing official statistics and heard nothing back. He tried to recall the stories of the dying patients in their hospital beds, and the clues they provided. He saw first-hand how radiation destroyed the body's defensive mechanism and its legions of cells and how this correlated to the prevalence of infection, the poor repair, the high mortality rates.

When he called the children into his ward, while he tended healing wounds or checked old scars, he was looking for signs of long-term contamination, of diseases yet to be detected but carried in arteries and bones. The nuns did not know but he tested for cancers in the lungs, thyroid and blood. He was trying to chart the course of this sickness through the evidence it left behind. Two toddlers abandoned by their families were crucial: Izumi and Kasumi, aged thirty-two and thirty-six months. He measured their heads and limbs; he checked their muscle tone and their facial features, the slope of their forehead, the distance between their eyes; he took pictures of their limbs and their faces. His observations, he believed, suggested that both girls showed signs of abnormal growth of the brain. Those two babies were not the only ones to be poisoned in their mothers' bellies that day. He was not compiling a report for where pikadon had been but where it might take us. This was what kept Sato on the island; he was looking for things that could not always be seen. He told Yuko he had begun to write a book, which he said would chart the medical conditions of foetuses contaminated by radiation in the womb.

Come 1949, the routine of his life was *'reassuringly uneventful'*. He rose early most mornings and walked through the grounds, past a patch of trees where dolls made by the children hung from creaking branches. These dolls were little more than balls wrapped in squares of cotton with faded outlines of faces swinging in the breeze, *'as the trees scratch out a morning lullaby. See what a poet you still make me?'* He would continue down to the shore to watch the sun rise and seep colour back into the island before he returned for morning surgery. In the afternoon, he worked on his research and after an evening meal, while the nuns fell to their knees in contemplation, he wrote up more notes in his room.

Life at the orphanage may be without much drama but we had one incident of note a couple of months ago. During one of my morning walks, I found the boy Ko standing near the pond, naked. He was wet, as if he had swum in the water, which was still congested from the disease that had killed all the fish. The red slime coated his skin. I called out his name and he turned to me and pointed at the water. I asked him, 'I don't understand. What's wrong, Ko?' He started to cry. 'What is it, Ko? Where are your clothes?' He looked at the water once more. 'I don't understand, Ko.' He opened his mouth and then he did something extraordinary: he spoke. His voice was high-pitched. It belonged to a boy younger than his years. 'Miki is in the water. Please help her.' I asked who she was. 'My friend.' I had heard of no Miki. He grew agitated. 'Help her, help her.' I told him to wait and I went to fetch the caretaker. We dredged the pond that morning and he watched us, wrapped in a blanket, Sister Abe by his side. Ko shivered as he watched the caretaker and his son pull the empty dragnets into the boat. I told him how sorry I was but no one was there. He shook his head, more angry than sad. 'Miki is in the water.' Sister Abe put her arms around his shoulders. 'Ko, there is no Miki. No one of that name lives with us.' He drew still at this and the nun held his chin, made him look her in the eyes. 'You're speaking, Ko.' The boy looked at her, cowed. 'My name isn't Ko.' She ran a finger over his face. 'Who are you then?' He looked at that dead pond. 'Miki.' And then he stopped talking again.

What to say of Ko? He is my most regular visitor and, with the exception of the two toddler girls, my most curious case. We sit in genial silence as I check his burns and fill out my forms. A surgeon from America has performed some plastic surgery on him and the doctor is keen that I report on the healing process. There is talk of more procedures taking place, perhaps in the US, although the logistics involved make that difficult. Ko's file is thick with medical assessments. The first notes were made when he was admitted to Nagasaki Commercial College on August 18. The burns are not those from the thermal rays of the explosion but some localised fire. Still, his survival is a rare thing. Ninety per cent of survivors exposed to the blast who I saw died by the fortieth day. Think of the care available to him. There was no zinc oxide oil; we used whatever we could get our hands on to treat burns: rapeseed oil, cooking oil, castor oil, even machine oil. The same thing when it came to disinfecting the burns. We used what we could find: iodine tincture, mercurochrome, Rivanol, boric acid solution. His life was immeasurably improved by the American doctor, that is for sure, but we humans, we do so like to create our Frankenstein monsters.

I can only imagine who this Miki might be. A lost sibling, an imaginary friend, maybe even the thing the boy might like to be. Days later, I was sitting on a bench in the orphanage's front garden. Children were playing catch on the lawn and Sister Abe and Ko were sitting on the veranda, shaded from the sun. Ko watched the other youngsters run around the grass and then he looked beyond them, down the gravel path. I followed his gaze but could see nothing save for the usual flowers, bushes and the gate. He turned to the nun and I saw his mouth move and then she smiled and held his hand.

His name is Hideo. He remembers little else at the moment, not the name of his parents, where he lived, the school he attended. The Mother Superior reported the scant information back to the head office in Nagasaki. They said they would check the missing persons register and various other records for any possible candidates but no one could see a happy ending to this search. We don't even know how many people were in the city at the time. Maybe 240,000, maybe more, maybe less. How many Hideos, of Ko's estimated age at the time of pikadon, were registered missing and how many parents left alive to find them? Eight weeks later I learned the answer: twenty-three.

I scanned the list the church's head office had sent

us. I turned the first page and then the next until only one more was left. And then there you were. I confess I wept as I read the date of birth, school, parents and next of kin: Hideo Watanabe; February 22, 1938; Yamazato Primary; Shige and Yuko Watanabe (née Takahashi); Kenzo Takahashi (grandfather), Mitsubishi Corporation (shipbuilding division). I think this is when the thought began, a kernel of hope, of possibility. As the days passed, this seed began to grow in my mind, burst open and push its way to the light until it became more than a shoot of possibility, but a living, fragile new life in the dead soil. Could this Hideo be your Hideo? Your mother told me he had died but could she have been wrong? And if she was mistaken about Hideo, what about you?

I waited for Sister Abe to bring Ko to my office. She held his hand as I explained we had been trying to find out more about his family. I told him we had a list of boys, all called Hideo, who went missing on the day he was injured. There was a chance he might be one of them. Could we read the details to him and see if anything sounded familiar? He said nothing and I began to read the names. By the fifth one he began to cry. Sister Abe said we should perhaps stop, but I asked to try one more, and when I read out Yamazato Primary, he looked up. I promise I did not imagine his reaction. 'Do you recognise the school, Hideo?' He wiped his eyes and nestled into the nun. 'Can you remember your mother's name?' He thought for a moment. 'I called her Mummy.' Sister Abe kissed the top of his head. 'Can you remember what other people called her?' He looked up at the nun. 'Can I leave, please?' She glanced at me and I said, 'We have plenty of time.

This is hard, Hideo, I know. Don't worry. This might help us find your parents.' He shuffled off the chair and touched Sister Abe on the wrist. 'Miki says our parents are lost, but they're coming back.' The nun smiled as she led him away. 'Miki sounds kind.'

Over the next days and weeks, I replaced brittle evidence with malleable hope. I study his mannerisms, the signs of the boy before this trauma. There are moments when I begin to see you in him. Why not, Yuko? Why not? But then I give myself a shake. That would be too miraculous for this world. He is no doubt just another orphan. That would be much simpler to comprehend, would it not?

I stopped reading. Sato had always been a foolish man, too ignorant of the damage he unleashed with his musings and desires. He had outdone himself here, playing a god to some boy. Why drape a past on a child that did not belong to him? My grandson would not be the only Hideo with lost parents. This boy could have been found at any number of schools destroyed that day. If Sato wanted to give this Ko an identity, he could have chosen any name pulled from that missing persons register, but he chose our Hideo Watanabe. Why? To ease his own grief, not to help one of too many orphans left behind. His selfishness was obscene.

The man had said he would return today. What to tell him of the letters? I felt soiled by their contents. I wanted to slough the words off my mind, cleanse myself of Sato, but as always the lure of him was relentless. With the coffee long cold by my side, I continued to read.

By 1950, he wrote, the church had managed to contact eleven of the families on the list. They were asked to provide facts that might help prove the boy's identity: a birthmark, blemishes or other features peculiar to their son or grandson or nephew. Some parents were even brought to the island to meet their possible child. Sato explained Hideo's injuries to them and the Mother Superior took them to a spot so that they could view him from a discreet distance. If there was any hint of recognition or desire to meet the boy, Hideo was brought to them and they stared at him and asked questions that he seemed unable or unwilling to answer. 'Do you recognise us? Where do we live? Do you have any brothers or sisters?' The process seemed crude and ineffective. The couples would fidget and cough and look to the Mother Superior and lower their heads, and she would thank them for making the long journey and apologise for wasting their time. They would catch the ferry home and another name would be struck from the list.

Then Sato mentioned someone who had been understandably absent from the letters: Natsu. He revealed his wife visited him regularly on the island. She had grown fond of the children, and she was particularly moved by Ko, or Hideo, as people now called him. She admired his quiet stoicism and how accepting the other youngsters were of his burns.

Forgive me for writing about my wife, but you will see my reasons. She came to mark the anniversary of pikadon with us. I watched her stare at my city map, flick through pages of my textbooks, pick up scribbled notes. She called my work an obsession, asked if I would come home for good. 'You belong in the city.' We talked about the children, what would happen to them. Suddenly, as if the thought had only just occurred to her, she asked how easy it would be to adopt one of them. The question was posed too casually. I think alone in Nagasaki, she has given this idea plenty of consideration. A child might have helped our marriage over the years, maybe. A child would have drawn me home sooner, certainly. She is a good woman and she would make a fine mother. My absence has been a cruelty to her but I could not grieve for another woman while she looked on. Our separation was a necessity, a kindness of sorts, but I realised if I was to return to Nagasaki permanently, I couldn't leave Hideo behind, not when there is a chance he is your son. I told her I did have someone in mind. She seemed uncertain, worried that Hideo would be better off here at the centre, safe from all those prying eyes. Natsu ran her hand down the map. 'Will people, strangers, look beyond his scars? If you don't see people as human, it's easier to hurt them.' I told her if one city could accept him then it would be ours. What I tell you is this: I look beyond his scars, and all I see is you.

I broached the subject of adoption with the Mother Superior. She tried to hide her surprise. I told her the chances of finding Hideo's birth family were reducing by the days and weeks. We had some responsibility to protect him from this further disappointment. She looked at the list of Hideo's possible parents. 'Do we not owe the boy a thorough search?' I offered her a cigarette but she declined. 'Mother Superior, I should have said earlier

136

but I know one set of parents on the list, the Watanabes, on the last page. They did not survive; it is likely the other names will prove fruitless too. I want to offer Hideo a future, stability.' She asked if the Watanabes had other family members still alive and I explained my wife had made enquiries. I told her that one set of grandparents had moved from Japan, their destination unknown. No other relatives had left contact details. 'You think this Hideo is Hideo Watanabe?' I waited a beat before I replied. 'I think we will never know.'

What to do with anger that can go nowhere? Kenzo and I had left contact details with the authorities but only for our Nagasaki address. There had been no need to make contact from America. But surely we could have been found, somehow? What if the orphanage had contacted us? Would we have believed in the possibility? It felt like hope had died so quickly and absolutely back then. Sato's letter made me try to comprehend the joy and agony of us being reunited with Hideo. How would he have fared in this country with those scars and the reason for them? How would we have coped as his grandparents turned parents? I imagined only good. I saw him sitting in a classroom in a baseball jersey, playing in the street with friends, going to summer camps, heading to university. We would have told him about his parents, how they met and fell in love, the sacrifices they made in the war. He would have had a better understanding of who he had been, where he had come from, maybe where he was going. This Hideo Watanabe would have been a blend of Japanese past and American future. We would have drawn such comfort from his presence. Our lives in this new country would have made more sense; the three of us would have known what we were supposed to be after pikadon: a family.

But the doctor and his wife took away the opportunity for us to know if this was our Hideo. On Natsu's next visit to the island they went for a walk in the woods with the boy and found a shaded spot for a picnic.

We explained that we had tried our best to find his real family but we had been unsuccessful. He asked why and I said that the likeliest explanation was his parents couldn't find him because, as Miki had said, they were lost. I showed him the list of names. 'It's likely these were your parents, Hideo.' I pointed to your name and Shige's. 'Will they find me again?' Natsu took his hand in her own. 'If they can, I'm sure they will. But until then we thought you might like to live with us, in Nagasaki.' He raised his hand to his cheek. 'What will people say about my face?' Natsu put her arm around his shoulder and drew him to her. 'We'll just tell them you were hurt but now you're better. We'll tell them how brave you've been, how clever you are, how proud we are of you.'

As the day drew near for them to leave the island, Sato could see how nervous Hideo was about the departure. He had been so closeted at the orphanage. The children seemed almost blind to his scars. His schooling, his confidence, they had thrived on the island. Natsu and the doctor were worried about how he would adapt to a busy

138

city, strangers' eyes, new classmates, but Hideo would have a future in Nagasaki.

The island has been a good place for both of us to heal but we cannot hide here forever. For a doctor, I have done so few kind acts in my life. He can be one. I will love him as my own and raise him as my own. He will have a good life. He will be the child I never had. I cannot shift the thought that you and Hideo are connected. I imagine him to be your son, not only to keep you close but to push other memories away. And even though I cannot see the marks of you in his face, his presence is as close as I can get to you now.

I checked my watch and skipped ahead. I wanted to know how Hideo had adapted to life in the city. Had he struggled, had he been tormented by bullies at school, had he pined for the safety and seclusion of the orphanage? On August 9, 1951, Sato and Natsu took him to a commemoration of the bomb. Crowds had gathered near what remained of the hypocentre. Survivors huddled together under umbrellas, sheltering from the heat. People wore garlands of paper cranes and carried doves made of paper. They listened, heads bent, as men and women took to the podium to talk of compensation and tolerance and medical assistance. A group of former Korean prisoners had gathered silent by a fountain. Hideo was enthralled by the spectacle; inspired was the word the doctor used. Sato said perhaps it was the one date in the calendar when Hideo could be accepted and embraced not as something to pity but a testimony, a caution, a living will.

We stood next to widows dressed in black, hair scraped back, eyes damp with tears. In front of them were sombre children, summer-fresh in white cotton dresses, shorts and straw hats. Surrounded by one-storey wooden buildings that had risen from the rubble, we watched a procession of women as they danced in peach and coral kimonos. Next came a black-and-gold silk dancing dragon, its writhing body held aloft on poles by men. Buddhist monks followed covered head to toe in white, and then toward the end of the parade, survivors held aloft canvas placards, painted with the word 'Peace'. Later we walked down to the river, its surface shattered by sunlight. We followed the tramlines to Tsukimachi and I found myself only a short distance away from the place where we began. I could not help myself; I had to go and look; I had to see the building once more.

I told Natsu and Hideo I knew a short cut to avoid the crowds and traffic. We headed past the rows of champon and sara udon restaurants, their red lanterns still in the heat of the afternoon. Women hid from the sun under parasols. They gossiped as they walked under sheets dripping wet from the lines that stretched across the street from balconies. Housewives bartered for live eels wriggling in wooden buckets; they smelled the wart skin of bitter melons for ripeness, picked among the baskets of lime-green silk squashes and swollen purple eggplants. Rotten fruit abandoned in the dirt soured the air as men in aprons strung plucked ducks on hooks and greeted passers-by with the trading prices of the day. Remember that scene, Yuko? Remember what it meant to us? I searched for our apartment, but it is gone. A pachinko parlour stands in its place. Even if the building is no more the memory of what happened there taunts me. I think back to that last afternoon we spent together in that room, your father standing there, telling me to go. I hate myself for not staying, not fighting, not telling him what we meant to one another. The family left to me, Natsu and Hideo, walked on ahead. I felt unworthy of this second chance. I do not deserve to have the burden of your loss eased by Hideo's presence. But he allows me to create new memories. He is the living wreckage I pull from the flames of August 9.

I was glad that blackened facade of rooms to rent by the hour was gone. For that hovel to have survived and Yuko to have not would have been too cruel. Hideo had soothed the sorrow of Sato's past. Kenzo and I had been denied such a gift. We had left Nagasaki so that the city might not torment us but, even in my American sanctuary, Sato was making me do what I had tried to avoid for so long: look back. I had mostly managed to keep my mind's eye on only the good from the life we had abandoned, the days spent drawing with Yuko when she was a child, the mornings passed watching her try to play the shamisen as her teacher quietly despaired at her clumsiness, the trips shared with her to the markets to choose Kenzo a gift, the joy of hearing her singing to herself in the garden, her voice trembling at the high notes. These recollections were sweetly, desperately bearable if I tried not to think on them too long. Harder memories sometimes pushed their way through, but if they dared, I trained my mind to fight back. Go to the shops, clean that cupboard, and if all else failed, pour that drink.

Sato's letters were dragging me back, forcing me to unearth all that I had kept hidden, but I couldn't tear myself away from his version of the past we shared. I wanted to hold these letters up to the dark light of my own memory. He had asked the same question that haunted me. Why was I still here when Yuko was gone? Why should we survive? I could not answer for him but if I believed in a god, my deity would have been a vengeful one. He would have ruled my death alongside my daughter too easy an outcome. My punishment must never stop being dispensed. My life was my sackcloth and my ashes. Sato must have reached a different conclusion. Maybe he thought he had been kept alive to save that boy. In turn this Ko, or Hideo, or whoever he was, would save him. Yes, I could see the reasons why Sato had needed the boy to be Yuko's son, but I felt the opposite: my grandson was too pure for any world that would keep Sato and me alive but claim my daughter. Only scavengers and liars and cheats survived. The best of us died young back then.

Humility

Kenkyo: Modesty is one of the most important concepts of virtue in Japan. People are expected to be humble and modest regardless of their social position. They are supposed to modulate the display of their ability, talent, knowledge or wealth in an appropriate manner. Self-assertiveness, aggressiveness and ambitiousness are all more or less discouraged, and consideration for others encouraged.

The knock was timid, unsure, as if he expected me to ignore him. I opened the door and we said cautious hellos to one another, shy without the whiskey. He stepped inside and removed his shoes and padded through to the kitchen in his socks. By the time I joined him, he was sitting in Kenzo's seat.

'I've made tea, and there are doughnuts, or I can make you a sandwich. You must be hungry.'

'Please, don't rush around for me.' He seemed exhausted.

'How did the conference go?'

He undid the knot of his tie. 'Speaking in America can be a challenge. You don't want to be seen as lecturing or hectoring about the evils of the atomic bomb but also you have a duty to speak up, to say, this is what happened, not what you think happened.' He gestured at his face. 'And people find this too much, sometimes.'

I did not know how to respond so I set the cups and

saucers on the table, brought over a knife for the doughnuts and two napkins. I realised I had no side plates and
looked for them in the cupboard nearest the door. Even
these small chores flustered me, the simplest task of
preparing refreshments for two people, not one, a trial.
I sat opposite him, his face so close, the red lids with no
eyelashes, the mottled yellow and pink ridges, the scars
from surgeons' incisions. Despite the lack of expression,
his face was fascinating. If beauty was uniformity, he
should have seemed abhorrent but the blasted skin around
his eyes just made them seem brighter, more inquisitive.
'Have the contents of the package been helpful?'

I answered as honestly as I could. 'They're letters from
Jomei. He mentions your orphanage and the adoption of
a boy called Ko. That's you, yes? And a girl called Miki.'

'Ko is me, yes, and Miki, well, how to explain her?'

He told me the story of when he arrived at the
orphanage, how the doctor who worked at the centre
before Sato made him sleep in the ward, in isolation.
They were worried about infections and they didn't want
him to alarm the other children. His injuries were thought
to be too shocking. He didn't like being left in the basement on his own at night. He became convinced there
was a demon stalking the corridors when everyone else
had gone to bed. He believed this creature wanted to
return him to the day of pikadon, or at least carry him
off into the mountains. One night, he heard the creak of
floorboards and he thought, this is it, this is the end, and
he said he felt relieved. He was so lonely. At least the
demon would be company. Who would miss him apart
from his favourite nun, Sister Abe? The children would

144

not care. They would not know. At that point in his treatment, his burns could not be exposed to sunlight. He was little more than a rumour to them. He watched the door handle shake and then move down as it released on the catch, and he thought, here he comes, I'm ready. But it wasn't a monster, it was a little girl. This was Miki. She was a little younger than him, with short hair and scabby knees. She visited him most nights, even when he was allowed to sleep with the other children. She would climb into his bed and they would whisper, dream and plan adventures. Sometimes they sneaked outside and ran through the woods, or swam in the pond, or lay under the tree of dolls and Miki told him stories. She had no fear; she did not believe in demons; pikadon had killed them all. Her own parents had been too close to the light, but they were not dead, only lost. They were coming for her. She told him to be patient, his family would return as well. When Miki drowned in the pond, no one believed she had existed, but he kept telling them that Miki had gone in the water. He finished talking, and looked at the floor, maybe embarrassed.

'Was she real?'

'Oh, I suspect she was only imagined, but she seemed so real at the time.'

'She was a comfort.'

'It's silly, but I still think she's going to come back one day. Like it was a game of hide-and-seek that just got out of hand.' We looked at one another, his blasted flesh, my soured spirit, and I felt an impulse to hold his hand but I did not. 'So how am I to convince you that I am your grandson, eh?'

'It is true that I had a grandson and his name was Hideo Watanabe. He would be forty-six years old, but . . .' How could I tell him that Sato appeared to have intertwined a missing boy and an injured one, melded them to ease his conscience, soothe his own loss. 'Can I ask, when were you told that you might have a grandmother alive?'

'In my teens. Father told me how he had been close with Grandfather when they were young, how he had worked with Yuko during the war. He learned you had moved abroad. In the chaos of the occupation, a search for you proved impossible.'

'We moved a couple of times when we came here, yes, in 1947 and 1956, but wouldn't there have been some trail to follow?'

'Maybe my parents thought you would find us?'

'And Sato gave Natsu the letters?'

'She didn't say.'

'Has she read the letters?'

'I don't know. Mother gave me the package shortly before she died. She told me the letters were for you and, should I find you, to tell you they were sent in good faith.'

Natsu had burdened me with this final duty: to seal her adopted son's identity or destroy it. Everything he believed himself to be, everything he had imagined his life to be, rested with me and those letters. He was looking to me to join the pieces together and make him whole – the irony of the request. How could he expect me to fill in all those years? The Hideo I had known was not this man. He never would be.

Suicide

*Shinju: The most usual case is that of a man and a woman
committing suicide when they believe that their love for each
other cannot be fulfilled in this world. Other cases may involve a
family suicide as the result of the parents' financial failure in
business. Some people might also resort to a family suicide to
protect their honour.*

Kenzo's office was little more than a cupboard crammed
with shelves of books and a writing desk, a chair and a
chaise longue. One window looked out on to the trunk
of a pine and bushes, black with lack of sunlight. Mrs
Goto led Shige into the room. She asked if he would like
tea or coffee. He shook his head and sat down on the
chaise longue, then got up and walked to the window.
Yuko stood hidden in the shadows upstairs. She watched
her father come from the direction of the kitchen and
close the door behind him. Yuko went to a dark recess
beside the office and listened through the wall. The alcove
had been a place where she liked to hide as a child.

Shige said he had come that day to ask an important
question. He spoke with humble intonation. He wondered
if Kenzo would pay him the honour of listening to his
request. There was a scrape and a cough, and a 'certainly'.
Next Yuko heard a squeak of leather, and she imagined
Shige leaning forward. He said he had enjoyed the priv-

ilege of spending time with Yuko over the past few weeks. He said he realised Kenzo might have hoped for a suitor more equal in status to him, but he was 'very fond of Yuko'. Kenzo's voice grew bigger as he told Shige, welcoming to hear as this was, fondness got them nowhere. It was a start, but not an end. There was another squeak of leather. 'Mr Takahashi, please do not think me presumptuous, but I come here today to ask whether you would have any objections if I asked Yuko to marry me?'

Yuko knew this question had been coming, for weeks now, but still its arrival left her breathless. *I feel an actor in my own life story.*' There was a sound of a drawer opening and the thud of an object on the desk and then something lighter, followed by the glug of liquid. Yuko pictured her father passing a glass to Shige as he said such rites of passage must be marked with good malt. They toasted each other's health. 'So, let me understand. You want to marry my daughter?' Silence followed, which perhaps was some gesture of agreement. 'And how does she feel about you, I wonder?'

Kenzo's voice grew smaller as if he were looking away from Shige. 'You seem a good man. You have a brain, I can see that. I will not embarrass you and ask about love. I was very much in love with Yuko's mother. That young love, as if the world would end if we weren't together, you know?' Shige said nothing. 'The question I must ask, as her father, is this: is there more to this declaration of yours than love? We are practical men, you and I. As employees of Mitsubishi we find ourselves at the forefront of our nation's imperial and domestic ambitions. The years ahead will be busy ones with much opportunity for both of us.'

'I do understand a union with Yuko offers more than just her beauty and kindness, but sir, I assure you, if you will forgive my frankness, it is her love not my own advancement that I seek.'

'As I said, you are a practical man. I would only hope you had considered the other benefits of marriage to my daughter. But, of course, romantic fool that I fear I am, I'm glad it is not your priority. So, how should we advance this personal matter of yours? Should I ask her to join us here?'

Shige said he'd like permission to take Yuko out, just the two of them. A clink of glasses and Kenzo told him to wait in the hall. She fell back into the darkness as the door opened. Kenzo wished Shige luck and told him he would bring his daughter to the front door.

'I waited for Shige to leave the study. The grandfather clock ticked away the seconds as I walked from my hiding spot to the kitchen corridor, turned and then headed back toward the hall, pacing myself against those metronomic clicks. Shige looked around and I said hello. I sounded shy, an uncertain child's voice in an adult's body.'

A noise of footfall came from upstairs and Kenzo came halfway down the stairs. 'Ah, Yuko, Watanabe is here. I understand you have an excursion. Is that not right, Watanabe?'

'Father retreated back upstairs and Shige managed to look at me. "I thought we might visit Inasa Cemetery." He knew it was one of my favourite places to sketch. How could I say no?'

They took a taxi, sitting in silence. Yuko watched Shige fidget. His expression hovered somewhere between unease and despair. She tried to smile to reassure him but her dry lips formed more of a grimace. *'We must have looked unlikely lovers.'* They arrived at the entrance and Shige paid the driver. He walked in front of Yuko through the wet mud and grass toward the gravestones inscribed in Dutch. They stopped by a tomb cut into a slab of hillside with an iron railing across the entrance. He touched one of the metal posts and his fingers came away stained with rust. He apologised, called the place morbid, but Yuko told him she found it fascinating. Shige rubbed his forehead and said with a weak smile that they were walking in the oldest foreigner cemetery in Japan, but she probably knew this.

'I'm not sure whether practicality or kindness made me ask if he had brought me here for a reason. We had been circling the only question that mattered between us since our first meeting on the Dutch Slope. Maybe when I heard the question, I would know the answer. He cleared his throat and moved toward me. We stood face-to-face. "I wanted to bring you here because I knew you liked it, but it seems wrong somehow. All these dead people." I said it was a fine spot and he seemed to consider this for a while. When he spoke he addressed his feet. "We have spent these past weeks together. They have been most enjoyable. And you know, of course, how I feel about you." I told him I did not. He seemed confused. "You must know that I admire you." We were friends, yes, I assured him. He stared at me. "Well, yes, friends, but I see you as, well, more than a friend."

'"A sister?" I was not teasing him. I had to be sure. This time I needed a guarantee that I was more than a convenience. How could I know I had his heart as Jomei had captured mine? False words were no good to me.

'He glanced away, appalled. "No, no. You need me to say it? That I love you? I'm no poet, Yuko. My words are clumsy." He took hold of my hand. "I am happy when I see you, I miss you when

you are gone. You make me see my own failings but also how I might better myself. Is that not love?"'

Yuko could not say. Her understanding of love had been something different, more brutal and demanding and cruel in the way that one day it was there, the next gone. She thought of those doomed lovers who chose to leave this world rather than one another. Could she? No, she loved life too much to reject it. She had spent her young years capturing the beauty of living: the tensed muscle of a horse, a bird in flight, a mother and child walking hand in hand. Small moments of a glorious whole. She could not turn away from existence however much pain it caused her. And she told herself this: if Jomei was turmoil, Shige was calm. His presence soothed her as did his words. He spoke plainly and in good faith. *'I trust him. I am lucky to have found Shige. He will give me freedom that I cannot imagine with my parents. I can see how life can be: a home, a job, a family. Could Jomei have given me any of these? Besides, if he had cared for me, he would have found me again. Shige is a precious gift when I thought my heart dead. Move forward, Mother says, and so I will. It is too painful to live in the past.*

'I looked into Shige's eyes, still so physically shy with him. I pressed his fingers as encouragement and the world drew closer. Everything is in focus, even now, hours later. The shadow of a leaf falls across his face, a robin calls somewhere behind him, the damp fungus and soil scent the air. Shige lifts my hand up. He unfolds my fingers until my palm is open in his own. He lowers his mouth until his lips brush the surface of my life line and love line. He stands back up and I see the pulse of blood beat in a vein in his neck. So much life, just there. I raise my head and with one more beat of our hearts his mouth is upon mine. We stay that way until I am breathless and

151

must pull *away*. His question talks around the proposal but I know what he is asking. "Do you want to live in the same grave as me?" I answer yes, and we smile and kiss again and I think, at that moment, in Inasa Cemetery, we are both happy with all that the future might bring. And the truth must be faced: Jomei is gone.'

The Pearl Divers

Ama: Japanese women working outside the home is not a new phenomenon, especially in farming and fishing villages. Among them the most conspicuous workers, far more famous than their male counterparts, are women divers known as ama. They dive into the sea to collect shellfish such as awabi (abalone) and sazae (turban shell) or edible seaweed. When they appear from the water, they let out a deep breath, making a whistle-like sound called isobue (beach whistle).

Before we settled down to married life, Kenzo took me away for a vacation to a ryokan just outside Hirado, in the north-west tip of Kyushu. The city's history reminded me of Nagasaki. Sakikata Park had once been the site of stone warehouses constructed by Dutch traders before they were forced to Dejima. A white castle, three tiers of grey roof, looked out to the steel waters of the Korea Strait. We took a sailboat with other tourists around the coastline and anchored in a bay that teemed with blue fire jellyfish drawn there to mate. On another day we hired a car and drove to a nearby fishing village. We walked down to the coarse sand littered with white cockle shells and empty horn snails. I took off my yukata and sat in a black bathing suit and wide-brimmed cream straw hat to shield my face from the sun. Kenzo wore black swimming trunks. We stared at the sea, too hot to bother with conversation. A group of pearl divers arrived, wrapped in short kimono jackets, carrying wooden buckets, black nets and masks. They busied themselves collecting driftwood and dry seaweed to build a fire. As the flames took hold, they stripped down to small white cotton briefs decorated with printed bluebells, daisies and pink moss, unembarrassed by their tanned breasts, whether young or old. They chatted and giggled as they spat onto the glass of their masks and tied knives around their waists with rope. We watched them run into the breakers with the buckets, which they used as buoys. They disappeared beneath the water, for minutes it seemed, then rose with a whistle of dead air and dragged their catch from the pull of the tide. Later they warmed themselves by the crackling fire. I envied their lack of self-consciousness, the freedom and strength of their bodies, their acceptance of this hard job in freezing seas.

On the final night of our stay, Kenzo and I lay naked on the rumpled sheets of the futon, our bodies entwined and wet with sweat. An oil lamp by our side cast shadows over the tatami mat and sliding doors that led to a courtyard of walnut seedlings. Kenzo reached for something under the bedding. 'This is for you.' He placed a polished teak box in my palm and I prised its lid apart. Inside was a pendant shaped like an open oyster shell. A white pearl nestled near the hinge. I slipped the gold chain over my head and the oyster fell between my breasts. I thought of the diver who had found it, the fire in her aching lungs as she rose to the sea's surface, the joy when she found that gleaming gem amid the oyster's flesh. I thought of the girl I had been and the woman I might become. I felt

I did not deserve Kenzo, his love, his faith, his loyalty. I worried that some terrible part of me would ruin or damage this pearl of happiness he offered. I made a silent promise to be a good wife, a good mother, freed by marriage if also contained by it. I was the grit in the oyster, growing layers of worth and value, if I tried hard enough.

Seventeen years later, here we were, preparing to hold the betrothal ceremony for the child I had pledged myself to protect in that ryokan. Yuko was worried about the expense and the burden the ceremony would place on her future in-laws. She had tried to tell Shige the formality could be avoided but he had insisted. When she argued there was no need, he was Christian after all, he would not hear of it. Shige's parents had taken the ferry over from Iōjima and they would be joined by Mrs Kogi and their son. We knelt on the floor of the living area and waited for Mrs Goto to let us know all four had arrived. I slid the screen back. They walked barefoot across the floor, careful not to step on the edges of the tatami mat, and we took our places in the alcove. Kenzo and Mr Watanabe sat at the head of our party, followed by me and Mrs Watanabe then Yuko and Shige and finally Mrs Kogi settled nearest the entrance.

Shige, dressed in a suit, led the introductions, his face flushed with the effort. His father, Katsu, wore a dark blue yukata. His face was lined and brown from his life outdoors; his fingers were grazed with rope burns and old scars from fishing knives. He said little but his gruff voice had the quiet authority of a man who had fought raging seas and searing hot days and knew as a result of these encounters that nature was all that he had to fear. Shige's mother, Sonoko, wore a pale blue kimono, which had once been beautiful but the silk had lost its lustre; the odour of dust and sea damp clung to the threads. They presented gifts wrapped in hexagonal envelopes, white on the outside, red underneath. The rice paper was knotted with gold threads and decorated with designs of the crane and turtle, signs of longevity. Inside the packages there was dried cuttlefish to symbolise pregnancy, seaweed to represent a child-bearing woman, a piece of hemp to wish for the couple's hair turning grey together, a fan for prosperity, and money. The final gift was a tea plant, impossible to transplant and thus a wish that the marriage would last forever.

The formalities dispensed with, we dined on trays of yellowtail and tuna sashimi and squid and shrimp sushi delivered from a nearby restaurant. Kenzo poured sake and plum wine and we began to relax. The men talked of Japan's activities overseas, the increasing number of members of the armed forces appointed to positions usually held by civilians, such as ambassadors. They noted these developments without expressing an opinion that could be viewed as negative. We women spoke of the wedding, the minutiae of where to source the food, the most suitable restaurant to hold the reception, the best material for the dress, and the name of a good seamstress. I watched Yuko for signs of unease or doubt, but either she was indeed excited or, like me, she was learning to hide how she truly felt. The alcohol had made us all giddy and giggly, even Mrs Kogi. As the night drew to a close, Sonoko admired my necklace and I explained it had been a wedding gift from Kenzo. She smiled, her cheeks rosy with plum wine. 'The pearl divers on our island have a song to celebrate a good catch.' She looked coy. 'Would you like to hear it?' Kenzo clapped and said, 'Sing, you must sing.' She closed her eyes, a tremulous soprano filling the hot room.

> 'Hear our song of the sea, Susano-o
> Quiet the angry storm, Susano-o
> Keep our fire warm, Susano-o
> Make the oyster grow, Susano-o
> The pearl is my child, the shell my heart, Susano-o.'

She finished singing, touched her cheek and smiled at Yuko. We applauded and Kenzo cheered. I discreetly moved the sake away from his reach. Perhaps embarrassed by the silence that followed, Sonoko turned to my daughter.

'Shige tells me you are an exceptional artist.'

Yuko shook her head. 'It's just a hobby.'

I could not hide my pride. 'She is being modest.'

Sonoko reached for my daughter's hand. 'May I be a nagging mother-in-law already? You must not let your artistic talents go to waste. It is such a lovely thing to be able to show the world how you see it, the shadows and the light, and the spaces in between. We miss those details in everyday life. Art reminds us of what we have no time to see.' She tipped her head. 'I apologise. Perhaps that sounded far too grand? Come to the island. We can draw together.'

'She studied me with those artist eyes. What does she see? Does she think me good enough for her son? Am I good enough?'

As I stood up to serve strawberry-and-chestnut steam cakes Kenzo burst into song. 'The pearl is my child, the shell my heart, Susano-o.' He put his arm around Shige's father and they sang the lyric again. We lifted up our glasses in a toast. Suddenly sober, Kenzo declared: 'To our pearl, Yuko, and her oyster shell, Shige.'

The two of them laughed and nodded their thanks, carefree and unguarded in that drunken moment of celebration. Sonoko and I looked at one another, and in the polite smile we exchanged we acknowledged a mutual appreciation that this union, for whatever reasons, suited us all.

Filial Piety

Oyakoko: In old days, filial piety was one of the most valued codes of ethics binding children. In their childhood, they were taught to be obedient and loyal to their parents. On a daily basis, they were encouraged to help parents with various kinds of errands. If parents were too sick to work, elder children were supposed to take their place to support the family.

Yuko chose a Western-style dress for her wedding, high cut at the neck, the sleeves long, a fishtail gathering of crêpe silk at her feet. She had seen the design in a magazine and a seamstress had drawn up the pattern. The fabric clung to her thin frame as she stood in front of the mirror. She wore a veil of silk tulle decorated with mother-of-pearl butterflies along the trim. I told her she looked beautiful and Shige would be proud. Later that night she must be careful not to show her experience. I looked at my own black kimono, twisted around to check the embroidered plum blossom. 'I assume he thinks he's getting a virgin?'

'I said nothing. What could I tell her? We had kissed just that once. Mother watched me as I stared again at my ghost reflection. She told me to follow his lead. I must react and not act. Did I understand? Little did she know, the rousing of desire is not what I fear, but its absence.'

I had suggested holding the ceremony at Urakami

Cathedral but Shige felt it too ostentatious. I thought this a slight to Yuko, but I said nothing. Instead they had chosen Oura Church. I walked to Yuko's bedroom window and looked out at the palest pink flowers that adorned the trees in the garden. As planned she would be married by spring. I allowed myself a brief moment of congratulations until Mrs Goto entered the room with an envelope in her hand. A boy had just delivered the note. Yuko reached for the message and I felt a flare of apprehension. I stepped forward, warning her not to get ink on her dress and took the letter from Mrs Goto's grasp. I scanned the contents, nodded and smiled. A school friend of her father had sent his congratulations, I explained, before I put the letter in the dresser drawer. 'You can read it later, come, we'll be late, we must go.'

In the street Kenzo opened his arms wide and moved to kiss Yuko's cheek. 'Exquisite, hey, Mother?'

'Her make-up, husband.'

He kissed her fingers instead and gestured to the waiting car. 'Well, shall we deliver you to your groom?'

The butterflies trembled more visibly in the wind as Yuko stood surrounded by a crowd of bystanders. *'There I was dressed in wedding finery for a man I hardly knew, a good man, yes, but a stranger with a gentle mouth and still unknown hands. I try to imagine how life could be. Shige and I will build a home together; our days will be busy and productive; I will stay in the present, not the past. Jomei will become a memory, softened and healed by time.'*

We arrived at the white church and the few dozen guests were seated inside. Shige was dressed in a black tuxedo and bow tie, his hair shone from the oil combed through the short layers. He beamed as he watched Yuko come toward him, held steady in Kenzo's hand. Her white satin shoes clicked against the stone floor and there was a ruffle of movement as an organ creaked into a hymn and the heads of those gathered rose and turned.

'I saw them stare at me and then my mind went blank. I remember nothing of the priest's words, or the songs, or even the vows spoken or the kiss granted.' The wedding reception at a hotel near Mount Inasa was when memory came sharper into focus, if still fragmented and drowned by the noise of voices, champagne bottles popped and glasses clinked. Guests pressed envelopes stuffed with money into Shige's hand as Sonoko approached Yuko. *'My mother-in-law smiled and said, "It's overwhelming, isn't it? All the people, all their goodwill? Don't worry, my dear. They will soon get drunk and forget you are here." I smiled at her, conscious that we had never spoken privately. I told her I wished I could draw this moment but it was just a blur. She seemed to think about this for a moment before replying, "Shige is happy, this makes me happy. I hope you will let him make you happy?" She nodded and moved away to speak to Mother, who glowed, triumphant and relieved.'*

The newly-weds sat on two high chairs at the top of the room and dined on a banquet of snails and sashimi, steaks and Chinese noodles, and rice with red beans. More drinks were served and the guests grew even more lively. *'Shige turned to me and asked, "How's your throne, wife?" I told him, uncomfortable, and he agreed. "Let's go." Could we leave? He laughed. "The guests are waiting for us to do just that." We made our way out through the throng of people who offered three cheers for a good life. I looked for my parents but could only see the red, black and pink smudges of faces and clothes before we poured forth* from the confines of the hotel into a waiting taxi. Shige reached for my hand in the darkness of the interior and his palm was hot in my own. He leaned toward me and whispered so the driver could not hear: "Remember the day we met on the Dutch Slope?" Of course, I told him. "I've been in love with you since that very first moment." He could not see me but still I smiled. "Thank you, Shige." "For what?" he asked, his breath gentle against my neck. I turned my mouth to his. "For you."'

Inner Feelings

Honne-to-tatemae: An opinion or action influenced by one's true inner feelings and an opinion or an action influenced by the social norms. These two words are often considered a dichotomy contrasting genuinely held personal feelings and opinions from those that are socially controlled. Aiming at peace and harmony, the public self avoids confrontation, whereas the private self tends toward sincere self-expression.

Kenzo stood weaving from side to side in our garden as he looked up at the moon breaking through black clouds. A night heron called out in the dark. He sighed. 'The blossom will soon be over for another year.' I watched him make his way, loose-limbed with drink, to our door. He was a sentimental if practical man, and both traits had been good for me. My life since marrying him had been about control, constancy and loyalty. I had never once strayed but the chaos of the years before our married life echoed through me. I thought of Yuko and Shige alone somewhere in a ryokan. I could still remember that burn of fresh desire and the agony sometimes of its surrender.

We took the stairs to our bedroom and he stumbled forward for a kiss. I stroked his cheek and told him I would take some tea, I was still too excited by the day. 'You looked beautiful.' We kissed again and he smiled, satisfied by some unspoken thing. I waited until he slid shut the bedroom door before I made my way to Yuko's room. The letter sat pristine white against her sketchbooks, pencils and boxes of charcoal. I had not allowed the note to ruin the day. Its presence had reassured me. It proved Sato had heeded my warning and would stay away. This was the closest he could get to Yuko. I turned the envelope in my hands. No address, no seal, only her name. I sat by the window and read his words by moonlight.

Dear Yuko,

I apologise for not writing sooner. I wanted to do so, many times. News of your wedding has reached me and I must speak out. I hope it's not too late. I cannot believe that this union is anything but one of convenience and I beg you to find the courage not to go through with it. Know that I love you. If you ever had any doubt of this then with all my heart, I am sorry. I am no longer in Nagasaki but I am close enough for you to join me, should you wish. Do you love as I love? If you do, write to me at the address below. The recipient will be a friend who can deliver your response to me safely, without fear of discovery. Please forgive me for the manner in which I left you. I broke my promise. I said I would never let you go. Those words haunt me. Believe me, I had no choice. I did it to protect you. But it is not too late for us, Yuko. We can be what we once were. Is that what you want? Write and set me free.

Jomei

The arrogance of the man. How dare he threaten the wedding day. I had worked so hard to give Yuko this opportunity for a stable future with a good man. He would ruin Yuko, for what? Some vague promise of being together. This was typical of him. Status and self-regard came naturally to him. He would not have thought of the shame involved in the wedding being called off and the reason for it. All that mattered was his happiness, no one else's. He did not know what it took to build a life from nothing nor how it felt to live in fear of that security being taken away. I had followed the rules, I had buried my past for my daughter. He would destroy all this with a few hastily written words and some pathetic appeal for forgiveness.

I took the letter downstairs to the kitchen and stood in front of the hearth, where embers still burned. I held the paper to the white coals and watched the edges blacken and glow red and burst alive until all Sato's promises were taken from the world. The floorboards creaked with my footsteps as I made my way to Kenzo's office. I sat in his chair and placed a blank sheet of paper in front of me. I wrote *Jomei* in black ink. How hard could it be to mimic the voice of a heartbroken girl? Had it been so long since I was one myself? I had to convince Sato that further pursuit was futile. He was too late. Yuko had married Shige. She would have a comfortable, secure life with no more lies, no torment, no vows broken. This would be her future. I waited for the words to come and when they did I wrote not only for her but for me. I told him of hurt fossilised to anger, of rejection turned to hate, of truths that could not be ignored. Maybe I had loved him once, yes, but no longer. His actions proved what I had meant to him. Nothing. He let me go. That had been his decision. He could blame no one else. He must never have loved me and no paper promises would convince me otherwise. I begged him not to torment me again. He must stay away. He had made me desperately sad but I had found a husband who would be faithful and who made me happy. He was a fool if he thought I would risk a better man for him. This was my letter to Sato.

Decency

Seken-tei: One aspect of the national character of the Japanese is shame culture, in which people are more afraid of shame than sins. Fear of being held in disrepute by society gives the individual an adequate reason for refraining from acts offensive to public morals. Sensitive to criticism from others, Japanese people take much account of the public eye and mind what the world says about them.

The doorbell rang and I felt a rush of anticipation. My days had been so ordered, so devoid of interest. The man who called himself Hideo had brought possibilities of unknown hours and unexpected endings. He seemed loaded with energy. 'Get your coat, I'm taking you to lunch.' He waited outside, stomping his feet against the cold, while I put on my jacket, a knitted hat and fur-lined boots. I could not find my gloves so I shoved on Kenzo's black leather mittens. I had a canvas bag in one hand and he took my free arm. 'Here, it's slippery underfoot. Where's good to eat?' Kenzo used to like a small diner three blocks away so we headed there. The morning lectures and workshops had gone well, he said. A local TV station had given them good coverage and he might even make the evening news. Tomorrow would be the last full day of the conference. He had the morning free and then he would make one final speech before he flew

167

home the following day. The hours were leaching away and still so little resolved.

We reached the restaurant and he pushed open the door. A few customers turned their heads to look at us before a waitress led us to a table near the back. Her green uniform strained against her chest as she handed us laminated menus sticky with past meals. 'This is for you.' I handed him the bag. 'It belonged to Kenzo. I thought it might interest you.'

He pulled out an edition of the magazine *Life*. Kenzo had collected stacks of the publication, with its images of Marilyn Monroe, Queen Elizabeth and Eisenhower on the front covers. When he died I had thrown them all away apart from the issue from September 29, 1952, which featured blonde girls tap-dancing in leotards and fishnets. Above their heads were the words: *First Pictures – Atom Blasts Through Eyes of Victims*. Kenzo had been uncertain whether to show me what was inside. 'You might find it too distressing?' I had, of course, but also those images were validation of why we had left Nagasaki. The horror was real, not imagined. Five Japanese photographers had taken the shots in those first hours after pikadon, but US military censors kept their pictures hidden from public view through the duration of the occupation. On January 1, 1946, the Emperor had given his humanity declaration. He was no living god. The following year, the country outlawed war as a means to settle international disputes. In 1951, Japan had renounced its position as an imperial power by signing the San Francisco Peace Treaty. Only now could these photographs be shown. There was a child soon to die after her first sip of water, a baby, burnt by the flash, held to its mother's breast. Other wounded survivors hopelessly waited for aid among the corpses under the caption *The Walking Dead*.

Hideo turned the pages and after a while he looked up. 'I wonder about the weather, sometimes.' I did not understand him. 'Those clouds over Kokura that morning, the smoke from the fire bombs that drifted from Yahata, the fact the crew needed a visual marker, the fact they had a fuel problem, the delay waiting for the observation aircraft, the Japanese fighter planes drawing closer. All those details that made the plane divert to Nagasaki.' He closed the magazine. 'Think of the air currents that made those clouds part over Urakami just at that moment, at 11.02 a.m., so Fat Man could be dropped.' He shook his head. 'Fat Man. What sort of name is that? A bad joke.' He looked at the menu. 'Hideo Watanabe. It's just a name. Two ordinary words . . . but for those damned clouds. What will you eat, Grandmother?'

I would not be manipulated so easily. 'Hideo, I can manage to call you that, but the last time I was called Grandmother was thirty-nine years ago. I'm not ready to be that person again.'

He nodded his acceptance. 'Well, Hideo is a start, at least.' He turned his head in profile as he tried to catch the waitress's attention. His left ear had melted away, his nose, still small like a child's, must have been burnt to the bone, skin grafts had stretched the skin around his mouth. And yet those scars that had so shocked me seemed somehow less disturbing in the few hours we had spent together. The waitress arrived and he ordered a steak, rare. I chose corn chowder.

I stared at the yellow plastic water jug on our table, the ice cubes bobbing on top. 'Do you know what I think about that day?' He looked at me with those inquisitive eyes of his. 'I hear the children, crying out their last words. Not "Mother", or "help" but "water". *Mizu, mizu.* Every time I drink a fresh, cold glass of water that's what I hear, *mizu, mizu.*' He stared out of the window. 'Can I ask you a question, Hideo?' He nodded. 'Why have you no memory of life before pikadon?'

'At first the doctors thought I must have been knocked unconscious or suffered a brain injury when the bomb fell. They said it was perhaps some kind of retrograde amnesia. I was expected to remember, eventually. When I didn't, they decided it must have been some sort of emotional amnesia, a reaction to the trauma. Again they thought my memory would return. It never did.'

'So you remember nothing of your parents?'

'I have a memory of a green canvas bag, a grey ship. I'm standing by boxes, possibly at a harbour. A man, it must be my father, is saying something but I cannot hear him. I see the ship pulling away and the woman next to me is dressed in a nurse's uniform and she's crying.' He shrugged. 'I suppose every child had a story like that back then. Who knows? Is it even a real memory? Do I imagine a nurse because I was later told my mother was one? We tell ourselves stories and they become our history. I can't say what's real.'

'But you remember pikadon? The flash and the bang?'

'Yes.' He sat back at this, stared out of the window again. 'But I can't talk about that here.' The waitress brought our food, and when she left, he said, 'I'm not sure how

170

I can prove who I am. I guess I'm hoping there will be something, some small thing that you will recognise, some detail that confirms I am who I say I am.'

Maybe he spoke with sincerity, maybe I believed him, but I could not trust the doctor. 'You should know that Jomei's letters are written to Yuko. Why would he do that?'

He took his time with this revelation. 'Well, I can guess one reason, but I don't want to distress you.'

'Please, don't worry. I'm made of sterner stuff than I might look.'

'Well, if I survived, perhaps he thought there was some possibility she could have done so too. He was keeping a record of all those missing years.'

'But that's ridiculous. She died. I promise you. She died.'

He held his hands up. 'I can understand your suspicion. No word for years, and then I turn up. I'm not sure I'm what anyone would have in mind as a long-lost grandson. I understand that. But why is it so difficult to believe that I am Hideo? Can't you see how wonderful this is? How rare? How lucky?'

I looked at his poker face, made for neither deceit nor truth. I'd taught myself to hide my emotions over the years, while translating what a flicker of the mouth, an arch of the eyebrow, a tilt of the head meant in the faces of others, but his was an unreadable mask. I looked into those clear eyes of his. 'I'm not a great believer in luck.'

Pathos

Mono-no-aware: A feeling of sympathetic pity aroused by the pathos of things. In its more technical sense, it refers to an element in experience or in artistic representation, evoking compassion, and/or to a capacity for appreciating such an element. Mono-no-aware constitutes reflective contemplation and aesthetic appreciation of natural beauty and human existence.

Hideo arrived ten months after the wedding on a February morning filled with peach and lilac clouds. He was a gift of happiness for us all; a way for Kenzo and me to heal our relationship with Yuko after Chinatown. Watching her gently cradle him to her chest after he was born, I thought back to the time I had first held her in my arms. The midwife had passed me this wriggling, screaming, bloodied creature. I had never known such a mix of fear, joy and relief. Here was a tiny being wholly dependent on me but I had no idea how to be a mother. There was no example to follow, no parent of my own to go to for advice. I had stumbled along through motherhood, terrified when she gagged on milk, worried when I put her to sleep in her crib, concerned more by her silence than her cries. I had made that child so many promises: to love her, to shelter her, to fight for her. The fierceness of my love came as a shock. She was all that mattered. I looked for dangers everywhere, ready to attack any threat. I had felt that same raw animal need to protect Hideo, our crying, giggling, falling wonder. Yuko was good with Hideo, more relaxed than I had been with her, but still she felt the primitive fear experienced by mothers. We cannot help but imagine the hungry predator in wait outside our cave.

The rain is falling, soft drops that make the world seem clothed in wet silk. Hideo is asleep in his cot, fists scrunched in balls, eyelids flickering. What can he be dreaming of? What's frightening him at so young an age? He fascinates me: his skin, those tiny feet, his blinking eyes, what does he see or feel? Joy? Fear? Dare I think of his future, what his life might bring? Shige and I chose the name Hideo. Excellent Man. Such a mature name for one so young, but none of us are old. I'm only eighteen, already a mother and soon to be a qualified nurse. Shige is twenty-three and a mining engineer. Sometimes when Hideo cries, I can't stand the noise. I pick him up and pace, pace, pace around our home, anxiety rolling in my stomach. Shige takes Hideo from my arms, tells me to rest, tells me to eat, tells me he is proud of me. I can see how he cherishes this small life we have carved in the world. His happiness is infectious. He knows how to make me smile but sometimes the sadness does visit me. At night, when the house is still, or Hideo is feeding, I cannot help myself, I think of Jomei. I try to push what remains of him away, but the agony of his departure flares up, a salvo across the firmament of my mind. I tell myself Shige is the one here in the flesh by my side. But this love I have for him and for my child scares me in a different way. I have already lost one person I loved. What if I were to lose them too? The pain would be impossible. The thought leaves me breathless with fear. Today I listened to men on the wireless talk about the China Incident and I asked Father what will happen. He says, don't worry, we will be safe. But soldiers are dying, our nation's ambitions are killing them.

More volunteers head overseas to do their duty, more young boys are drafted to active service. I pray our family will be spared. But why should we be? Why would God help us and not others?'

I, too, look back and wonder: did we know where we were heading? The year of Yuko's marriage, 1937, we entered into an undeclared war with China that raged from Manchuria in the north to the borders of French Indochina in the south. That August, our troops landed near Shanghai; by December they had entered Nanking, China's capital. Kenzo would read the paper and frown. 'China is too vast, however many troops we send. What will the West do? Sit back, smile and say, please, Japan, help yourself?'

Nagasaki was the nearest major port to Shanghai and Japanese emigrants who had fled the fighting returned home through Dejima Wharf. So many came that the authorities had to set up white refugee tents at the train station. As the returnees waited for their new lives to begin beside the rail tracks, conscripts gathered alongside them ready to leave. Loved ones waved them off with flags and loud farewells on the long platforms. The boys and their families seemed thrilled and excited by the job at hand, the bettering of a nation. Even safe within our own island borders we were readying for the fight. The military police, the Kempeitai, warned people that speaking recklessly about military affairs would lead to punishment. New organisations came into force: the Civil Defence Headquarters based in the City Hall was established to prepare for air raids. The following year the National Mobilisation Act came into effect, commandeering factories and government budgets for war production and

nationalising newspapers that told us of our successes.
Rations were imposed on petrol, leather and coal. In 1939,
as war broke out in Europe, we watched newsreels of
Adolf Hitler address crowds, arms raised in salute. Wage
controls came into force, the price of cigarettes rose, their
names changed from the language of the enemy, Cherry
and Golden Bat, to their Japanese equivalents, Sakura and
Kinshi. The message was clear: not only our government,
or our municipal leaders, but all of the Japanese people,
even our young, were to unite in a great battle. In 1940,
dance halls closed. By September, Japan had joined the
Axis Pact, becoming an ally of Germany and Italy, and
our forces entered French Indochina. In December,
America banned the export of scrap iron to our shores;
the next year, oil and steel joined the list. Authorities
and the press talked about the Greater Co-Prosperity
Sphere, which called for more space to ease our populated
lands. Japan lacked natural resources, we needed more
oil, rubber, tin and coal. Shige was sent increasingly to
Gunkanjima, the coal-mining island off the coast of
Nagasaki. The tower blocks and concrete walls made it
look like a battleship sailing to war. Sometimes he would
be gone for weeks. Between departures he and Yuko would
take Hideo on a day out, building memories as a family,
even if their son would be too young to remember them.

'Yesterday, we drove to the Shimabara peninsula and went to a
beach. Hideo clambered to his feet on the flat sand and grinned.
We have named this look his naughty face. Suddenly he was off,
half walking, half running his way to the water's edge on those fat
legs, his head bobbing from side to side. We ran after him and each
took hold of one hand, lifting him up and then dropping his feet

into the surf as he laughed. Later we cooked oysters on a fire, their sea juice spitting as we watched smoke flow from Mount Unzen. The volcano has not erupted since 1792 but still I stared at that black, smouldering peak, wary. As Shige packed this morning, he told me not to worry. The mine is safe, the work important, how else will we build ships or fuel homes? He kissed me, held me to him, told me he would be home soon enough. Now he is gone, and I'm alone again. I hate it when he is not here. I have Mother and Father, friends at the hospital if needed, but I miss the solidity of him. His presence keeps me calm, reminds me always of what happiness can be. I circle the date he says he will return, December 14, 1941.'

But first came December 7 and two words changed the world: Pearl Harbor. The news came over the radio at around 9 a.m. I listened to Prime Minister Hideki Tojo telling us we would have to sacrifice everything for our country's cause. *'Our adversaries, boasting rich natural resources, aim at domination of the world. In order to annihilate this enemy and to construct an unshakeable new order of East Asia, we should anticipate a long war.'* The Battleship March blared out and I phoned Kenzo at his work, asked him what this would mean to us. He said Shige would be safe, his work on the domestic front was vital, there were other men to send abroad. In those first few months, our family seemed protected. Shige came and went to Gunkanjima as we watched neighbours' boys receive their call-up papers. At first the news was astonishingly, perhaps unbelievably, good. Films were made of our great triumphs in Hawaii and Malay. We held lantern parades to celebrate and lines of people waited outside the cinema desperate to hear of more victories. In news reports our pilots stood

176

proud and handsome in white mufflers as they drank their farewell cups of sake. 'Banzai,' the audience would shout, cheering in the dark. When footage flickered on captured enemy soldiers, humiliated in their surrender, we felt a quieter pride. The authorities described our forces as 'invincible' and our men were 'military gods'. But we could not deny that these results seemed to come at terrible costs: many men never came home. And now we had the combined beast of America and Britain straining at the leash.

At home we lauded our lost. Black streamers fluttered outside homes for a father, husband or son killed; placards declared here is a 'house of honour'. We reminded ourselves that great courage was needed to win the war, not just from our soldiers, but from ordinary citizens. We followed the rules, put up air-raid curtains, handed over gold jewellery, bought more government bonds as every six months a new cabinet came to power. Metals were collected from Shinto shrines, ancient bells melted down, Christian graveyards and Buddhist temples were plundered, businesses stripped of rain troughs or window grilles. Even the hangers for mosquito nets were handed over.

Early in 1942, the rations became more severe. Shops shut and the black market flourished. Women traded kimonos for rice. We called those grains our white silver. People in the streets began to look unkempt, harried, thinner than they had been. Instead of lessons, students carried out volunteer work. This was education enough for them, parents were assured. On excursions to nearby forests, they cut pine roots, which were turned into fuel. We lost more weight, shadows darkened under our eyes, stomachs growled their complaints. The euphoria of those first few months of dazzling success in the Pacific began to fade in our collective memories. In June came the Battle of Midway. US torpedo planes and dive-bombers destroyed four of our carriers and a cruiser. Kenzo shook his head. 'We are too exposed, Amaterasu.' Then one spring morning in 1944 Yuko was awoken by a knock in the dark just before the break of dawn.

'A military affairs clerk stood at our door, with red call-up papers in his hand. He needed to speak with my husband. I stood in the shadows as the man told Shige he must report for officer training by 10 a.m.; it would be pointless to contest. An address would be forwarded to me. Shige had a class-A physical and his engineering skills were needed more now at the front. The man bowed and made his way to the next home on his list. We stood in our kitchen and Hideo, alerted by the noise, joined us. His hair was standing on end, a crease of cotton imprinted on his cheek. "Is it morning yet?" Shige picked him up and swung him around. "It's a special day today. Help your mother make us a big feast to celebrate." He went back upstairs to pack and I made red rice for breakfast. While he and Hideo ate, I went to Shige's canvas bag and hid a senninbari I had made under the few possessions he planned to take. A thousand stitches on a belt, could they ward off bullets? The hours went too quickly and soon we were standing by the rail tracks and I was saying goodbye to my husband. "I'll be back," he said. "The training will only be for a few months. We can go to the beach when I return, eat okonomiyaki, get drunk on plum wine, give Hideo a brother or sister, what do you say?" I tried to smile but I felt as if he had taken hold of my heart and *was squeezing it in his hand. Hideo did not understand what was happening but my tears brought on his own. Shige knelt down, whispered in his ear, "Look after your mother." Then he left. I looked at my son, still too small, too vulnerable, and I thought, "How am I to look after you?" I've just found the envelope Shige must have hidden under our bedsheet before he left. I unfold his note and hold his words to my skin: "I promise you when this is over I will never leave you again."'*

Three months later he did come back for ten precious days before he left for the front line. He seemed changed, harder, more distant. He was still Shige, yes, but a soldier now. While he and Hideo played in the park one day with a kite, Yuko and I watched them from the shade of a maple. She whispered of Shige's late-night confessions, the prisoner he had been made to kill as proof he was ready to fight. He described the way his commanding officer had unsheathed his sword, scooped water on both sides of the blade and said, 'This is how you do it.' He remembered the officer's anger when he realised his sword had been bent by the force of the cut. I asked Yuko why he would tell her this. She said, 'He had no choice. I found him crying.' Shocked, perhaps more by the tears, I looked at my son-in-law, who was unwinding string from a branch. 'Did he do it?' She looked at me, one sharp nod of the head. 'He was following orders,' I told her and we forced the conversation on. He shared one final goodbye with Yuko and Hideo, this time down by the harbour. More tears were shed, more promises spoken, more plans made for when he returned the next time. We never saw him again, but at least, at first, she had the comfort of his letters.

179

'Hideo keeps asking where Shige has gone. He gets confused, asks if his daddy is back on the coal rock, his name for Gunkanjima. I explain Shige is a soldier now but he does not understand. Neither do I. His letters are jigsaw puzzles. I try to read what he really means in those cheery lines. He always sounds so light as if he, like a child, is playing at war. He writes of drinking bottles of Tiger beer on the boat that took him to his destination and the food they eat wherever he is stationed. "Honestly, lizard is delicious. Such pink meat, such a juicy taste, but tell Hideo, water buffalo is not good." I showed some of the letters to Father to see if he can find clues. He looked at the map in his study and pointed at Burma. "He's maybe here with the 15th Army. That would be good. He'll be safe there. Wherever he is, don't worry, Yuko. Your priority is Hideo now." In December Yuko received a postcard from Shige with a printed list of statements. He had circled the most appropriate: I am very well, I am confident of victory, this fight is a noble one. Scribbled in his own hand, he wrote: 'Be proud of me as I am of you. I think of you and Hideo always. The thought gives me strength.'

Then six months went by and she heard nothing. No more letters, or postcards, no word from the military either. I told her she had to believe him alive until she was told otherwise. Communication lines were challenged by the fighting, yes, but surely, if he had been killed, she would have been informed by a telegram or a death notice. The newspapers were full of our men who had sacrificed themselves for our country. His name never appeared among them. But Yuko needed proof of life, some hint of Shige alive in the jungles or seas or prison camps. 'He's dead, he's gone,' she said, her body doubled over with the anguish of that thought. Those months of silence were filled with more military defeats, more hunger, growing fears of the enemy's retribution if we failed. Decades later, reading Yuko's diary, I learned this was when Sato returned: January 4, 1945.

A Spirit

Hitodama: According to folk belief, if the spirit of a dead person is not satisfied with the way it is treated by the bereaved family, it hovers around in graveyards at night in an effort to locate the right place for a peaceful settlement. The form it supposedly takes when travelling is a reddish, yellowy or bluish-white ball of fire with a tail.

What to say of the moment you see a living ghost? The day was ordinary, the sun did not shine any brighter, the ward did not look any different, but in a heartbeat her world transformed and her fate was sealed. The shock coursed through her body, along quickening blood to eyes that doubted their vision, even her sanity, but Sato was no illusion. He stood surrounded by a group of nurses who were listening attentively as he dispensed instructions. I imagined the panic in her lungs, the strafing in her stomach, the scream in her mind when she recognised him. She waited for him to look up, but still he checked a clipboard and smiled at a patient and walked to a bedside.

'He must see me. Had I grown so invisible? Was I so much changed? Finally he glanced up and stopped talking. Across the ward we stood, only forty feet but eight years apart. I felt as if I was standing on a precipice, staring down into the waves below, the urge so strong to fall. Step back, Yuko, step back. One step and then another and more

until I was out in the hospital grounds, my breath ragged, my heart so alive it might break free from my chest. I pushed past a screen of shrubs, walked over fallen branches and damp moss. I heard footsteps and the rustle of leaves behind, but I did not turn around. I kept going until I came to a clearing encased by trees. I waited for him to arrive, terrified and thrilled in near equal measure. I see him, standing in front of me as if we had never been apart. All that love, that desire, that pain floods over me. Here is Jomei. Not in my head. Here. I cannot speak at first, I can only stare. The mouth, the mole, his is such a cruel beauty. "Is it you?" He says nothing. I walk up to him. "Are you real?" I dare to touch him, hold my open palm to his chest. "You've been gone so long." I lay my head against his shoulder, allow myself these few moments, and then I think of Shige. I tell myself to hold on to the smallest possibility he is still alive. I move away. "We cannot be the way we were. Do you understand?" He seems wounded by these words but not surprised. He cannot look at me when he speaks. "I had no idea you were a nurse. If I'd known, I'd . . ." He shakes his head and I close my eyes. When I open them he is gone. I listen to the sounds of the world beyond this cloak of trees. I hear a woman's laughter, a rumble of traffic, signs of life. I say a prayer to my husband. Please, Shige, send word. Remind me I am still a wife. Tell me those vows still matter.'

Those first few days Yuko kept her distance as did he, but they were two caged animals prowling around the pen. She caught him watching her sometimes, staring at her as if she were a riddle to be solved. She had her own questions, ones that had gone unanswered for too long. Why had he not contacted her? Why had he sent no word? Why was he back now? The gossip did the rounds quickly. Sato had been posted abroad for a couple of years, had been up north somewhere and had been seconded to the medical college, which was desperately short of staff. His reputation proceeded him and the nurses frothed around the handsome doctor with the disarming smile and flirtatious manner.

'I count the days as they pass. Jomei has been back two weeks. I try to ignore this desperate need to be near him. Instead I scour the death lists in the newspaper to reassure myself that Shige's absence from those pages is a sign he is still alive. He has to be, for Hideo, for me, for him. Every day that I don't see his name, I tell myself, stay true, have faith, be strong. But some days all I can imagine is a rotten body abandoned in a jungle. This morning as Hideo prepared for school, he asked, "Is Daddy dead?" I looked at him, shocked by his bluntness. What a question for a son to ask. What could I say? "No, he's just away somewhere being brave, he's being a soldier." Hideo scratched his nose. "Tadashi's daddy is dead." I passed his clothes to him. "Tadashi must be sad." He nodded and clambered into his shorts. When I arrived at the hospital later that morning I heard Jomei had been called to the prisoner-of-war camp near the foundry. He needed an assistant and there was no shortage of volunteers. I watched the chosen nurse talk with him before she disappeared into the changing room to collect her belongings. He left the building and, iron filings to his magnet, I followed him. "Take me instead, Jomei," I said. He looked at me, cautious. "Why? You made it clear to stay away." I could not tell him of the lonely nights passed and those still to come. I could not tell him of the nightmares I have of Shige's death. I could not tell him my body has forgotten the touch of another's hands. Instead, I said, "I need to feel happy today, Jomei, just for a few hours. Spending time with you used to make me happy. Let's see if it still does." He looked at me, silent. I don't know what he saw.'

When they arrived at Fukuoka 14 Camp the prisoners stood in groups behind wire fences, emaciated and burnt by the sun. Some grunted words at Yuko, or whistled, but most said nothing, their wide eyes watching in silence. Sato and Yuko passed two men emptying latrine cans onto the officers' tomato plants, the fruit as big as apples. Two hundred prisoners had arrived days earlier, all of them survivors of a cargo ship, which had been sunk as they were being transported to Japan. Injured men needed treatment before they joined the other POWs working at the Mitsubishi foundry. The camp commander led Yuko and the doctor to an examination room and the first patient was brought in, limping from a hernia. He was young, British, a shock of red freckles across his nose. Sato talked to him in English and the boy began to undress, blushing as he glanced at Yuko. He eased himself onto the table and lay back and she placed gauze over his eyes. Beads of sweat lined his upper lip. She took his hand in her own, squeezed his bony fingers and Sato began to operate.

'I don't know how but I kept myself from shaking as I passed instruments and administered medicine. We worked in silence, in synchronicity. I took pleasure from watching his hands work and listening to his broken English. When had he learned to speak the language? The afternoon was a perfect moment, a dream realised after eight years of hoping for it. Dusk had fallen by the time we left the camp. We stood outside the gates and Jomei asked if he could drop me off anywhere in the taxi when it arrived. I did not plan what happened next. I'm sure I acted spontaneously. Hideo was staying with my parents that night, I had some free hours. Did he want to have a drink with me? "I thought we might be friends," I told him. He reached for a cigarette in his pocket and repeated the word as he flicked open the lighter. "Friends? Can we be friends? You think it

likely?" I told him possibly, if we try. "What would your husband think?" I felt shamed by his words. Who was he to judge me? I started to walk away but he called out, "OK, one drink. I know a quiet place."'

They took a taxi to Maruyama and the buildings and paving stones seemed much dirtier than she remembered. The lanterns that advertised the bars still shone, but the paper was torn, grubby, lopsided. They passed prostitutes who flashed their red under-kimonos as they called out to a group of sailors, gleaming bright in their navy whites. Yuko and Sato walked down a less frequented alleyway to a black entrance painted with a white chrysanthemum. The dull thud of a gramophone began to leak through the walls as they climbed the stairs. They reached a door decorated with a poster of Greta Garbo as Mata Hari.

Inside, beside a small wooden bar, two men stood dressed in blonde wigs, red satin evening gowns stained at the armpits and scuffed gold heels. The shorter and rounder one ran up to greet Sato. He gave Yuko a critical eye and introduced himself to her as Greta. His friend was called Simone. Greta led them past the other clientele, Mitsubishi workers and more sailors on leave, and found them a table near a stage. An old lady in a US soldier's uniform placed two bottles of beer on their table. The opening bars of 'I Get a Kick Out of You' poured out of a speaker and Simone and Greta shuffled onto the raised platform. They began to sing the song in tortured English as they high-kicked their way across the stage. The audience clapped and Greta worked the crowd, sitting on Sato's knee, wrapping a feather boa around his neck. Another song, 'You're the Top', was followed by more beer, the brew weak and mouldy, but potent enough to provide the illusion of intoxication. The cabaret show clattered to a close with 'What a Joy to be Young' and Simone and Greta disappeared behind a silver lamé curtain, ripped down one side.

'I asked Jomei how he had found this place and he said Greta had dragged him off the street. How had she and Simone avoided the attentions of the Kempeitai? He did not know. He said we could go somewhere else if I felt uncomfortable. No, I told him I liked the bar. It was so far removed from my own life. He ordered more drinks and I watched him pour cloudy yellow liquid into two glasses. I wondered how different the man in front of me was to the one I had known in Chinatown. I am so changed, how can he not be too? I had been a young girl and Jomei had been new and thrilling. I felt a similar excitement that night to be out in the city, drinking and laughing. For a few hours, I could be young again, not a mother, or a nurse, or a wife who might well be a widow. I wanted to get drunk, to lose myself. We downed the drinks and I poured more. I had conjured up nights like this one, many times, over the years. Jomei and I together once more, how it might be, how it might feel. I had imagined joy and fear and vindication. Our reunion would confirm that we should never have parted. Only we were different. I am not Cio-Cio-san. I am not even Yuko Takahashi. I am Yuko Watanabe. I reminded myself the man sitting opposite me in this cheap bar had abandoned me. How can I not be angry? But what I felt was more forgiving, more complicated. What about him? Maybe he felt nothing. I reached for more drink. The liquor loosened my tongue. We gossiped about which doctors were having affairs with which nurses. We knew to keep the conversation light.'

She told him about training to be a nurse, the day she had been handed an amputated leg in a bucket and had tried to throw the bloody stump out in the garbage before a janitor pointed her in the direction of the incinerator. She felt flattered when Jomei laughed, more so when he told her she was skilled at her job. They moved on to tales of Hideo, the day he had stuck a wasabi pea up his nose, the morning she found him reaching for a fat black mukade centipede, drawn to its yellow legs and unaware of its bite, the expression on his face when he ate his first salt plum. The laughter felt good, a release of tension. She could feel herself unfurl, like a nadeshiko at dawn, pink and slender on a strong stalk. They never mentioned Shige.

Carelessly they found themselves talking about Iōjima, the elderly couple who always squabbled on the ferry over to the island, the sound of the sea lice scuttling over rocks. Yuko cringed. 'There must have been millions of them.' Sato slapped the table in amusement and shouted above the second act of the stage show, 'And remember the sea urchin? The way you kept clasping your leg, "Am I dying, Jomei? Am I?"' She pouted. 'I never said such a thing.' Still she laughed, remembering the pleasure she had felt when he carried her in his arms. But Iōjima wasn't just about Jomei. The island belonged to Shige too. Yuko stood up, excused herself and made her way to the toilet. She peered in the mirror. Her face was red with the alcohol, her eyes bloodshot. 'Remember who you are,' she said to her reflection. 'Remember the pain this man caused.' She walked back to the table, suddenly more sober.

'Jomei seemed quieter too, subdued. We looked at one another. I could not avoid the question any longer. "Should we talk about what happened?" He took a long time to reply. "Does it matter now?" This

angered me. How could he be so indifferent? I persisted. "What if the affair hadn't been discovered? What then?" He grimaced as he swallowed more drink. "It's impossible to say. It's probably best not to think too much about it." How could I not? Where would our lives have taken us if Chinatown had never ended in that way on that day? I felt foolish for expecting some kind of explanation, some show of regret. Mother was right, it seemed. He had not cared for me. I tried to conceal my hurt. I smiled, nodded my agreement. "You're right. The past is better kept where it is. And look at us now. Two old friends catching up." I clinked my glass against his. He gave me another wary, sad smile. "I'm surprised you even want to talk to me." Why would I not? I had so many questions to ask. Now it was his turn to look confused. "When I saw you that first day in the ward, I thought about the letter, your anger. I thought you would be furious." Suddenly I felt sick as I leaned forward to ask above the screech of Greta's laughter, "Jomei, what are you talking about? What letter?" He said the words slowly as if he could not believe he had to repeat them. "The letter you sent after your wedding." "How could I write a letter? I didn't know where you were." It only took seconds for us both to realise what had happened. Mother. I asked him what the letter had said. He just held his head in his hands for a long time. "It doesn't matter. It's in the past. Let's forget it." I looked at him, appalled. "If you don't tell me, I'll ask her." He considered this and reached for my hand. My desire was like a light bulb crackling to life in the dark. "You can't. If you do, she'll know I'm back in Nagasaki." Our fingers intertwined. "Neither of us wants that, do we?"'

Sato stood up, unsteady on his feet, and said he would walk her home. She held onto the edge of the banquette for balance and looked around. Greta's wig had slipped even farther back as she loaded dirty glasses onto a tray with exaggerated care. They headed to the door and Simone waved a dishcloth in farewell. Outside the streets were wet with rain and the only sound was their feet on the cobbles. They traced the route along the river to the doorstep of her home, hidden behind a wall. Sato looked up at the two-storey house and sighed, as if resigning himself to his next disclosure. 'The letter I wrote, it was an apology, for the way I left. I wanted you to know how sorry I was.'

Yuko leaned against the door. 'And you believed the letter you received back?'

'Why would I not? The feelings were so heartfelt. Your mother left no room for doubt. I believed you hated me.'

She sighed. 'What if I'd seen your letter? Would we be here today, like this?'

He stared off into space. 'It's too late to ask these questions.'

Yuko said he sounded sad but angry too. What more could he expect? What more could either of them expect? Eight years is nothing to the world but something to the human heart.

'Where did you go, Jomei? Where did you learn to speak English? Abroad?' He shook his head, looked to the ground as if wrestling with some moment of confession. 'Maybe I'll tell you one day, Yuko, but not tonight, not now.' She had one more question to ask then no more. 'I loved you, Jomei. I learned not to over the years; at least, I thought I had. When I never heard from you, I decided Mother was right, I meant nothing to you. You never loved me. Is that true?'

Sato shook his head and took her chin in his hand, tender with the truth. 'Yuko, how can you say that? I've never loved anyone but you.'

Not my letter, not their forced separation, not marriage, not even the war could stop what happened next.

'We kissed on that doorstep, with caution and care. No more words were spoken. We had found one another again. I took his hand and led him through the house to my bedroom. Of course I thought of Shige but I stilled my mind long enough to see only Jomei in front of me. I could not resist him, I never could. He is my drug, my opium. Chinatown and Iōjima seem foreign countries. We are no longer those people. We are new and different. I am grateful for his return. The dawn is rising and Jomei has just left. We did not talk of love when we parted. We will not speak of love when we meet again. There is no need. He is the secret I stitch into my heart.'

An Awakening

Satori: In the Buddhist philosophy, spiritual enlightenment constitutes attainment of transcendental wisdom by intuitive insight. According to Zen sects, it is the realisation of Buddhahood inherent in human beings. They believe that the attainment of this wisdom will lead one to the state of freedom from karma and suffering (bonno), or to the state of nirvana (nehan), which is the ultimate goal of Buddhism.

I knew from Sato's letters that he learned to speak English in China. No wonder he did not tell Yuko where he had gone after he left Nagasaki. His silence just proved the moral coward he was. Confessions to a dead woman are meaningless. In 1937, he and Natsu had moved back to his home town of Kumamoto, a few hours east of Nagasaki. His father-in-law had found him a position at a hospital, where he specialised in immunology, specifically in organ transplantation. Four years passed before the war caught up with him and he was dispatched to Shanxi in the north of China. He was part of a medical team preparing doctors on their way to the front line. Some of the medics had never seen a bullet wound or had never had to treat mass cases of dysentery, typhoid or tuberculosis. Sato was expected to help make them battle-ready.

On my first day in the operating theatre my superior, Masaru Hayashi, told me we would run through some basic surgeries, while a group of ten doctors observed. He would lead and I would assist. Two guards brought a Chinese prisoner to the room. He was young, in farmer's clothes. The nurse told him to lie on the table and she administered anaesthesia to his spine. 'Can you feel your legs?' she asked but he did not reply. Next she tried to give him chloroform and maybe then he realised what was about to happen. He began to struggle and some of the men held him down until he became still. Then we began our procedures, first with the removal of his appendix, next a leg and finally we lacerated his bowel and tried to repair it. When he was dead we let the men practise dissections. My hands were shaking as I scrubbed down. Hayashi noticed and this embarrassed me. As he left for the canteen, he said, 'It gets easier, don't worry.' Yuko, he was right.

This might have been his war had it not been for a visitor to the hospital at the start of 1942 who went by the name of General Shiro Ishii. Sato had shown the general around the facilities and, a month later, a letter came and, as instructed, he took a train to Harbin city. The stench of manure in the streets from the horse carts was overpowering as he walked to the bus station past opulent carved facades and shining domes built during the time of the Russian tsars. The trip to the village of Pingfang, past fields of red sorghum, took an hour. Inside an innocuous-looking building of yellow stone with a red-tiled roof a professor from Osaka led him through his induction: division one researched the bubonic plague, cholera, anthrax, typhoid and tuberculosis; division two developed warfare and field experiments; division three was the factory that produced biological agents in artillery shells; division four made other agents; division five looked after training; the last divisions were responsible for equipment.

The professor told Sato he would be placed in division one. He opened a filing cabinet thick with files and explained how their patients came marked for special deportation as 'die-hard anti-Japanese' or 'incorrigible'. Most were Chinese civilians but sometimes enemy soldiers were used. He said the locals had been told the site was a water plant or a lumber facility. The professor rapped the metal cabinet with his knuckles. 'These are our little logs.' Sato had ended up at what was officially known as the Epidemic Prevention and Water Purification Department of the Kwantung Army. He and his colleagues called it Unit 731. Here his knowledge of immunology and transplantation was tested to its limits. If Shanxi had been the descent into hell, Pingfang was the final destination.

At first he only worked on animals. He administered shots of cyanide, nitric acid and strychnine nitrate to rabbits and made notes on their seizures. But a month after he arrived he was given a security pass to two buildings inside an inner court, separated from the rest of the complex by an iron gate. Here he found bacteriological scholars from prestigious universities who showed him their studies, explained what they had learned, what hypothesis they hoped to test next. He watched researchers culture bacteria or breed fleas. He helped technicians, naked apart from white gowns, flash red lights in black rooms to coax the fleas into the dark of a waiting cylinder. The parasites would then be released in cages among rats infected with the bubonic plague. Later the prisoners would be selected. Every night he took baths in disinfectant, his skin stinking and bleached, but his mind could not be so easily sterilised.

I told myself this was science, the advances made would benefit all humanity. Breakthroughs in medicine take extraordinary measures. I tried to see the prisoners used as one might those lab rats. But I could not escape the question, how to live with all the suffering we inflicted? How to face the memory of those shouts of 'Japanese devils' from the prisoners when we came for them? The screams followed by silence. How to live with all that knowledge we acquired? I promised myself one day this would be over. I would take what I had learned and leave. And I did but I could never forget. What would you have said had I told you who I truly was that night on your doorstep? You could not have loved the man I was and so I hid the devil from Pingfang from you. But I cannot undo these deeds. The monster is me.

On days off, he would take the bus to a place where he could forget the work he did for his country. Customers chose their women from photographs displayed on a wooden veranda. They all had flower names: Peony, Chrysanthemum, Lotus, Plum Blossom. They even had a Western woman at the pleasure palace, Rose. He found her lying on a filthy futon, coiled up, foetal. She flinched when he knocked and entered, drew her knees higher. Her soles were bare, black with the journey she had taken. Her calves were thick and stained with dirt. He could not see her face but her hair was worn loose, dirty brown, knotted down her back. He imagined lice laying eggs in those unwashed follicles. He moved to the window and began to smoke. The tobacco roused her and slowly she turned around. He could not determine her age but he learned later she was thirty-four. She had two children, alive somewhere, she hoped. Her cheeks had the hollow mark of malnutrition, her mouth stretched in a mock smile, the grimace of starvation. Her nose was long and thin. Her forehead and eyes were too large for her head, like a fly, but her body was solid despite her hunger.

'Cigarette,' she said in English and then she repeated the word in Japanese.

'You speak Japanese?'

She held out a palm and he moved toward her and gave her the one in his mouth. 'A little.'

'Your name is Rose?'

She considered the word for a moment and shook her head. She pointed at his pocket and he handed her another cigarette. She took it, moved from her bed and placed her prize on the windowsill, where she perched looking out through the shreds of an orange curtain.

'My name is Alva.'

They smoked in silence and when she had finished her cigarette she undid the buttons of her dress, once patterned with pink rose buds long turned grey. She stood up and pulled the fabric over her head. Bruises were patterned yellow and green and purple and black over her breasts and hips. Teeth marks were pressed into her back. She took his hand and led him to the squalor of her bed. He would never forget the smell of sweat and blood and other men. She took his hand and pressed his fingers between her legs, until she was wet enough to be ready for him. When he was done, she walked to a bucket of water, wrang out a cloth and wiped herself down. 'Next time, bring me a packet of cigarettes.'

Sato worried about diseases carried by the other men but he couldn't resist the foreignness of her. He did not want to be reminded of home. He bought her cigarettes and medicine and once a new dress he found at a street stall. Alva never wore it. She told him she would do so when she left the comfort palace. She wanted to look pretty when she met her children again, if she ever did. He never found out. Sato left Pingfang halfway through 1943, first to Tokyo for a time, and finally he arrived back in Nagasaki at the start of 1945. But he carried China with him. The cries of the prisoners, the staff sheathed in white safety suits, that iron gate to the inner complex: they haunted him.

Rumours of the dark acts committed there had surfaced in the years after the war and Sato expected for many years to be prosecuted for his work. But the authorities never came for him, nor many of the others. They knew too much, their knowledge of bacteriological warfare was too important. Many returned from China to senior posts at hospitals, universities and research laboratories, both in Japan and America. Others were not so fortunate. In 1946 he read of Hayashi's imprisonment for war crimes.

He looked at the picture of an innocuous man in round metal glasses and a neat moustache and thought, 'Why you, Masaru? Why not me?' I began to understand why Sato had hidden away at the orphanage for five years after the war. Not for fear of exposure, but guilt. Those children and his studies, perhaps Hideo most of all, were his attempt at atonement, but could they ever make up for all those lost logs at the lumber factory? He waited until 1968 to publish his research on the effect of the atomic bomb on child victims. He wanted his case studies to have turned twenty-one years of age so that the work would be definitive, thorough, indisputable. If the book was another bid for redemption, he seemed strangely unmoved by its poor reception. He reasoned he could not force people to face what he had concluded from the wards and X-rays and medical samples. Experts lined up to dismiss the data he had collated in the orphanage and Nagasaki. They argued his case studies, those two marked toddlers in particular, would have developed their conditions regardless of August 9, 1945. A few voices backed him up but their support was muted. He understood the negative reaction. *Yes, we mourn our dead, and we campaign for proper health care and compensation for the survivors of pikadon, but we seem more resistant when it comes to accepting how that day carried forward in our bones and in our offspring. Is it not safer to contain the horror to one day? How could we parade these children, now adults, to the world, and say, look, this is the legacy? And who was I to do this?'*

In 1970 he had just turned seventy-five when he began to suffer from night sweats, fevers and aching muscles. Natsu forced him to go for tests and the results came back: leukaemia.

Of course, I wonder if I have always carried these sickly cells since that first August 9. Maybe this ending was always my fate. So many other survivors have had multiple cancers, I'm surprised I haven't fallen ill sooner. Natsu and Hideo want me to treat the disease aggressively. I go through the motions of chemotherapy and other treatments for them but I do not much care for the fight. My illness has had one side effect, however, perhaps not so unexpected. Last week I found Natsu searching for the adoption papers we filed twenty years ago. It did not take much of an interrogation to find out why. Hideo did not want to upset me so he had gone to her with new questions about his biological family. I am not offended. I understand the motivation. She asked me, 'Could we have done more when he was still young? What if he has living relatives out there somewhere in the world? We've kept him from them.' Too many decades have passed, I assured her. The search would likely end in failure. Best not to give him false hope.

But here is the truth I will tell only to you. Yes, of course I could have looked for Kenzo and Amaterasu with more determination after the war. I could have tracked down mutual acquaintances, written to newspapers or A-bomb organisations or contacted migration authorities here and abroad. I did none of those things, gladly. I fulfilled the cursory official obligations for the adoption process and then I stopped. And this is why: I was punishing your mother. I was keeping Hideo from her, deliberately. She had kept you from me; I would keep her from her grandson.

I thought when Hideo started to become known for

his peace work, she would hear of him and come looking. We never hid his family name. How could she stay away? I am glad for all our sakes she never turned up. Her opinion would have been definitive, as it had been on all matters. She would have claimed him as her own or refused to believe he was her grandson. I had to shield him from both possibilities. I had to protect him from her.

The Rising Sun

Hinomaru: A red circle against a white background symbolising the rising sun also represents the Japanese national flag. It was officially selected as the Japanese national emblem by the Meiji government in 1870 because it had been one of the symbols of authority granted by the preceding Tokugawa Shogunate. The symbol is very popular in Japan. Hinomaru-bento is a packed lunch with a red pickled Japanese apricot in the middle.

Hideo and I left the restaurant as an ambulance howled its way down the road. We started to walk to the train station. I cleared my throat, awkward with the question. 'The letters mention Jomei's illness. Is he dead?' He nodded. Hideo said it had been hard to watch the man who had raised him end his life in so much pain. I asked when. 'Ten years ago.' I had thought so many times about what I might feel when I heard the news of his death, but there was no sense of victory, quite the opposite. I felt cheated somehow. What to do when the enemy is defeated and not by your own hand? I was glad his passing had not been easy, but death does not discriminate; even the most undeserving leave this world in unimaginable agony.

Sato's victims would have known this as they took their last breath. Natsu must have found the letters about Pingfang and presumably read them. How must she have felt to read this outpouring made not to her but another woman? Or maybe in a moment of remorse, some deathbed confession, he had told her what he had done? Either way, surely, her instinct must have been to burn the letters? What a risk to keep them and then give them to me. Had she feared what I would do with this information?

I paused in the street to get my breath. 'So now you have no family?'

'Well, Angela's parents live in Chicago.' He noticed my confusion. 'Father hasn't mentioned her?' I told him no. He took a photograph from his wallet of a Western woman, thickset, with hair the colour of rice ready for harvest. She was sitting by a pool, laughing, dressed in a sunflower-print swimsuit. Beside her were two children grinning at the camera. 'These are my children: Benjiro we call him Benji, and this is Hanako.'

I noted with diplomatic care the mix of American and Japanese blood in their genetic make-up. I could see little of Yuko in either. 'Your children are beautiful. How did you meet your wife?'

'Angela's a teacher like me. She came to my school to work, a sabbatical for a year. We became friends. I took her to peace rallies, showed her the countryside, picnics on the beach. We got to the end of the year and I real-ised I didn't want her to go home.' He paused.

'So you asked her to stay?'

He laughed. 'We married in 1972. Father died a few months later.'

I looked again at this family of his. Why wait until now to mention them? He too must have had doubts about me. Why would he share his children, this life with some stranger? His company had been a welcome oasis in the desert of my small world. That was the truth, I think he knew this. Our final hours were nearing. What a gift to give him an identity, and me a grandson. But there had been no moment when I thought, yes, there you are, there's my Hideo. Natsu had set me an impossible task. How could I put an imprint of a seven-year-old boy on this grown man? I gave the photograph back to him and reached into my own purse. I handed him a black-and-white image of Yuko and Hideo sitting under a tree, smiling at the camera. 'Why don't you have this?'

'I couldn't, it's yours.'

Here was a kind man. Had the scars made him so, had Sato? 'Please, keep it for now.'

'Thank you. When was this taken?'

'Hideo was six. Shige was just home from training. He left a couple of days after that was taken.'

He looked at his watch and hesitated. 'I've got time before I need to catch my train back. We could talk some more, if you like.' I caught my reflection in the mirror, a lonely woman with nothing of value to fill her days. Did he feel sorry for me? 'I know he died in New Guinea. I don't know much else.'

We were standing by a bar with no windows, just a red neon sign that said 'BAR'. I knew I would need a drink to tell him. 'Let's go here.'

Inside, a green lamp hung above a pool table. Two customers, in baseball caps, sat hunched over beers. Behind them there was a toilet for men, and a poster with a picture of a cupid on a condom and the headline, *Don't aid AIDS*. Hideo asked, 'Is this OK for you?'

'It has character, certainly.' He laughed and I enjoyed the long-lost sensation of amusing someone. Once that talent had come naturally to me. We hung our coats on metal pegs and chose two stools near the entrance. A bartender, pockmarked at the neck, hair falling long in chemical waves, nodded at us and we ordered a beer and a whiskey. We clinked our drinks together. I thought back to July 9, 1946, the day Kazuyoshi came to tell us about Shige as we packed for a new life. There had been no word from him but still we heard stories of men held in prison camps and of soldiers who refused to surrender. The possibility of life did still exist.

Kazuyoshi stood at our door in a dark suit and tie that seemed tailored for a shorter, stouter body. He had been a first lieutenant of the 20th Division of the 18th Army, recruited on our island of Kyushu alongside Shige. They had become friends, two of the 170,000 men sent to New Guinea. Embarrassed, he told us he had been one of only 10,000 to make it home. He seemed to find this shameful. He apologised for taking so long to find us but he had been detained as a prisoner of war, then he had become ill with malaria and only recently recovered. Shige had asked him to deliver a letter to Yuko, in the event of his death. He blushed furiously. He was also sorry to hear the news about our daughter. Reaching into his pocket, he handed over a small bamboo box. 'This is from Shige. I don't know what to do with it now.'

We invited him into our home, fed him steamed vegetables and broth. When he had eaten, I brought what alcohol I could find to the table and poured three cups of sake. He thanked us both and we drank. I refilled our drinks. 'Please, what happened to him?' His mouth trembled. I glanced at Kenzo, who lifted up his own cup as encouragement. 'Drink up, then tell us.' When the bottle was nearly empty, he asked, 'The truth?' My husband nodded. 'Shige would demand it.'

His voice was so quiet we had to lean forward. 'During those last weeks we saw so much death. Friends and strangers killed by hunger, disease, enemy bullets, their own hand, that stinking coastline. There were bodies everywhere, we had no time to cremate them, we just kept moving. We knew we would be expected to make some last stand, one final sacrificial battle. But Shige would whisper to me, what was the point? Why die in some foreign place? We needed to surrender, to get home. There was no shame in this, he said. Sometimes at night we would hear our enemy calling out. It was always the same man, speaking perfect Japanese in a Tokyo dialect. "Surrender and you will be treated with due consideration under the guidelines of international law. You have fought well but the battle is lost. We have food, medicine, blankets. Come forward and soon you will be home safe with your families." This went on for days. Then one night Shige handed me the letter and stood up. Before I had a chance to stop him, he dropped his rifle and began to walk. Others watched him, some started to follow.' Kazuyoshi stopped, looked at the bottle, poured another drink. 'The shot came from over my left shoulder, hit him in the back of the head. He must have died instantly. He didn't suffer, I'm sure.'

Kazuyoshi fell silent. My husband took his time to find his words. 'Thank you for coming here today. We are grateful.'

Our guest nodded. 'Shige was a good man, a fine soldier, my friend.'

When he left we sat side by side, staring at the box. Finally, Kenzo picked it up and opened the lid. He pulled out a folded piece of paper and handed it to me. 'I can't, Amaterasu. You must.' I opened it carefully, worried those creases and tears might disintegrate to nothing. Shige had used a blunt pencil, the letters thick and fat.

Yuko,

I broke our promise. I said I would never leave you again. I tried my hardest to come back to you. I'm sorry I failed you and Hideo, but there is comfort in knowing some part of me lives on in him. Don't let him forget me. Thank you for the happiness you brought me. I wanted to spend my life repaying my debt of gratitude. Now that I cannot, promise me you will find joy again. Don't let this war define your life. Be happy, Yuko. We are here to love, so love.

Your husband, Shige

I looked up and saw Kenzo's face, tears falling down his cheek, but then he faded from view. In his place was Hideo, sitting in the gloomy bar with music churning out from a jukebox. 'Do you still have the letter?' I nodded. 'Would you let me read it? Just to see, not to keep.' I reached spontaneously for his hand, but he pulled away.

'I know what you're going to say. But what if I'm right, what if I am Hideo Watanabe?'

A clock next to a row of upended bottles of spirits ticked forward to 3.12 p.m. 'Isn't your train due?' He looked at my empty glass and signalled to the barman. 'I'll get the next one. Amaterasu, I understand your suspicion, your caution, I do, but what I struggle with is your total resistance to the possibility that we are related. Why would you not want this . . . well, miracle . . . to happen? This armour you wear. I don't know how to pierce it.' The barman put our drinks in front of us and Hideo took a swig of beer. 'My good looks don't seem to be working.'

I found myself laughing at this. He did too. 'Tell me more about Angela and the children.'

He knew he was humouring me but he began to sketch out their lives. He told me how Benji was more like his mother: lively, boisterous, a joker. Hanako was quieter, more sensitive. She was older, nine. He was seven. They had terrible fights but loved each other fiercely. I listened, nodded and smiled and thought back to my own childhood. No one knew about my life before my marriage. Not even Kenzo. At least, not the whole truth, just carefully chosen excerpts. Unlike Sato, I had felt no need to confess my past even if I could not forget it.

Professional Entertainer

Geisha: Around the end of the seventeenth century, geisha girls replaced an earlier class of 'courtesans' who were skilled in such arts as music and dancing. Geisha no longer carries the sexual implication that is often suggested by the English use of the word. Dressed in kimono and often with their hair done in the old Japanese style, they entertain a group of men by playing the shamisen, singing, dancing, serving food and drinks, or through light-hearted talk with a sympathetic smile. Some are highly educated and are intellectually stimulating enough to entertain elite businessmen.

Mother took me to Bar Printemps when I was fifteen. Father had died of an impossible mix of black lung and rice wine. She was too fond of sake herself. She said we needed the money and there was no shame in the work. She was too old but I was the perfect age. Maybe in time I would be introduced to a decent man, unlike her. She would bemoan the cruel fates that had thrown her in the path of my 'feckless' father. During slurred rows and thrown cups, I learned neither had wanted to marry the other, but my impending birth necessitated the union. She said her beauty had cursed her life with the attentions of this good-for-nothing but my looks could be put to better use.

We lived close to Maruyama, the red-light district of

Nagasaki known as Shian Bashi, or Hesitation Bridge. Anyone wanting a night of pleasure would have to cross this first point of entry. Once they had, they would then pass over, guilt-free or not, Omoikiri Bashi, Made Up Your Mind Bridge. Safe among the rows of wooden homes, where women lounged from balconies, visitors to the area had their choice of entertainment: tea houses, bars or dance halls. The customers came not just from Japan but Malaysia, Europe, China and India. Traders, sailors, merchant seamen, local workers and foreign diplomats could all be found drinking, talking and doing deals behind shoji screens. The modan gaaru, or modern girls, of the jazz age had not yet arrived, nor had the cafe girls, dressed in their kimonos and aprons with their fast flirtatious chat, but the men found plenty of variety to distract them. There were geishas, skilled in musical instruments or dance; there were women who could laugh and pour drinks; there were concubines to love and prostitutes who expected no such commitment. Girls driven from poor rural areas, or the textile factories with their low pay and harsh discipline, would head to this part of the city, targets for traffickers who would take them to the docks for transport across the water to the brothels of Shanghai.

Rain battered the cobbles the day we arrived at the bar. The mama-san was looking at a ledger of accounts as she sat on one of the maroon velvet banquettes. She was probably older than Mother but with her gleaming hair pinned high, careful make-up and trim figure, her age was an elegant mystery. She saw us and checked her watch then closed her book. She gestured for us to come closer. Mother bowed very low and said, 'This is my daughter, Amaterasu.' Mama-san looked at my mother's stained kimono and unwashed hair and then checked me up and down as you might a beast at the cattle market. She pointed to the seat opposite her and we sat down. She asked Mother questions, confirmed my age, my schooling. She studied me once more, asked me to turn my face to the side. She told me to smile and frowned when I did so. Did I know how to pour drinks? Could I light cigarettes? Could I hold a conversation? Mother said I was a quick learner. Mama-san said she would be the judge of that. She nodded as if she had come to a decision. She would loan me an initial sum to pay for kimonos and make-up. She expected rigorous hygiene. She looked at Mother when she said this. I must go to the baths more than once a week. She had a doctor she could recommend if I fell ill. If she found out I had been meeting customers on my own time, I would be fired. She wanted to be clear about these punishments. Mama-san told me to come back that evening. I could observe proceedings from the kitchen, which had a view of the bar.

When I returned some hours later, Mama-san was perched at the mahogany bar, positioned so that she might keep a discreet eye on most of the tables save for the few designed to be more private in a smaller back room. The girls began to arrive and greeted her with careful respect. They were a rainbow of silk kimonos, their coils of hair glossy with oil, powder heavy on their faces. The lights were dimmed and they began to shimmer like a shoal of koi wriggling over one another for food. Some of them spotted me standing behind the glass beads that separated the main bar from the kitchen and I could hear them whisper and titter before they began to clean glasses or prepare jugs of sake. A girl, not much older than me, came up and introduced herself as Karin. She said not to look so scared; I would soon get the hang of the work, and the customers. Then the men came and with them the smoke, and noise, and transactions shrouded in low-lit lamps. Most of them stayed in the bar but some headed to the recess at the back and only after a long time would they return.

I watched the girls smile and serve drinks and light cigarettes and flit around the bar gentle as butterflies freed from the cocoon. The hostesses held their hands to their mouths and giggled as their companions emboldened by alcohol slapped kimono-clad thighs if they dared or their own if they lacked the courage. The girls were able to chide them with taps of their folded fans on the end of a nose or a careful exit to replenish the men's drinks. I saw envelopes passed and gifts exchanged and arrangements whispered.

Later still a man dressed in the dark green cavalry uniform of the Kempeitai arrived with a woman on his arm in a rush of night breeze from the entrance. He wore the white armband of the military police on his left arm but his katana sword was missing. Mama-san wriggled from her seat and led him to a reserved table. She told girls yet to be assigned to a customer to bring bottles of spirits. I watched the man's companion as Mama-san fussed around him. She wore a gold kimono emblazoned with red-and-white koi, her hair was pinned in coils, but her face was free of make-up.

They sat down and the man in uniform studied the line of the woman's neck and the patch of skin between her hair and the top of her kimono. He said something and she twisted around and gave him a look of faux annoyance. I saw how she held his gaze for longer than necessary until she turned away as if the bar was imbued with new interest. She scoured the room and saw me, not quite hidden behind the glass beads. The man watched her and turned his head until they were both staring in my direction. Then my view was obscured by one of the hostesses carrying a tray of glasses and corn snacks. I stepped farther back into the kitchen and a few minutes later Mama-san rattled through the beads. 'Someone wants to meet you.' My heart thumped. I did not want to go into the bar, have eyes upon me in my drab clothes and clogs and the cheap scent my mother had insisted that I wear. Mama-san opened a cupboard and checked her face in a cracked mirror that hung on the inside of the door. 'Just an introduction, nothing more. Even hidden away you have caught a customer's eye. And not any customer . . .'

When I walked up to them, the man was holding the woman's wrist upwards and tracing the white line of an old scar with his thumb, a reminder of some childhood mishap, maybe. The woman smiled and her eyebrows arched up as she spoke to him.

'Maybe not good, but I can be bad.'

'Have you been bad, little one?'

'Very,' she replied, frowning with mock sombreness. She looked up and smiled. 'Ah, your little guest.' She patted the seat next to her and I sat down. She smelled of peony. 'What a sweet young thing you are. How old are you?' I told her. 'So young. I remember that age. I was a little younger when I started working. And your name?' She listened and smiled. 'Most fitting. I'm Kimiko and this is Captain Sakamoto.' I must have looked then. He was sitting back, watching me through a fug of smoke, an amused smile on his lips. He was not a handsome man, but I soon learned that he did not need to be. Wealth and his position secured him the best tables and girls in the bars and brothels of Maruyama.

Kimiko poured a drink. 'Here, little one, you must be thirsty.' She offered me the glass and I put the liquid to my lips. Suddenly I was coughing and spluttering and Kimiko was laughing. 'I'm sorry, I should have said. That isn't water. Still, if you are to work here, you will need to acquire the taste.' She poured from a different jug. 'This is water.' I knew Mama-san was watching and that I should smile but I just kept staring at the table. 'Do you like my kimono, Amaterasu? A present from Sakamoto. He is a very generous man.' She drank some sake. 'Captain, do you like Amaterasu's dress?' He tapped his cigarette into an ashtray.

'You're teasing the girl, Kimiko.'

She lit a cigarette. 'I'm doing no such thing. I think you look beautiful, Amaterasu. A moth dancing too near the flame. Wouldn't you agree, Sakamoto? Isn't our new little friend adorable?'

The captain, obscured behind a haze of smoke, lifted up his drink in a toast, but said nothing.

A Subordinate

Ue-shita: One of the most important patterns that Japanese people are expected to recognise in human interaction is the relationship between the superordinate and subordinate. A subordinate is supposed to be respectful to a superordinate and the latter caring in a paternal way for the former.

I bought three kimonos with the money that Mama-san lent me. They came in shades of amber, teal and coral pink. I had never owned anything so exquisite and as I ran my hands over their silks I began to understand how beautiful possessions could change how you saw yourself and how others viewed you. The night I next met the captain, I was swathed in amber. Mother sat on a stool by our hearth as she watched me prepare for my night at the bar. I had been doing shifts for a month, with one day off a week. Mama-san had told me to wear minimal make-up and put my hair in a simple bun. My youth was the only decoration I needed, she said. I wound the cords and sashes around my body. Reflected in the mirror, I could see Mother looking at the kimono, an unhappy smile drawn across a face prematurely reddened and lined through too much alcohol and too little rest. She drank from a glass and told me her favourite story, how she could have been someone if my father hadn't trapped her in the wrong part of Nagasaki. Poor as we were, she could

214

still imagine another ending for herself. She was still alive enough to dream. She believed I had the chance to take us both from this place we were forced to call home. She talked of saving up what I earned and moving to a better part of the city. Bar Printemps was a tunnel to freedom, one she expected us to take together.

I looked around our cramped, damp quarters, the dishes of half-eaten food and the piles of unwashed clothes next to the futon where I slept in the main living area. She saw me as a way out when, in truth, I wanted to escape from her. Could she not see me pulling away? Wealth, class, culture, they could all be mimicked and perhaps even acquired; the hostesses had given me such hope, but I feared if Mother clung to me, I would end up like her. When I was ready to leave for the night I handed her some money. The evenings went better for us both if she could afford to spend some hours at the shack masquerading as a bar at the bottom of our street.

I arrived at Printemps and began collecting glasses from the previous night's business. One of the girls, a bitter melon called Akiko, began to bait me about Sakamoto. The hostesses had noticed the captain's interest in me and teasing me about his intentions became their new game. Akiko smiled conspiratorially at her dumpy stooge, Mika.

'Hey, Amaterasu, how's that captain of yours? Has he placed an order yet? You're just his type. He likes his meat raw and bleeding.'

Akiko and Mika laughed as Karin arrived through the main door. Mika picked up a fried shrimp from one of the bowls and began eating with her mouth open. 'Don't worry, Amaterasu. Kimiko is more pimp than mistress these days, she'll be delighted with the rest.'

Karin shooed them away and Akiko sloped off with a bored pout. 'You're no fun, Karin. Tell Amaterasu she should be grateful if Sakamoto shows any interest. He has power and wealth; he isn't some drunken merchant sailor or factory worker.'

Mika wiped her fingers on a cloth. 'Yeah, tell her, she should be grateful.' She shot a sly glance at Akiko. 'No matter if he smells of fermented soya bean or his skin is like wet tofu or he carries more fat than a farm pig.'

Karin collected a tray of dirty glasses. 'Well, Mika, you've got that in common with him.'

Mika scowled but before she could respond Mama-san entered the bar. I followed Karin into the kitchen and helped her stack the glasses by the sink. 'Don't listen to those girls, Amaterasu. They're jealous, that's all.'

I lit the stove. 'I don't understand why.'

'You could have anyone you wanted here, if you learn the game. Don't look so uncertain. It has happened. I've heard of hostesses living in fine apartments, wives in all but name. Why not you, Amaterasu? Or me?'

'It sounds a fairy tale.'

She laughed. 'Maybe, but let's just say, a certain client is coming here tonight, and he's asked for your company.'

Mama-san had made it clear I was not ready to sit with the customers. I filled my nights with cleaning duties, or making simple snacks for hungry clients. When I could, I studied the hostesses, the cadence of their voices, their posture, the way they refilled glasses with playful atten-tiveness. 'I'm not able to entertain.'

Karin smoothed down her kimono. 'Mama-san isn't keeping you away from the tables because you aren't ready. She's keeping you for the highest bidder. You're her latest prize. Make the most of it while it lasts.'

When do hopes of a different life crystallise into plans? Was it that night or later? I know that I kept myself busy, not sure how I would react if the captain did appear. The hours ticked by until the customers stumbled to their beds. I felt a relief that Sakamoto had not come. Mama-san began to send some of the hostesses home as the bar emptied. I was working in the kitchen when she appeared at my side. She sighed as she surveyed my work. 'Too many nuts, this is not a feeding zoo.' She ran one hand over her coiffured hair and then poured alcohol into a glass. She handed me the drink. 'Swallow this. Sakamoto is here.' I walked to the curtain and peered through the beads. I saw him through the smoke, a cigarette hanging from his mouth, a half-smile on his lips. I looked back at Mama-san. 'Don't look so nervous. Just follow his lead. And remember, smile.'

I made my way through the pirouettes of smoke past the figures shrouded by dimmed lamps. He stood when I reached his table. He told me to sit and poured me a glass of sake. I thanked him as he said, 'Let me play hostess.' He asked what made me come to Printemps and I told him my mother had thought it a good idea. He asked if I liked the work. I said I felt like a bat, the late nights, sleeping through the day, the hours getting ready. 'I can't remember the last time I saw the sun.' He asked what I made of the clientele. I hesitated and he answered for me. 'Old and drunk?' This made me laugh, or rather,

I already knew to laugh at the joke. He asked if the men were well behaved. I told him the other girls were teaching me how to temper their excitement. He indicated that I should replenish his glass.

He shuffled nearer. 'Let me tell you a secret, but if I tell you this secret, I will expect payment. This is a valuable gem of wisdom I offer you. Do you promise to repay me this kindness?' I giggled as the girls had shown me and said yes. 'Good. A good deed for a good deed. Here is the secret you must learn. The hostesses are the ones in control, not the customers. These men and their wallets are at your mercy. Mere puppets. You pull their strings, remember this. Love and bars do not work well together. Mix the two, and you invite a broken heart. Try to keep your heart like stone. The men here are not looking for love. They want to drink and kiss the necks of pretty, young girls. They are not looking for wives. This is fantasy. See the men who come to these places? Some are lonely, some are thirsty, some are hungry, and not for food. Be warned: they will do anything to win your affections. They will buy you presents, they will tell you that, oh, they have never known such beauty, that they have never felt such love. Do not believe them.' He sipped some sake. 'Take their gifts but do not believe them. Well, believe me, you are beautiful. That colour is exquisite on you.'

I recall this conversation now as an old woman with too many years behind me. He was telling me all I had to know about the city's entertainment district, but no doubt, like too many other young girls before me, I thought these rules would not apply to me. So while

I thanked Sakamoto for his kind words and advice, I did not appreciate them. He looked me over, as if he were in a shop, considering a purchase. He took a fresh cigarette from a gold tin and held the tobacco to his lips. 'Please, let me.' I picked up his lighter but my fingers were clumsy and shaking and he held my hand in his to steady my hold.

'You must call me Tetsu.' He leaned back in his seat, looked around the room and stretched. 'Amaterasu, I am hungry. Would you mind making me some rice porridge?'

I nodded and slipped away, annoyed that I had said or done something that had displeased him. I dipped through the beads into the kitchen, where Mama-san was counting a pile of money. She glanced up as I moved to the sink. 'Sakamoto wants some food.'

She looked at the clock behind her and tutted but continued her calculations as I opened a cupboard to find the rice. A minute, no more, must have passed when the smell of tobacco infiltrated the room. I turned around, and there he was, the captain, in the kitchen. He stood next to Mama-san but said nothing and I saw her look at me and then the money. She opened her mouth as if to say something before she gathered up the banknotes and, head bowed, left me alone with him. He walked up to the sink and dropped his cigarette with a fizz against its wet bottom. He smiled.

'My apologies, I'm not hungry any more. I'm in the mood for something else. Good deeds deserve good deeds, don't you agree? Would you kneel for me, Amaterasu?'

I remember pushing the rice away. 'I don't understand.'

He repeated the question. 'I'd like you to kneel, just there, where you are, on the floor.'

I must have looked at the wooden floorboards. 'But my kimono, it will get dirty.'

He moved closer. 'I'll buy you a new one, a nicer one.' He ran his fingers over a crate of empty sake bottles stacked next to the sink.

'But Mama-san?'

'Don't worry, little one. I'll show you what to do. Now, would you kneel for me?' The captain stood in front of me. I could smell his liquor breath. He stroked my face. 'Don't be scared.' I could see the pores on his nose and the spider veins on his cheeks. 'I'll play teacher. Kneel for me.' I did not think to say no. Perhaps I could have done so. Perhaps I could have run home, told Mother I would find another job. Perhaps I could have paid Mama-san back somehow. Perhaps I could have lived as my mother had and numbed myself with cheap sake. Perhaps those options were available to me but in that small kitchen, alone with the captain, I could not think of them. So I knelt. And as he promised, the captain showed me what to do. I never wore that amber kimono again.

The Whore Spider

Jorogumo: A mythical creature from the Edo period of Japan. A spider, usually an orb weaver, is given magical powers when it turns four hundred years old. The spider grows into a beautiful woman who lures men to a quiet spot by playing a Japanese lute called a biwa. She then ties up her victim with her silk threads and feasts on him. Sometimes she takes the form of a woman carrying a baby, which may be her egg sac. The word is also the name of a species of spider called Nephila clavata, or golden orb-web spiders such as the joro spider.

The captain sent a flurry of gifts to my home after that first night. Each parcel marked a new lesson dispensed by him, a new acquiescence on my part. Mother would watch me receive them, the air rancid with her envy. Much of the jewellery and furs she pawned but she let me keep a coral necklace. The present arrived in a tortoise-shell box with a white rose. She seemed to understand its significance. I was not yet sixteen but Sakamoto had given me a full education. His friendship improved our living standards. We ate better food, sat at a better table, but Mother was hungry for more. She wanted to know when we could move to a bigger home. I need only ask the captain nicely and he would provide, she said. Mother did not understand the game. Neither of us wanted to break the illusion that this physical contract was more than some cheap transaction. Yes, I might move beyond the label of Maruyama companion if I was patient and clever but to force his patronage would be to ruin the false tale we spun: of a man and woman in love. Why would he set me up in a home when there were so many other hostesses to whet his appetite? I spent those first months trying to satiate his desire so he would need only me. I was a child but children learn fast, and Sakamoto had no hesitation in showing me where his tastes lay.

Of course, I did not love the captain, nor like him, but I appreciated his presence in my life, what his interest, sexual and therefore financial, might mean to me over the coming years. Our companionship had mutual bene-fits. He was the possibility of flight made flesh. The more he sought my company, the more the other hostesses dangled tales in front of me of women who lived in grand apartments paid for by their Maruyama lovers. Some had children and were de facto wives; others had saved enough money to run their own bars or businesses. The hostesses all saw what Sakamoto held in his hand: the key to doors beyond the entertainment district. Yes, he had claimed me too young but I refused to see myself as some victim. He sought satisfaction; I sought benefaction.

Timing was important. His companion, Kimiko, had disappeared, but vain as I was becoming, I suspected this vanishing act had little to do with me. I sensed the captain's interest had an unspoken time limit attached. I began to worry at some point Sakamoto would tire of me, as he had Kimiko. I had to show him due respect and consideration while I warranted so much of his atten-tion. It would be folly to risk his patronage by allowing another man into my bed. Few were held in higher regard than him, and what he had or owned, other men envied and coveted. I learned to spurn persistent admirers that nipped at his heels with a gentle diplomacy. The balance between not bruising their egos while encouraging their company was a delicate one. I could have had some fallback plan, some other man to pursue, but Sakamoto was the most likely, and the best placed, to take me from the streets of Maruyama and my mother. All I had to do was ensure he judged my companionship the finest to be found in the night bars. This is why I tolerated his hands and mouth and those other parts of him. I entertained all his predilections. I became a good actress. I faked desire to the point that I could almost believe myself in love with him. I learned to hide my yearning for something more than the captain's attentions underneath layers of insouciance and disregard of all matters serious. I was light as a Chinese windmill butterfly carried on a summer breeze.

Between my time spent with the captain and at the bar, Karin and I would visit the city's bathhouses and scrub ourselves clean. We would hang our kimonos on pegs, buy small towels and soap from an assistant, and find stools next to one another. We gossiped about the clients we liked, the ones who could not hold their alcohol and those with straying hands. We created a code language. Sakamoto was *dango*, dumpling; Mama-san was *kitsune*, fox, or benevolent guardian; Akiko was *mimi-kaki*, ear pick, because her laughter was like a stabbing pain in our ears. Karin was from Sasebo, in the north-western tip of Kyushu. Her family had worked in the coal fields that fuelled the naval base. She had fallen in love with a metalworker and run away to Nagasaki. When I asked what had happened to him, she would shake her head mournfully. 'I don't know. I woke up one day and he was gone.' Mama-san had found her loitering outside a restaurant, with no money for food, and had taken her in. As we talked and imagined the lives we could lead outside Maruyama, I poured buckets of hot water over my skin and wiped off Sakamoto's saliva, his sweat and his semen.

Clean once more, Karin and I took walks by the harbour before our shifts. We would stroll to the water to watch the sun set. Nestling between lamp posts and pallets of cargo, joro spiders would sit in their orb nests, which shone gold in the low, dying light. Karin hated those creatures but I loved their beauty, their stomachs marked with a flash of red, legs striped yellow and dark blue, the unashamed boldness of them compared to the ordinary brown spiders that scuttled around the ground. I admired their patience and cunning and began to understand what it took to tease the silk from hidden glands and build a home that was also a trap. I thought of the Jorogumo, a seducer impossible to resist. She was the one who feasted on men, not the other way around. Could I be her? I dressed for work in my bright kimonos and tried to see a different future. Be irresistible, patient and resolute, I told myself. Become a joro spider.

A year passed and still the captain favoured my company but not enough to free me from the bar. When he did not visit Printemps, other clients courted my attention. One night, a literature professor who thought himself more in love with me the more brandy he drank slouched forward, his body chastised by alcohol and whispered, 'How is my Clarissa this evening?' I asked him what he meant and he smirked but said no more. On his next visit he brought me a book, *Clarissa* by Samuel Richardson. 'Here we go, my caged princess.' He had bookmarked one page, with a quote highlighted in pencil. *'I am but a cipher, to give him significance, and myself pain.'* I asked the professor if the book was a love story and he laughed. 'Depends on your point of view.' I understood that he was mocking me. Unrequited desire had that effect. 'Come now, Amaterasu, you must be an expert in love. You see it bloom here every night.'

What I saw in the bar was not love. The hostesses were paid to be surrogate wives, or lovers, or even mothers, only we fed our charges with sake not breast milk. Most conversations consisted of sexual innuendo or bawdy jokes. We spent hours listening to our customers' woes, nodding sympathetically while pouring more drinks so that they might abandon their fumbled attempts at seduction and forget what grievance had brought them to our door. I told the professor I could not begin to know what love was, although it seemed to make people more miserable than happy and was probably best avoided. He shook his head, muttering, 'My sweet girl, you know nothing. Love is wondrous, rainbows, sunlight on a waterfall, dew on a petal, a wild horse galloping on an empty beach. What a sad little thing you are. I will show you what love is outside this dreary bar.' I told him that sounded delightful but he should realise I was only a figment of his imagination, a night spirit conjured up by alcohol when the sun set. I did not exist in daylight. I refilled his drink and he asked if I was happy. I replied as gaily as I could, 'Why would I not be? You are here to keep me company, to tell me about love even if I am cursed never to know it.'

'You are admired, yes, but will you recognise love when it arrives? Will you allow it into your life?' He put down his glass of brandy. 'I am drunk. I must abandon you to these foul beasts, dear princess.'

The professor stood up with exaggerated care and made his way to the exit, no doubt in search of other Clarissas in nearby bars. He bumped into a man as he walked through the door and raised his hand in apology. The professor drew my gaze to this new customer but something more than his strong features and bearing held my attention. How to describe that feeling? The bar drew still and I felt sucked into a vacuum as I watched him walk toward Mama-san. He did not arrive with wild horses or rainbows, but a companion, a little shorter and stouter than him. If I had not seen this man at that moment on that night, what would have happened? Would Sakamoto have moved me to an apartment? Would I have become another mama-san? Would I have ended up another version of my mother? I cannot say. This new customer came and scored his presence indelibly in my life. I did not know his name. Later that night he would introduce himself. Jomei Sato. His friend? Kenzo Takahashi.

Sacred Day

Ennichi: Old people believe that if they visit a shrine or a temple for religious services on such a holy day, they will receive special divine favours. Less religious townspeople will enjoy these days, as street pedlars set up fair stalls. The 8th of each month is observed as ennichi of Yakushi Nyorai (god of medicine), the 18th as that of Kannon (goddess of mercy), the 24th as that of Jizo (guardian of children), and the 28th as that of Fudo (god of non-movement).

This was their first visit; the signs were easy enough to spot. They tried to act nonchalantly but still hovered by the main door. One scanned the room and the other could only look at his shoes. Mama-san hid her surprise when I signalled that I would attend to them. Karin joined me and we greeted the two men and led them to one of the less requested tables near the kitchen. Until we could ascertain the spending power of a new customer, the rule was to reserve the better tables for the men who could afford the best sake. The men looked rich enough but hostesses knew more than most that this was not an indication of wealth. We brought them drinks and learned their names and occupations. They were both recent graduates; Kenzo Takahashi was a nautical engineer and Jomei Sato had studied medicine. Karin talked with Takahashi and I attended Sato. I was still only sixteen but practised enough in conversation to talk to most clients with a light assurance. Some of the older, more educated, sombre men were harder to put at ease but I had not been intimidated by a customer for a long while. Sato was different. I had never felt an attraction to any of the men that came through the doors. Desire was an unsettling new sensation.

I poured him a drink. 'Medicine is a fine profession. Your family must be proud.'

He smiled mischievously. 'And your family must be proud of you too?'

I did not like his tone but I was not paid to take offence. 'This is your first time here. Are you new to the delights of Maruyama?'

'No.' He clinked glasses with his friend. 'But this is Kenzo's first visit. See, Kenzo, I told you, did I not?' His companion's cheeks flushed and he gave Karin a shy glance. 'So, ladies, I promised my friend a fine time, drink and beautiful women and the best shabu-shabu in town. When you are done here, you must join us. Listening to all these men droning on must work up an appetite.'

I laughed, out of habit. 'That is a generous offer, but I'm afraid we will be here long after you are asleep.'

Sato gave me another impish look. 'Is there room in your bed for two?'

I pretended to look at a watch. 'Most customers wait at least ten minutes before asking that question.'

He laughed now. 'I apologise for my lack of originality.'

I began to refill his drink when Akiko came up to our table and leaned down to whisper in my ear. I looked to the table at the back. The captain had arrived and requested my attendance. I stood up from the stool so that she could take my place.

'Gentlemen, it has been a pleasure. I hope to see you back here again. I'm afraid I must leave you for the moment.'

They both bowed and as I turned to leave Sato took hold of my hand, pressed it to his lips. 'It really has been a delight. We will eat shabu-shabu, I am sure, one day.'

I walked across the bar to sit with Sakamoto. The captain touched my coral necklace. 'I don't like you talking to other men.'

'Tetsu, it's my job.' I lit a cigarette for him. 'How else am I to pay my bills? Besides, those men are boys.'

'I don't like how they look at you.' He moved his hand under the table and lifted the hem of my kimono, pushed his way between my legs. I tapped the end of his nose with my finger, chiding. 'Naughty, Tetsu. Not here.'

'Here.' The captain and I were in the corner but I feared if I looked up over the bar I would see Sato watching me, and this thought caused me shame. He kissed the side of my neck and, frustrated by the restrictions of the kimono, moved his hand away. 'Let's have Mika join our table tonight.'

I sighed. 'Must we? I dislike her so.'

'She's not so bad. You have nothing to be jealous about. Besides, am I not good to you?'

Mika came to our table, all giggles and flushed cheeks and wet lips, so eager to please, like a dog freed from the leash. When the captain was not looking she shot me an expression of satisfaction. She could see, everyone could: the captain's affections were on the move. An hour or so passed before Sato and Kenzo stood up and made their way to the exit. The young doctor was too handsome for this meat hall. He had no need to sit among hostesses feeding him false compliments. His looks alone could have tempted any one of them into breaking Mamasan's rules about entertaining clients outside the bar. Such a pity he was not older, or wealthier, or he would have been a perfect substitute for the captain. Sato bowed to Mama-san and as he was about to leave he glanced back, just for a moment, and smiled. The captain did not see our silent exchange but Mika did. I felt a flare of alarm and exhilaration, as if dipped in a freezing cold pool while the sun shone overhead. I felt alive, and just as quickly as the elation rose, I was left back in the shadows of Printemps, the high followed by a crashing low.

Later that night, long after Sakamoto and I had left the bar and found a room at a nearby inn, I lay next to the captain. I watched him snore and scratch his folds and dimples, a contented pig in a poke. I thought more on the professor's question. Would I recognise love when it arrived? Up until this evening I had not dared imagine how it might feel. My head, once so full of ways to keep my dango happy, became overrun with the image of Jomei: that mole, that mouth, that silly promise of shabu-shabu anywhere outside Printemps. Was this love? Or just desire? It did not matter. Sato was too young, too unknown, too unpredictable to risk my future on him.

High Spirits

Iki: An aesthetic and moral ideal developed by urban commoners in the late Edo period (1603–1867). This idealises not only an urbane, chic or bourgeois beauty but also the sophisticated life of a person who enjoys sensual pleasure. A lady possessing iki is highly spirited and always willing to make sacrifices for her lover.

A month later I saw him again. Monsoon showers had kept most of the customers away but as the rain finally subsided the door clattered open and his face appeared from beneath a roll of dripping newspaper. He peered across the empty tables and I felt as if he had shot a flare of light over the bar. He smiled and walked up to me. 'Your captain is not here?'

Sitting alone, I must have looked like a market trader waiting for a sale. 'He's not my captain, but I am expecting him.'

He gestured at the seat beside me. 'May I keep you company until he arrives?'

'Of course. It would be a pleasure.' What else could I say? And the truth was easy.

He sat down next to me, too close, but I did not move away. I lit a match and he leaned forward with a cigarette in his mouth. He surveyed the room as he smoked.

'You live a curious life, Amaterasu.'

I smiled. 'I do? How so?'

'All these beautiful young women stuck here with these old men. What a waste.'

I shook my head in remonstrance. 'Our customers are attentive and generous. We are lucky to spend time with such educated, charming gentlemen.'

He nodded, maybe in agreement. 'I had not thought of it that way.' He looked at my coral necklace. 'And that Kempeitai officer is the finest of companions, I imagine?'

Was he trying to embarrass me? I lit a cigarette to steady my nerves, breathed in deep to settle my stomach. What to say of Sakamoto? I saw myself naked, the captain pouring sake laced with gold leaf over my body until my nipples were yellow beads shining in the room. I felt him lick me clean and tell me I was his chrysanthemum as he poured the chilled liquid down my spine and eased my body open. What to say of that? 'The captain and I are friends, nothing more.'

'And is that what you want, Amaterasu, only to be his friend?'

What a casual and cruel remark. How little he knew of the choices available to me. 'You cannot judge what you do not understand.'

He considered this and then responded: 'I've lived a privileged life, I know. But I'm not immune to how we might be forced to do things we would rather not.'

I hated that my laughter sounded bitter. 'Money makes such compassionate judges of us.'

'Forgive me, Amaterasu. I may be young but I do realise this is a job for you, nothing more. How you must tire of our company while you indulge our poor jokes and tickle our fragile egos.' He picked a stray shred of tobacco from his lip and I found myself wondering again what it would be like to kiss that mouth. 'If you get the opportunity, will you leave all this eventually?'

I smiled. 'You make it sound as if I'm trying to escape.'

'Well, aren't you?' I could not reply and he nodded as if he understood my caution. 'I'd like to think that outside this place there is a handsome lover waiting for you. I see you both walking around a park, the sun on your face, or the rain, whatever you prefer. You are on your way to a concert, or a restaurant. He has bought you a small gift, but you cherish it.'

I shook my head playfully. 'You have a poet's tongue for a man of science.'

'I am not a sentimental man, I promise you. I'm a new customer here, I know, but it's impossible not to care for you girls.' He looked at me as if I were the only object in the room. 'I just wonder what happens when you are no longer girls?'

Even if I could have answered him I did not get the chance. The captain walked through the door and Sato, aware of my sudden alarm, turned to look. The two men exchanged some silent understanding and the doctor gathered up his cigarettes. 'Thank you for your company.' Mama-san went up to Sakamoto to alleviate any potential embarrassment, and Sato turned to me, the picture of relaxation. 'Tell me, Amaterasu. Can you see yourself walking in a park one day?' He paused. 'With me?'

I could not say what I truly thought. 'Mama-san does not allow private meetings.'

Sato tutted. 'How cruel. I imagine you look very different in sunlight. I'd like to see that.' He bowed, but before he

233

left, he teased me once more. 'Kazagashira Park is lovely this time of year. Tuesdays at noon are particularly pleasant, I hear.'

He brushed shoulders with the captain as they passed one another. If Sakamoto was angry he did not show his displeasure. He asked Mika to join us, but she only stayed a few minutes before he whispered some words in her ear and sent her away. We left the bar soon after. Later, when I finally thought him done with me, there was a knock at the door. In that lost light between night and day, a woman entered the room and as she drew closer I saw it was Mika. I went to stand up but Sakamoto held my arm.

'If you can make new friends, Amaterasu, so can I. That's only fair, don't you think? Are we still friends?' He smiled first at me and then Mika and moved the sheet from our bodies. 'Well, little one, why don't you prove it?'

A Foolish Parent

Oyabaka: This term refers to a parent who is so fond of his/her own child as to do a foolish thing for its sake. For example, some may buy their children every toy they show interest in, however difficult it might be financially. Many are willing to sacrifice themselves in their own way for the well-being of their children. Neither can those parents punish their children for any misbehaviour, although they often know that they should.

The first Tuesday passed and I did not go to the park, the second came and went and one more, but still I stayed away. Then one night at the bar a face from the not too distant past paid us a visit as Mika regaled the captain with some dirty joke that made her forehead shine with the telling of it. She stopped seconds from the punchline when a woman walked up to our table drunk and unsteady on her feet. It took me a while to realise this was Kimiko. The loss of the captain's patronage had taken a toll. Gone were the golden silk kimonos, replaced instead by cheap blue cotton. Her skin seemed pitted with dirt. Sakamoto said nothing but indicated that she should sit down. She fell into the seat next to me and all I could smell was stale alcohol and sweat. Mama-san was watching from her usual spot at the bar and the captain looked at her for a moment, some message sent and received.

The captain twirled his cigarette case on the table. 'This is a pleasure, Kimiko.'

She snorted and poured herself a drink. 'I'm sure it is.'

'What brings you here?'

'That's rich. I brought you here, or have you forgotten, little Tetsu? Little, little Tetsu.' She sang his name as she held up a finger and waved it in front of his face.

'You should go home.'

She laughed at this. 'Home? Home, you say. Where's home, Tetsu? Where's home, little, lying, little Tetsu?' She turned to me. 'Is this why I'm homeless?' She shook her head and studied my face and laughed. 'I know you. Little moth with the clogs. My, look at you now.' She took a drink and shook her head sadly. 'I wonder who he has lined up to replace you?' She made an exaggerated survey of the bar. 'Let me see, oh, what about her, Tetsu? No, you're right, too old. Who else?' She smiled at Mika, whistled and slapped her knee. 'My, aren't you a big one?' She pointed at Sakamoto. 'I never knew you liked them so large, Tetsu.'

Mama-san walked up to our table, her voice as melodic as a wood chime. 'Dear Kimiko, so good to see you. It's been too long. We have had so many requests for your company. You've disappointed our customers with your absence.'

Kimiko closed one eye and looked at the captain. 'Have you missed me, Tetsu?' She started to sob. 'We had a pact, didn't we? We made promises, didn't we?'

Sakamoto stood up and gestured that Mika and I should do so too. Kimiko leaned back on the chair and drank, liquid dribbling down her chin. He bent down so their heads were close but I could hear what he said. 'Come to this bar again and I'll make sure you lose everything. You'll be so desperate you'll be spreading your legs for any diseased trash down the docks, if you haven't already.' He started to walk away and then stopped, spoke loud enough so everyone could hear. 'You disgust me.'

He offered me his arm and, as we headed to the door, I looked back. I could see Mama-san sitting next to Kimiko, a hand on her shoulder. Outside, the captain signalled for his driver to fetch the car but I could not move. Sakamoto turned to me. 'Amaterasu?'

'What happened to her?'

His irritation flared up. 'She expected too much, made too many demands. She grew tiresome. That's all.'

'I see.' I found the courage to speak. 'Will you grow tired of me too?'

He walked up to me, took my elbow. 'Sweet thing, how could I tire of you?' His grip tightened but I did not move. 'Amaterasu?' His voice was low, more a warning than a question.

'Mika can entertain you tonight since you enjoy her company so much.'

He looked surprised and then angry. He grabbed my neck and pushed me against a wall. 'Don't be so ungrateful. Let's go.' I rubbed my neck and a man caught my attention as he moved toward us. His face came into view under a street lamp. I thought for a moment to shake my head as a warning to keep walking but it was too late.

'Amaterasu, what a pleasure. May I accompany you inside?'

The captain did not look round. 'We're fine.'

Sato stood next to Sakamoto. 'Here, the cobbles are a little slippery. Take my arm.'

I looked at both men and there in that dark corner of the city I made my decision. I squeezed past the captain, and returned to the bar with the doctor. If Sakamoto complained to Mama-san I knew I would be fired but in that moment, next to Sato, I did not care. I allowed myself to believe that he would be worth this recklessness. I went to find Mama-san but Karin said she had left with Kimiko, having taken a roll of banknotes from her money box. I turned to look at Sato, sitting in the seat the captain had just left. I felt relieved and nervous as I joined him. We sat cloaked in a silence thick with the unsaid words that bounced between us. The particles of air around our table seemed to have shifted, this atmosphere drawing us closer than the distance between our bodies suggested. He smiled, and I prayed he would not talk of the captain.

'So, you must be famished?' I realised that yes, I was. 'Well, let's drink up here and go for some food. We can eat and talk without –' he raised a hand and gestured at the bar – 'all this pretence. Would you like that, Amaterasu?'

During our late supper, he asked me about my child-hood and my guard almost down I hinted at the truth, testing him perhaps to see his reaction. At the end of the night he hailed a taxi and arranged to meet me the following week at the botanical gardens. This first visit to a park turned to many. I adored those days. I had never spent time with a man before nightfall. We strolled past children as they played with beanbags or tried to tickle pearl koi hiding under water-lily leaves. Sato and I had not so much as kissed but I took this coy courtship as a sincerity of intent, a depth of attachment. All it indicated was patience. One day, while sitting on a stone bench, a picnic of bean curd and octopus laid out between us, he presented me with a box, smaller than my palm. Inside I found a brass key.

'It opens a door to an apartment, well, more a couple of rooms, clean enough and discreet.' He looked around the park and just for a moment it seemed as if he might blush. 'I thought it would be good to have somewhere private to go.' I picked up the key, held the lightness of it in my hand. 'It's not far from here.'

Maybe Kimiko, Mika and Karin would have understood what the brass key meant. I chose to see it as an unspoken promise. As I slipped the box into my purse, I dared to imagine its worth was more than small grams of metal. Fate had brought him to the bar, had it not? How could he not be mine? We took a rickshaw to Chinatown past stalls selling steamed dumplings to a restaurant lined with a mural of swallows. The apartment was in the building above. A Western-style iron bed with a bare blue-and-white-striped mattress dominated the space next to a bamboo desk placed under the window with a pine chair. The kitchen was in the next room with a square table, scratched with use, and another chair. Sato watched me as I walked around. 'It's basic, I know.'

'The bathroom?'

'Shared, down the hall.'

I nodded and that seemed to be all the reaction he needed. He walked up to me, put his hands on my waist where my obi was tied and laughed. 'I have no idea how to get this off you.'

And so Sato became my new Sakamoto.

My nights at work, and Jomei's rounds during the morning, meant we could often only spend time together in the afternoon. I counted down the hours until we could be alone. Those rooms were my escape from the bar and from my mother, a place, finally, to call my own, even if we only spent a few hours there a week. I could not help myself. I filled the apartment with cream roses in crystal vases, found two framed pictures of a horse and a heron at an antique shop, bought fine white cotton bedcovers and a lamp made of stained glass. I was trying to create a home. For two months I felt as if I was succeeding. But then Sato arrived one afternoon as I was standing on a chair, trying to hang blinds in the bedroom. They were the palest blue with a print of pink blossoms covered in snow. I asked without thinking, 'Can you help me?'

He looked at the blinds and then took in the rest of the room as if seeing it for the first time. He seemed annoyed and a chisel of worry tapped at my heart. 'Leave it for now.'

I stepped down from the chair, walked toward him and kissed him on the cheek. He picked up a small carriage clock from the desk, a gift from Karin, and then put it down. Next to the clock, on a piece of scrap paper, I had written my name next to his surname and my heart pounded with shame. Had he seen it? He smiled absent-mindedly and seemed to remember something. 'I forgot to say. I can't come on Friday. I have a lunch.'

'Can't I come?' I smiled coquettishly. 'I'll be on my best behaviour.'

He grabbed my waist and spun me around until I felt

240

giddy. 'What would be the point of that? I don't want you on your best behaviour.'

He stepped backwards as he led me to the bed. I pulled free from his grasp, not out of petulance but worry. 'Why can't I come? I know how to behave.'

He sighed. 'The lunch is with a surgeon and his family. It's a formal invite. It will be boring.' He sat down on the bed and patted the mattress. 'We only have two hours. Let's not spoil it.'

'When can we go to lunch then?'

He groaned. 'Soon. Isn't this place enough for us?'

I gestured at the room, testing him, perhaps. 'Do you like it?'

'Very pretty, like you.' He patted the bed again, smiled. 'Come join me.'

I glanced at the clock, Karin's sweet gift. 'Why don't I live here all the time?'

'What's wrong with you today?'

'The rent's paid after all.'

He looked around the room again. 'I don't think it's suitable to live here.'

Perhaps I should have kept my own counsel but I suddenly, stupidly, had the need to explain why I bought those blinds, why I filled that tiny apartment, why I needed more than a brass key, why I cherished Karin's gift, and lastly, why I imagined what it would be like to be called Amaterasu Sato. 'There's something I must tell you.'

He looked alarmed, as if he sensed what was coming. 'Don't say it.'

'What?'

'There's no need. Don't you see that, Amaterasu? Just being here is what matters. Come here, let me show you how much being here matters.'

Did he know what I wanted to whisper to him? As I undressed for him, did he know the words I repeated in my head? I had practised them at home in the mirror, blushing even when alone. I clung to him, felt the hardness of his body against mine and promised myself that I would find the courage to say my secret incantation out loud to him soon. *I love you, Jomei Sato. I love you, Jomei Sato. I love you, Jomei Sato.* This is the truth I ached to tell him.

Disownment

Kando: In the Edo period when the family system was wholly patriarchal, the parent could disinherit a disobedient, prodigal, or delinquent son. The disinherited son was to be dressed in a kimono made of paper (kamiko) and turned out of the house. Kando generally involved a moral as well as an economic sanction, for the disinherited son was branded as a disgrace to the family and cut off from it.

During those six months I spent with Sato, Karin had found her own companion, a politician from City Hall. He had not visited the bar for some weeks. I asked her why one morning after our shift as we walked through the deserted streets. Karin broke down in tears and confessed his vanishing act was a response to her predicament. She told me she had already made up her mind about what she would do. She was too young to be a mother, and too poor. Would I go with her?

Perhaps I had been more fortunate than Karin. Not long after that first night with the captain, he sent me to a doctor, who explained he was going to fit me with an object that would help stop pregnancy. He called it a womb veil. Karin would cajole her politician into buying condoms but often he refused to open up his pack of Heart Beauty. Instead, she would devour pomegranate seeds after one of the girls spoke of their contraceptive qualities. We would talk about other methods at the bathhouses. But the truth was abortion, despite being illegal, was often the chosen method of birth control among the girls, even if they risked prison and their health. When Karin realised what was wrong she tried home remedies: sponges soaked in alcohol, an aloe purgative, water so hot it was near boiling, but in the end she found a retired midwife, who ran her illegal business in a part of town the city officials tended to avoid.

We held hands as we made our way down cobbled paths, past houses made of little more than sheets of rotting wood and blackened metal. Children playing in the dirt, old women throwing cooking water into streets and a blond gaijin on a creaking bicycle looked up as if they knew what we were doing. Even cloaked, we stood out as girls from Maruyama. We carried the scent of the bars and rooms for rent. The house when we arrived was no different from the shacks that had lined our journey. A girl of seven or eight answered our knocks. Inside, the room had a low ceiling with a sunken hearth in the middle and an oil lamp placed on a wooden stool. The girl disappeared into a back room and returned with an elderly woman, dressed in a grey apron. Karin clung to me and then followed the woman and the door closed behind them. I took off my shawl and sat beside the girl as she played with a rag doll, soiled with grease.

When the operation was over, Karin winced as we made our way back to her lodgings. By the time I helped her onto the futon, she was feverish and bleeding. I stroked her damp hair and placed a cool towel around the back of her neck and every so often I would glance underneath the blanket. She told me the woman had said to expect some blood. When the bleeding did not stop, I said we had to call the bar's doctor. She tried to sit up and reached for my hand. 'Please, no, no. Mama-san will throw me out.' Come morning, she was barely conscious. I had no choice. Sato had told me in an emergency he could be contacted at the medical hospital and so I wrote a note and paid a boy to deliver my request. If he was angry when he arrived, he did not show it. He examined Karin, told me she had an infection and explained what medicines were needed. He would wait with her until I returned.

'I'm sorry, Jomei. I didn't know who else to ask. If Mama-san found out, Karin would be gone. And she has nowhere to go.'

'Why can't the man who did this look after her?'

'Hostess girls are only here to entertain. We're not paid to be an inconvenience.'

When I returned he stayed until Karin's fever broke and then I walked with him to the exit of her lodgings. The landlady peered out of her room but I shooed the witch away as I opened the door. The last of the afternoon sun bled into the hallway and we stood bathed in the orange light. I told him how grateful I was, how I could never repay him this kindness. He raised his hand as if he were about to touch me but seemed to think better of it. 'Sometimes I can almost forget what you do, what you are, what I am to you.' He looked back to Karin's door. 'And then I remember.'

I watched him leave and said nothing. I should have

spoken. I should have told him he was more than a customer, so much more. *I love you, Jomei Sato.* Why were those words so hard to say? Why did I hesitate? Would the sincerity of those words have mattered?

The metallic smell of bloody rags clogged the air when I returned to Karin's room. She was sitting up. 'Will Sato say anything?'

'You can trust him.'

Tears were in her eyes. 'I wish he'd never touched me. He told me he cared for me but he wouldn't like me all fat. Said he wasn't sure the baby was his.' Karin stared up at the ceiling. 'I told him I'd be thin again. He said the problem wasn't his, I should have been more careful. Some joke, huh?'

Karin scraped her fingers along her scalp and I came and knelt by her futon. 'What will you do?'

She shook her head but we both knew the answer. We bribed the landlady not to mention Sato's visit and we continued as before. She was back working in the bar a couple of days later, her absence explained by a stomach illness. Karin smiled and laughed and showed no discomfort, but some events leave a mark, even if they cannot be seen. Whereas before she had been a butterfly, lying her bright wings flat in the sun, now she held them close to her so that the customers could not see her colours within. She talked often of that lost foetus, her water child, she called it. She bought small statues, dressed them in red bibs and caps and took them to temples. Sometimes, rather than the figurines, she left round polished stones instead. She thought these offerings would ease her sadness but they did not. Her water child left its mark on me too but I don't blame Karin for what happened. I chose to ask for Sato's help. I chose to show him my life as it was, not how I wanted it to be, some room filled with roses and pictures of horses and herons. In the days that followed his visit to Karin, I waited at the bar, I visited the apartment and parks, I sent notes to his work, but Sato had disappeared. He was a conjuror's trick, one minute there, the next gone. I told myself he just needed time to adjust to this truer version of me and he would return. I did not have to wait too long. I saw him two or three weeks later, on the night of Shoro-Nagashi, August 15, 1919.

Mama-san had given Karin and me a couple of hours off work, knowing the bars would be empty while thousands of people gathered in the streets. The festival is unlike any other in Japan. Families welcome back their deceased from the spirit world or send them on their way. Joy and sorrow march side by side as drums bang and incense burns. We stood among the throng and watched the procession of bamboo and grass boats built for the dead, some as big as real ships. Men wrapped in white sheets were carrying the vessels festooned with lanterns down to the water to be lowered into the sea and pushed off into the darkness. Those glowing boats floated off while the bereaved placed gifts of fruit on mats and sent them also into the night. The city was a flare of colour, dragon dances and men drunk on rice wine. The shouting, the high-pitched calls to the spirits, the fireworks, the crackers, the gongs, the noise is loud enough to scare off the wild cats and wake up the dead. Our departed cannot rest. They cannot ignore us. They must leave or return to us. We are too loud to ignore.

Karin and I jostled among the people to find a good spot next to a stall selling grilled caramel. The smell of burnt sugar filled the air along with sulphur from the fire crackers. One of the men from the procession, his hand bleeding, his face dripping sweat, stumbled up to Karin and shouted at her, 'Hey, beautiful, marry me,' before offering her a bottle of opened plum wine. We moved away from him, and that was the moment, with the streets vibrating with music and voices and the air filled with smoke, when I saw him. Not the ghost of his face reflected in another, but him. What joy, that jolt of recognition, mixed with surprise. He was heading toward us and then I saw that he was not alone. A girl, taller than me and perhaps a little older, was holding his arm. Without thinking, I went to raise my hand in greeting and he looked up. Instead of a smile, he seemed furious. Karin must have seen him too. She pulled at my arm to move away but I was paralysed by that expression of anger and then disgust. I did not know what to do or where to go. There was no room among the crowds to slip past them. Instead the mass of people were pushing me directly into their path. He was only a step or two away when he whispered something in the girl's ear. She laughed and just seconds before they reached me they disappeared between two food stalls and joined the parade. Karin asked if I was OK and searched for a handkerchief in her purse, worried that I might cry, but I was too shocked for tears. I looked down and saw myself as he must have done. Too gaudy, too bright, too cheap. How to describe that moment of humiliation? How to paint the pain of his rejection? After all those months, after all that I had risked for him and hoped of him, I did not even merit an acknowledgement. That is Jomei Sato.

A Lordless Samurai Warrior

Ronin: In feudal times it often happened that samurai warriors would lose their lord in a war or social upheaval. These lordless samurai warriors were called ronin. Because they were poor, they had to work. Many taught children reading and writing. Thanks to their contribution, it is said, the literacy in Japan at the time was considerably higher than in Europe.

I am suspicious of nostalgia, pliable as it can be to our moods or needs, but sometimes I allowed the memories, however dubious, to take me to the bar before Sato, when the glow of the lamps was the only sign of time passing, or energy spent, or old jokes shared not just to fill the silence. The doctor had done a cruel thing; he brought light into this black hole of survival and then, just as easily, he withdrew into the shadows. Sakamoto was another absent face from the bar, much to Mama-san's displeasure. She never asked why he vanished but learned from a rival bar owner that he had set up camp two doors down. I thought Mama-san would blame me for the loss of his custom and send me away. The thought was not unappealing; too much had happened, too many opportunities lost, too many tears of self-pity shed when alone at night, but all I knew how to be was a hostess. Like Karin, I had nowhere else to go. I did not want to end up like Kimiko or the other women down by the wharves offering themselves for coins, a warm meal, brief shelter.

With Sato and Sakamoto gone, other admirers began to sniff around. Basho Arai was not so bad. He had a large head, small chin and skinny fingers, yes, but he was not without charm. He liked to talk politics, his eyelids half shut, one hand waving a cigarette as a conductor might, drunk on the music. His subject that September night was the Paris Peace Conference earlier in the year and the Treaty of Versailles. 'We've got the German Islands, Shantung, Jiaozhou. America and China might not be happy but they're ours. Do you know what all this means, Amaterasu? We're a first-class nation now. Good, eh?'

I smiled at his enthusiasm. 'Tokyo, I tell you, is the place where you need to be.'

'Why, sweet thing?'

'That's where the action is, my friend.'

'Not here?'

'Here?' I lit my cigarette, my voice dismissive. 'Don't be silly.'

He touched my knee. 'I'll go to Tokyo if you come with me. You can be my assistant. Think of the stories we will write together.'

I pretended to type on the table with my cigarette hanging out of my mouth. 'Like this?'

'Perfect. Why not? Now get me some stew. I need to sober up. I have a story to file.'

I stood up, dizzy from the drink, and as I neared the kitchen I saw Mama-san talking to someone by the entrance. I was surprised to see him, another lost customer.

He walked toward me, self-conscious. 'How delightful to see you, Kenzo.'

He bowed, smoothed down his hair. 'Hello, Amaterasu, it's been too long.'

'It has.' I gestured at the nearest banquette. 'Please, sit. You've been missed.'

He considered this. 'Work is busy. We have so many orders for ships, soon we will have more ships than people. You should come down to the docks. I can show you around.'

'Your boss would allow that?'

He smiled. 'Well, I'm my own boss and I give myself permission.'

I laughed and he seemed pleased by my reaction. But then he cleared his throat and looked embarrassed. 'Jomei sends his regards.' Hearing his name felt like a knife wound in my chest. I could not speak. 'We need not talk of him if you would prefer?'

'Please, do not trouble yourself.'

He studied my face. 'Amaterasu, you need not hide your disappointment. Jomei is discreet but we are good friends.'

My cheeks burned at the thought of them talking about me. Akiko placed two glasses and a sake bottle on our table. 'Here, let me serve you. Please tell Sato that I am fine.'

He watched me pour the drinks. I think my hands did not shake. 'I am glad, Amaterasu. I would not like you to be sad.' I offered him a cigarette but he declined. 'Jomei is my friend and so I don't say this easily, but he is not a serious man when it comes to women.' He took a drink.

'Perhaps his marriage will change all that.' My face must have betrayed my shock. Kenzo looked abashed. 'I'm sorry. I thought you knew?'

I lifted my hand as if the news were nothing. 'When?'

'A few weeks ago. A daughter of a surgeon at the hospital.' I did the calculations: his gift of the key must have coincided with the start of their courtship. Had his plan been to keep me as some unofficial mistress? For how long? Karin's pregnancy must have caused him to weigh up the dangers. He couldn't risk the same predicament with me.

'Forgive me, Amaterasu. You should not have heard that from me.' He seemed to wrestle with something, and almost as if in confession, he said, 'I know how charming Jomei can seem but I don't think he would have made you happy.' I drank to this and he moved a little closer. 'Sometimes it is easy to overlook what will make you happy.' He took hold of my hand. 'Perhaps you need to open your eyes, Amaterasu, to other possibilities, ones that have been there from the start.' He smiled and for the first time I paid proper attention to Kenzo Takahashi. And he held my wounded heart softly in his hands.

We married a month later. Neither of us wanted to wait. He wanted me to invite Mother to the ceremony but I would not. I had expected objections or tears when I told her but she shrugged off any hurt or anger. I needed to leave the past behind. I could not take her with me. I paid her off with cash saved from my earnings. I told her there would be more payments if she left me alone. Her voice was low as she looked at the box of money on her lap. 'I did the best for you, Amaterasu.' She shook her head, resigned maybe. 'I did what I could.'

'I was a child, Mother.'

'And look at you now. The bride of a respected engineer. You have me to thank for that.'

The Wind

Kaze: The wind as well as the rain has been more than a mere natural phenomenon with the Japanese. There was an ancient belief that the wind was caused by the comings and goings of invisible gods. With ancient people, therefore, all winds except ill and nasty winds were literally kamikaze (divine winds).

Hideo ran his finger down his glass and used the condensation to draw a circle on the wooden bar. Two eyes and a mouth. A smiling face. He glanced up and we looked at each other across the divides of time. I was the past, he was the future. By tomorrow night, he would be on a plane to Nagasaki. We had so few hours left to glue dead leaves to an infected family tree. What could I tell him? What parts of Sato's letters should I reveal? In his one from 1971, the kanji and hiragana had been whispery across the page, the writing of an ill man. Sato wrote he had hoped that the older he grew the more certain he would become of his life, the choices made, the mistakes, the few small triumphs. He had assumed they would all solidify into some kinder version of the past. Old age had tormented him with a harsher understanding. The years had made the pain of regret grow not lessen.

Who knew my body would rail so much against the dying of the light? Now I think I am nearing my destination,

I remain plagued by this thought that I should have fought harder for you, Yuko. Or maybe I should have never gone near you. Did you think of me in those final seconds with love, or anger, or at all? Increasingly, I play a dark fantasy game in the hours when my medication cannot kill the pain. I try to rewrite our last meeting together so that you did not leave for Urakami Cathedral that day. I ask myself what I would have said to have kept you from going. I had been ruled by the orders of your mother for one final, catastrophic time. Together we put you in the path of pikadon. Our love for you drove you to the cathedral. How has she lived with this knowledge all these years?

I will confess that I have, more than once, thought about ending my life. Such an act seemed not an indulgence but the only honourable step to take. What stopped me? An injured boy we brought into our home called Hideo. He was reason to continue. He was reason to fight to be a better man. Was I wrong for wanting all those years ago to believe that the scarred child we found in the orphanage was your son? We had expected his memory to come back and when it did not I began to give him the small facts I did know. Natsu warned me against giving him a label. What good was it being Hideo Watanabe? she asked. But I had wanted to give him a sense of self, of history, a line of ancestors from which to draw. His face can tell nothing other than that day of August 9, 1945. I wanted to give him more than one day. Was that cruel of me? And maybe, just maybe, I am right. Amaterasu will know whether he is your son. Maybe it is not too late to find her.

Can I let her near my boy? Will this be my last act of contrition?

Sato would have been too ill to look for Kenzo and me anew. No, Natsu had led the search. She had been the most selfless of all of us. That is why she had written the introductory letter. The lies, the tangled affairs, the hurt and losses; in the end, none of them mattered. She was concerned with only one element of our shared past: Hideo. In that dark bar, I smiled at her son, the pikadon boy. Was this my grandson? Or had my Hideo always been among the 75,000 dead?

I reached for his hand and caressed his scars. 'Tell me, if you can. What do you remember about that last morning?'

He shook his head. 'I don't think it will help.'

I squeezed his fingers. 'Try.'

He nodded but he could not look at me as he spoke. 'I was playing with some other children. We liked to use our magnifying glasses to set alight weeds or ants and we were waiting for the sun to burn through the clouds. Teachers were working in the rice paddy or on the school air-raid shelters. I don't remember the sound of an aircraft above but suddenly someone shouted to run to the shelter. I ran as fast as I could, my friends were behind me. I managed to reach the shelter when some force propelled me forward to the back wall. I blacked out, I don't know for how long, and awoke in the darkness. I called out for my friends but they did not reply. As I crawled my way to the entrance, creatures appeared out of the gloom. They must have been human beings but they had no skin.

They could not speak. They just made a terrible croaking noise. I was too scared to stay in the shelter with them.

'Outside the sky was purple. I looked for my friends, for the teachers, but they were gone. More people were heading to the shelter, naked, moaning, their torsos bloated. I ran away from them. I did not want to hear their cries. In the playground, the sandbox was full of bodies and the school was on fire. All I could hear was the blaze. I had never realised how loud fire is. Beneath the roar, I heard another noise, a voice in the fire, crying out for help. I knew I had to be brave. I can't remember how I got into the school, how I found her, but I did. A girl was cowering under a desk. I must have told her to come with me but she wouldn't move. Perhaps I begged her as the fire came closer, but she just cried out for her mother. I couldn't make her come with me, so I left her. I don't remember flames on my skin.' He held up his hand. 'But there must have been contact. My next memory is being in a hospital.' He stopped for a moment, his voice unsteady. 'The school had nearly 1,600 students before pikadon, three hundred survived. You heard such terrible tales in the months that followed, orphans foraging for food, searching for their parents' cremated ashes in the ground, the injuries that would not heal, the suicides. Children killing themselves. Can you imagine?' He took a drink. 'People feel sorry for me . . . but I'm the lucky one.'

He had described exactly the scene that had confronted me at Yamazato school. 'I remember a school building on fire. You must have been rescued by then, taken away. It is a miracle you survived. Truly.'

'The air-raid shelter saved me. Not God.'

Why could I not accept my own miracle of a grandson returned from the dead? Why could I not hold him to me and say, yes, I believe you now. I know I didn't deserve such joy. Was this why I hesitated? Guilt? If he knew what I had done, who I was, how could he not push me away? How could I bear that ending? And yet I couldn't leave us in this limbo. He needed to know one way or the other. I scrabbled for confirmation again.

'Do you remember the question I asked you when you first came to my door the first morning?' He cocked his head. 'About what we saw in the garden that last day?' I waited, hopeful, but he could only shake his head, apologise. I checked the clock behind the bar. His train was due. Next to the clock postcards from around the world had been pinned alongside a rainbow of foreign banknotes. I even spotted a one thousand yen among the francs, sterling and Deutschmarks. As I looked at that crumpled piece of paper, I knew there was one way to resolve who this man truly was.

'Hideo, I know you've been waiting for me to tell you whether you are my grandson. Thank you for your patience. But before I answer, I have one final request. I'm afraid it's rather a big one.'

A Female Medium

*Itako: These women are divinely inspired and supernaturally
possessed. They are supposed to be able to bring forth messages of
ancestors to their descendants, mediate between the spirits of the
dead and living persons, and divine the fate of a family or an
individual. Before these women become independent practitioners,
they live with experienced masters of these magic acts.*

An overlay of maple trees hung above our heads as we
travelled in a taxi from the airport to the city. They must
have looked glorious in summer, a lime covering of
sunspots and dazzled leaves, but that day the stripped
branches bounced above the road in eddies of air. I
lowered the window to hear them creak in the wind but
the car's engine masked their aria. The low sun lit the
underside of birds' wings on the dive. I breathed in the air
of Japan. Like no other. So ripe with possibility. So
cleansing. How I had missed it. Hideo was sitting next
to the driver and was wearing beige trousers and a
matching sweater. I was disguised as an old woman, navy-
blue crinoline pants, synthetic purple jacket, floral scarf.
We drove past the outskirts of Nagasaki toward its beating
heart and I clutched the door handle to steady myself as
the streets rolled by.

What to say of a city you haven't seen for nearly forty
years? The two peaks, the harbour, Chinatown and the

Dutch Slope were still there but modernity had left its mark. Pachinko parlours were everywhere, with their neon lights and beeping machines and silver balls. Newly built offices of metal and glass and concrete rose up above our heads, and the centre had been taken over by a covered central shopping mall. Despite those curiosities, I had come home. How to explain the feeling? Do you remember waking on a summer morning as a child, when you opened the window and the promise of that day flooded into your room? That was Nagasaki for me, a shocking sensation of hope. I had robbed Kenzo of that unexpected feeling of return, but I tried to tell myself I could not have come back any sooner. America was a place to heal as best we could. I had needed those four decades to find the strength to revisit the ghosts and the places where they hid.

Hideo's home was situated in one of the steepest parts of the city. You could only access the two-storey house by walking up flights and flights of concrete steps, or by finding your way to the top of the hill and then walking down. I had grown too used to the flat, uniform streets of my American home, with every address labelled and known. Here, houses and apartments were crammed one against the other, all different sizes and shapes linked by warrens of paths. Their home was a side of grey pebble-dash and a roof of red tiles, built against a moss-stained stone wall beside a river that ran past a medley of corrugated-iron shacks, wooden lean-tos and tarpaulin flapping against brick huts.

We stood outside his home and he told me not to be nervous but, of course, I was. He rang the doorbell and there was a clatter of feet and shouts of 'Daddy'. The door opened and Benji and Hanako ran into their father's arms. He held them tight. 'My little devils. How I've missed you. Have you been good for Mummy?' Angela stepped into the hallway, drying her hands on a dishcloth. She reached down and tickled Benji. 'They've been perfect monsters.' The children laughed and gave me curious glances. Angela took a step forward and kissed Hideo. She spoke in English, 'Hey, baby, glad you're home.' She smiled and kissed him again, switching back to Japanese. 'And you must be Amaterasu. We're so thrilled you could visit. Come in, come in. Where's your bag? The children have made you a cake, haven't you, kids? Go bring it into the living room.' They ran off, shouting, 'Cake, cake, cake.'

'Apologies, the kids are wild. Let me take your coat. The oil heater is on. You'll be freezing and exhausted. It's quite a flight.' In the living room we sat on beige sofas surrounded by bookcases crammed with books and walls covered in pictures drawn by the kids. A large glass door opened to a small courtyard. The children returned and placed a chocolate cake on the coffee table. Round red candies had been pressed into the brown icing. Hanako looked at me shyly. 'It's a ladybug.' I smiled. 'My favourite.' Benji knelt down next to me as Angela cut thick slices. Hideo told his family about his trip, while his daughter clung to him.

I looked at the children, greedy for signs of Yuko in them. Hanako's dark hair fell down her back and she was dressed in maroon corduroys and a grey jumper. She fiddled with a scab on her chin as she ate her cake. Benji had a rash of freckles and a fringe that fell in a heavy layer over his eyes. He wore a baseball shirt and denims that threatened to fall off his thin hips. His lips were coated in brown frosting. He whispered to his mother, who replied, 'Why don't you ask her?' He turned to me. 'Want to see your room?' Hanako stood up and reached for my hand. 'This way.' She held my fingers lightly, as if she was worried she might crush my bones.

First they took me to their small yard, next to a waterfall that trickled over rocks black with slime. They threw a ball back and forth while they asked me where I had come from and did I like America and had I seen *The A-Team*? The inquisition over, they led me to a door that opened to a small room, little more than a cupboard. We peered inside. A round hole had been cut into a raised wooden platform. Benji sneaked past me and looked down the open sewer. 'This is the toilet,' he explained, laughing as he revealed that during the monsoon season Hideo had to nail a board over the seat to stop the water shooting up into the house. Next they took me to the kitchen and Hanako scuffed one foot back and forth along the tiles as she told me in the summer the floor was overrun with slugs. She shuddered when she said this. I had imagined a modern home for them. Sato's wealth and Hideo's job as a teacher surely would have bought them a more comfortable property but the chaos of the ramshackle house suited the family.

Back in the hall, Benji warned me the stray cats liked to congregate outside their front step at night and I must not be worried by all their howling. We took the stairs and they waited patiently for me to climb each step. They showed me where they slept and then slid open a paper

263

door to reveal a square room, with tatami floors and a futon, already made up. 'This is where you're going to sleep.' I was thrilled by the prospect of sleeping on a futon again, even if my body was not. Hanako pointed to some plastic daisies in a vase. 'These are for you.' I thanked her and she shrugged but seemed pleased. 'We'll get your bag.' She ran out and Benji followed her but before he closed the door, he said, 'Let's play sumo wrestlers later, OK?' I smiled. 'OK.'

In the evening, while we sat in the living room before dinner, the children came running in, giggling. They had stripped down to their version of a sumo wrestler's mawashi fashioned out of their father's white T-shirts tied in knots. Hideo laughed. 'What have we here? Our own sumo match?' Benji nodded and ran to a clean pile of laundry and started pulling out socks to make the outline of the ring. Hanako came up and tapped me on the knee. 'You're the judge. You decide who wins.'

Later still, Hanako sat next to me on the low couch with a sketch pad. She chewed a pencil in her mouth. 'What shall I draw?' I thought for a moment and suggested a horse. She leaned against me as she drew and I marvelled at the ease of children in new company. Angela smiled as she played cards with her son. I put my arm around Hanako and rested the side of my head on top of hers. I smelled the fresh air caught in her hair and the sweet milk scent of her skin. Closing my eyes, I imagined Yuko nestled in my arm, the weight of her, all those hours we had passed this way. When Hanako was finished, she looked up to me, a slight furrow in her brow. 'Do you like it?'

'It's perfect.'

She held the picture at arm's length, admiring her work. 'I'm quite good at drawing.' She showed the sketch to her father, who pinned it to the wall and then ordered them both to bed. They hugged their parents and suddenly I felt a stranger again. 'Give Amaterasu a kiss,' Angela said. Before I could say there was no need they ran up and took turns to kiss me on the cheek, wet lips soft on my skin.

During those first few days, Angela and Hideo fizzed around me, hovering and anxious. I told them to go about their business as normal. I wanted to be left to explore the city, ease back to the point where I had left Nagasaki. I needed time to reacquaint myself with all that I had left behind. One morning I rose early and wrote a note to say I would return before dinner time. I took the tram past Hamaguchi-machi and got off near the post office. I walked five slow blocks to Sanno shrine, reconstructed after the bomb. To reach it, I passed through a torii gate, one leg blown away, the other upright. It had been left that way after pikadon as a memorial. I crossed flagstones and found one of the camphor trees that had survived all those fires that had raged across the city. I ran my hand down the blackened bark and felt our shared past in the cracks and charcoal fissures. We were still here, one growing, the other stunted, but both alive. I could not face going to Urakami Cathedral and Yamazato Primary, where new buildings had replaced those lost. Instead I went to the Peace Park. A statue of a man sitting in vigil stood at the head of the open square. Kenzo had shown me a picture in the newspaper after the site had been built in 1955. He had called it an affront, so ugly, but as

I sat on a stone bench and looked up at this muscular naked man, with his flowing hair and loincloth, I took comfort from his presence. We had a watchman for the city at last. His green bronze right hand pointed to the sky, the left horizontal across Nagasaki, his eyes closed in prayer. Paper cranes – red, yellow, white, orange, purple – lined fences and posts and benches. Schoolchildren, so neat in their sailor outfits, walked up to tourists and handed them postcards with handwritten messages of peace. One ran up to me and gave me a card and I looked at it for a long time before I walked down to the circular stone fountain, where jets of white spray shot up into the air. Here was the water the dying had begged for. A leaflet flipped by in the breeze and I stooped to retrieve it. There was a map of atomic bomb landmarks, the cover dominated by the cathedral. This new version built in 1959 was so red, so substantial. Here was the great solid entrance returned, those two towers rising tall once more. Only the original belfry remained, lying on the riverbank, blown thirty yards away by pikadon. *'Urakami had been a distinct Christian district since the second half of 1500. Under the suppression of Christianity from 1613, Christians continued to practise their religion by organising secret groups. The villagers managed to come back to Urakami in 1873. When they built the cathedral, it took almost 30 years to complete. The cathedral was also exposed to the atomic bomb and was destroyed. Around 8,500 of the 12,000 Christians living in the area were killed by the blast.'*

I read that last sentence and thought of Yuko, just one among all those thousands. Where had all the shattered bricks been taken? Where had they been buried? Where had she gone? Was she buried with those bricks? Could

I dig down into soil and unearth the black embers of her? I did not follow her faith but I was drawn to the stories of burning pits and boiling cauldrons and crucifixions. These were stories of pain and of loss that I could understand. The twenty-six martyrs of 1597, the 37,000 peasants massacred forty years later, the thousands arrested in the city and exiled not so long ago, those thousands more who lived and worked in the shadow of Urakami Cathedral; I admired the sacrifices made by them all to this religion, but no, I was not a believer. I looked again at the photograph, ran my fingers over a line of worshippers walking toward the great oak door. Those Christians who survived, how could they worship in that new building, how could they cross its entrance and not wonder: Why did we live? Why were they taken? Why did my god allow this?

Shade and Light

In'yo: The idea of these dual forces evolved from the cosmology of the ancient Chinese, and explains every phenomenon of the universe by shade (in) and light (yo). For example, day and night, heat and cold, and male and female all comprise in'yo, day, heat and male being yo.

My journey home had taken me thirty-eight years. The winter sun was beginning to set and orange lights appeared from the windows of the cathedral. I whispered my apologies to my daughter for my lateness and stepped over the threshold. The last time I saw Yuko, we met at the cathedral, two days before the bomb. The red facade was bleached coral in the sunshine but the darkness of its interior swallowed the daylight. I could see her sitting on one of the back pews, the outline of her shoulders and head shimmering from the golden shafts that spilled off the stained glass. I walked up to her, my feet silent on the paved stones, and touched her on the shoulder. She turned round and her face was pale and drawn. Call it a mother's instinct but I knew something was wrong. We moved outside to one of the stone seats west of the building. She opened a parasol and we sheltered under its white frame. I tried to fill her silence with chatter. I asked after Hideo and told her Mrs Goto had been unwell. She did not respond and stared at the ground. I waited, and when she finally spoke, she could not look at me. 'You know Jomei is back?'

The dread returned instantly. We had never spoken about the doctor since her marriage. What would have been the point? I tried to keep my voice light. 'No, I wasn't aware. Since when?' She said nothing. 'Your paths have crossed?' Fear coursed through my body. 'He has acted in good faith?' Again she did not reply but her hesitation was enough. She handed me the parasol, turned away and began to cry. Her tears fell in splashes and she reached into her pocket for a handkerchief. I'm ashamed to admit this but I often feel a swell of disgust when seeing someone in distress, especially someone I love. I need them to be strong, contained. Any show of weakness frightens me. I ran my palm down her wet cheek. 'Why are you telling me this today, Yuko? Why now?'

A minute or so passed and she grew calm. She folded the handkerchief into a square and wiped her eyes. She reached for the parasol and we drew closer under its protection. 'I need your help, Mother. I need to do something and I cannot face it alone.'

'Do what, Daughter?'

'This is not his fault, before you blame him. To see him again after so long, it was as if all those years, Shige, Hideo, had vanished. I was foolish, selfish, I know.' She sighed, ready for the confession. 'To keep the baby is a sin. To get rid of it is a sin. What can I do, Mother?'

'Baby?' The word fell from me in a rush of anguish. I said the word again and then dug my fingernails in my palm so that I would not cry. We sat in silence as the

269

sun began its slow descent behind the cathedral. My throat felt gritty with the dying afternoon heat. Finally, I found the strength to speak. 'Does Sato know?'

Yuko dabbed beneath her eyes with her fingers. 'I haven't told him yet, but surely I have to tell him?'

I gathered up my fear, sealed it away. 'You want my advice? Then this is it. You cannot keep the baby and he must never know.'

'Maybe I could have the child and have it adopted?' I looked to the sky, exasperated. 'I can't destroy the baby, Mother. What will God say?'

'It's not God you have to worry about, it's Shige. He's your concern. And Hideo. They are your family. This thing, this seed in your belly, it's nothing, see, nothing. The war will end some day. Shige will return. Hideo will need a father. And you a husband.'

'What if I could take Hideo away with me, start a new life?'

'And abandon Shige? You could do that?'

She started to weep again. 'He's dead. I know it. I feel it.'

'You can't believe it. This is war. This is what happens. He will return.' I took her hand. 'You asked me here today for help. Women have been dealing with this problem for centuries. There's a fishing village down the coast. Years ago now, before you were born, a great storm hit the area. It battered the nearby cliffs so hard that when the wind and rain passed on, the villagers noticed strange objects protruding from the cliff face. Bones, human bones, children's bones. For hundreds of years, the women of that village had gone to that spot to rid themselves of children

270

they could not keep because of disability, or hunger, or parentage. There are places you can go. You will not be the first woman to fix this problem.'

'So, it's that easy? Some trip down an alley and the problem's gone?'

'And Sato . . .'

She pulled her hand away. 'I knew you wouldn't understand.'

'I do understand, Yuko. I understand that kind of love, I do. But it doesn't make you happy. Believe me. You can't see beyond it now, but you will.'

'I need time to think.'

'The longer you wait, the harder it will be, the more likely you will be to tell Sato.' I forged the plan in my head. 'We will meet here on Thursday. I'll find someone who can help us. You have a break at eleven in the morning, yes?' She nodded. 'OK, two days, you have two days to accept what you have to do. We'll fix this, Yuko. But you must promise, when this is done, no more Sato, no more. You have your family. That is who you are.'

She looked up at the cathedral. 'I can't make that decision with God so near. Let's meet somewhere in town after work. I'll be finished by five o'clock.'

'No, here is better. Thursday at eleven o'clock. I'll be waiting.' I had thought maybe the presence of the cathedral would remind her of her vows to Shige.

She stood up. 'I'm expected back at the hospital.' She looked away briefly as if trying to contain her emotions. 'I'm sorry I'm such a disappointment to you.'

I should have called her back, gathered her in my arms, told her she had never disappointed, not once.

How could she? Yuko had been the one true joy in my life, the pearl in the shell of my heart. But rather than say any of this, I watched her walk away, her nurse's uniform shrinking into the evening as she returned to work. My biggest worry was that she would confess the pregnancy to Sato before our next meeting and he would manipulate her into keeping the child. As I sat on the bench my loathing for him poured over me. I felt the hatred prick my pores and pierce my stomach. I had tried to cleanse the doctor from our lives before. I had underestimated his resolve, but there was one final move I could make that would poison any feeling he might have for my daughter. I could see no other alternative. This is not my excuse, but an attempt at an explanation.

Lingering Attachment

Miren: A feeling one develops when, for example, one is forced to part with one's beloved due to the pressure of social circumstance. It is part of the emotional category of sorrow. A man is said to be effeminate and unreliable if he cannot suppress his lingering attachment to his sweetheart once he has decided he had better leave her.

Maruyama in the early morning resembles a geisha stripped of her fine kimonos and make-up. Empty beer bottles are stacked in crates, the shutters of the dim-sum and takoyaki stalls are down, the lanterns droop and the clogged drains ferment under the day's harsh judgement. The cracks and stains and decay are all too visible, but most delivery men, or cleaners, or hostess girls making their way home know better than to look too closely down side lanes or inside doorways.

I had chosen a bar where night workers could still find a beer or company come the end of their shift. I sat at a bench at the back wall and asked for a coffee. Except for two hostess girls, bleary-eyed with lack of sleep, I was the only female customer. I watched the door for Sato. When he arrived I felt that same pull in my guts of fear, anger and some feeling I refused to acknowledge.

He sat down opposite me and studied my face. Even in this forgiving light, I knew what he saw. The greying under my eyes, my skin still pale from the night's caress even after all those years. I remained a creature of twilight, blanched. He pulled a silver case from his jacket pocket and offered me a cigarette. I refused and he lit one for himself. I had left my name and the address of the bar with his receptionist the evening before. I did not know whether he would come but I had not dared go to the hospital in case Yuko saw me. The waitress came over and he ordered a glass of shochu. He tapped his cigarette carton on the table and waited until our drinks had been delivered before he spoke.

'Tell me, Amaterasu. I was thinking on the way over. How long have we known each other?'

I smelled the aroma of roasted acorns as I replied. 'Don't be cruel, Sato. Don't make me count.'

'Nonsense, we are still young, you and I. We're still game for the fight.'

Wisps of tobacco crackled near his mouth from his cigarette. I gave him a rueful look. 'Come now, Sato. You're not feeling nostalgic, are you?'

This amused him. 'You know me better than that.'

'We have known each other . . .' I began to count. 'One, two, three . . . no, don't make me do it.'

He leaned forward and touched my hand. 'In all those years, I have not been as forthcoming with my expressions of admiration.'

I fell into my former guise, pouted and fashioned a frown. 'I don't know what you mean.'

He half smiled at this. 'Did Yuko tell you I was back in Nagasaki?'

'She did. Perhaps I shouldn't have been so surprised.

Tell me, Sato. What is it about Yuko? Of all the women in the city, why do you keep coming back to her?'

'You're not jealous, are you, Amaterasu?'

'Don't be ridiculous. I'm not your wife, Sato.' I tried to keep my voice steady. 'My only concern is Yuko. Do you understand what you have done here?'

'I did not come here to explain myself. Only to tell you, unlike last time, I will not be ordered around like some housemaid. This matter between Yuko and me is unfinished business. And maybe more too.'

'What? You still think this love? You have no idea what that word means. If you continue to pursue Yuko, you will destroy her life, for what, your own selfish needs? A parent's love is selfish too, in different ways.' I paused. 'Why her? Anyone but her. Think, Sato. Think. Did you never do the calculations? Did you never consider how soon Kenzo and I began after you and I ended? Did you never think about her age?'

I watched the clouds of confusion clear on his face as he understood what I was saying to him. He stubbed his cigarette out in the ashtray as he shook his head. 'Amaterasu, don't do what you are about to do. If you love Yuko, don't say what you are about to say.'

'Yuko was a small baby. It was easy enough to pass her off as premature. No one guessed the truth.'

He sat back with a look of despair. 'Why would you tell such an unnatural lie? Don't you realise I know when you are lying? Even after all these years. You pride yourself on deception, but you are a terrible liar.'

I pulled some money from my purse. 'I'm sorry, Sato, I really am, but it's no lie. Who could make such a crime up?'

He sat back, as if stabbed in the chest. There were tears in his eyes. 'I don't believe you. You are nothing more than a Maruyama whore who would lie and cheat and say anything to get her way.'

I stood and picked up my parasol. 'I'm meeting Yuko at Urakami Cathedral tomorrow morning. You have until then to break off this foul union, or I will tell her everything.'

Sato gave me another look of revulsion. 'You would do that to your own child? I can see how you would lie to me, but her?'

'To keep her away from you, Sato, I'd do anything.' I walked out of the bar, turned down an alleyway, squeezed through lanes little wider than me so that he could not follow me – faster and faster – and when my lungs burned in protest and I could run no more, I bent over in a doorway and retched. Again. And again. And again. Until I had purged those words from my body.

India-ink Painting

Suibokuga: This style of painting was introduced into Japan from China together with Zen Buddhism and perfected by the painter and priest Sesshu (1420–1506) in the fifteenth century. As in many other Japanese arts and traditions such as haiku poetry and tea ceremony, there is a deep-rooted preference for simplicity and subtlety. Suibokuga abhors superfluous strokes of the brush and unnecessary splashes of ink. It is interested in the essence of the subject matter, usually mountains, rivers, plants, animals, etc.

Various shades of black and grey on the white background stimulate the imagination of the viewer far more than colours. The white space left untouched does not represent emptiness but embodies all meaning and possibility, thus playing as important a part as the painted object itself.

A couple of worshippers bowed their heads in prayer underneath Jesus on the Cross. The silence was calming. This was as close to a cocoon as I could find. I opened my bag and took out Yuko's journal and Sato's last letter, dated 1972. I opened my daughter's diary to her final entry and listened to what she had to tell me.

'Unlike Mother, I am weak but maybe I will have the courage to do the right thing, if only I knew what that was. I love Shige. I do. These words are easy to write. I love his constancy and his loyalty. He is a good father. I thought I would have to live with the pain of Jomei's departure forever. Shige helped me mend. He fixed me.

277

No word but maybe Mother is right. I must believe him alive. I would not wish to cause him pain. I do not wish to cause Hideo harm. What am I if I cannot be a good wife and a good mother? What else will be left of me? But there is the other side of me, a darker part where Jomei exists. He is a tumour who feeds on me and grows stronger every day until all of me, bones, organs, flesh, will be consumed by him.

'Mother says there is no choice to make. Shige and Hideo are my family. She says the role of mother and wife has been sufficient for her. She cannot imagine the alternative. She says to surrender to some foolish notion of love will hurt everyone. Sometimes women are the collateral damage, she says, but we can bear the agony of decisions forced upon us. Is killing one child forgivable if it saves two families?

'All these words mean nothing until I meet with Jomei again. Despite what Mother says, I must tell him about the child. He may not want me or this new life in my belly, but if he does, what then? I cannot have the child and him without losing Shige and Hideo. Surely then there is no choice to be made? Surely I must stay true to what I have and not gamble on the unknown? What would my life be without Hideo and Shige? What would have been the point to all of this?'

Had I acted too hastily in meeting Sato at the bar that morning? I had seen the move as security against any indecision on Yuko's part. I wanted to leave nothing to chance. I pulled out his letter from the envelope. His words were barely legible, scrawled in an uneven slope down the page. He must have taken great effort to write them.

I think about the child we would have had. For some reason I see a daughter. I imagine her born healthy, with screaming lungs and clenched fists raised at the rudeness of her delivery to the world. I call her Miki. I imagine her growing into a young child. She would be free from worries and fears. She would delight in her surroundings and laugh with abandon and cry with gusto. She would not shy away from her feelings but embrace and wrestle with them. As I write I can see the bushes in my garden, shaking with the sparrows that have gathered in them. Safe within the inner branches, they chirrup to one another all day. The sound cannot fail to make whoever hears their song happy. I imagine Miki listening in wonder to the singing bush, mimicking the sound of these delicate little birds. As she grew into a teenager and young woman we would have shown her wondrous places beyond her own country. She would learn other languages and other cultures. She would make her own way in the world, choosing a career, falling in love, having children of her own. I see you holding a grandchild in your arms. These images do not torment me. I take solace from them, this imagined other world.

And then I think of Miki as she might also have been, infected by the bomb. I know the challenges she would have encountered, the obstacles we all would have faced. I imagine strangers looking at her, turning away, asking ugly questions, rejecting what they see. But her life would still be a success, only different, her goals changed but still achievable, and our love for her the same as it would be for any child, fiercer maybe in our fight to protect her. And the singing bush? Can you imagine her joy at such magic? We would have been happy, just in a different way.

I used to think losing you both was punishment for China, but I deserved such retribution, not you. This cruelty I cannot reconcile. Hideo is no atonement for all my wrongs, but my pride in who he is, what he is, how he is, are as deep as the fires that flow under Japan. As my body and mind prepare for what is about to come, my doubts about him are gone. He is your son and I love him, Yuko. It was an honour to raise him on your and Shige's behalf. He is a giant among men. This is no surprise to me. He came from strong stock. We just provided shelter while he grew. The rest, all that he is and all that he will be, is down to you. To Hideo, my love. To your son.

I wept there in the comforting shadows of the cathedral, tears muffled by a hand over my mouth. I accept now that Sato loved my daughter but I will always struggle with what happened because of that love. I'm glad she did not take my advice and had told Sato about the pregnancy. The burden of a decision was not hers alone to endure. Sato had mentioned nothing of what they had discussed when he came to my home in those days after pikadon, desperate to believe somehow she had escaped. As he stood in my bedroom, he had only one other question to ask.

'What you told me the other day in the bar, was it a lie?'

I hesitated to tell him the truth, frightened about how he might react. The summer sun fell in hot streaks through the window and we were both stripped of age and duplicity in its harsh light. We were young again, unsullied by our schemes and ambitions, a young doctor and a hostess girl. I had been a fool to imagine a life with him. I could not picture our home, our children, our happiness. The greatest gift Sato had given me was Kenzo. I returned the favour. 'Of course it was a lie, Jomei. A terrible lie. I could not let you destroy her life.' Rather than seem angry, he looked relieved. 'Please tell me, you said nothing of it to Yuko?' I asked.

A cloud cast him in shadow and he aged before my eyes. He shook his head. 'Why would I say such a thing to her?'

I glanced out of the window as I watched a kite harry another bird in the white sky. 'But you met, reached a decision?'

'It's none of your business, Amaterasu.'

'It's just, I see her there, in the cathedral, alone. I want to believe in that final moment she had some peace.'

His was the saddest smile I've seen. 'We both wanted that for her. We both did.'

He walked out of the room. I never saw him again. Would it have helped if Sato and I could have mourned her death together? Ours was a shared loss but not shared grief. The only kindness we could afford one another was honesty during that last encounter. There was no need for deceit after the fires of pikadon. Her diary and his letter gave two endings. Which was I to believe? Had she made her way to the cathedral that morning to tell me she was keeping the baby or had Yuko told Sato she had chosen her life with Shige? I'll never know but I cannot contemplate the former. The second ending is the one I choose to believe. Maybe that decision would have been easier in those final moments of her life. I hope that was her choice. I can do no more than that. Hope.

I watched a woman, close to my own age, light a candle and place it next to others melting away to nothing. Candles burn, diaries and letters rot, memories weaken or die. When I am gone, what will be left of my daughter? What will remain to show the world she once existed? I had carried her with me through the years but the toll was a heavy one. I had felt dead inside for a long time. I knew why Sato wrote to Yuko and why he created a new ending for her, alive, with a daughter called Miki. I too sometimes conjured up my own fantasy that she had survived pikadon. She had not waited for me at the cathedral. This had been my hope, Sato's too. Had this been true, Yuko would be sixty-three years old by now. I try to imagine how she might look. I try to conjure up the colour of her hair, the pallor of her skin. I try to sketch a softened waist or protrusion of bone and veins. Even if I use my own face and body as a map, I cannot picture this other Yuko, but I guessed at the life she might have led had she chosen Sato, the joy a daughter would bring, the sacrifices this Miki would be worth.

The doctor's letters and Yuko's journals had forced me to accept that I must let this fantasy creation go. I did not need to think of other endings, only the actual one: my daughter was taken suddenly from me, before I had a chance to tell her that I loved her, before I had a chance to ask her to forgive me, before I had a chance to say goodbye. I wanted to mourn all of the woman in the journals and letters, not just the one trapped in the cathedral when pikadon hit. She had been so much more than the

282

Yuko of that day and that hour. Inside me, she will always be a baby, a young girl, a lover, a wife, a nurse, a mother. I told myself, while I had led her to the cathedral that day, none of us could have known the fate about to be bestowed upon our city and its people. I heard the great bell that had survived the war ring out, I watched the woman's mouth move in silent prayer, I looked up at that bleeding crucified carpenter. Yuko had believed him the son of God. She had come here to pray, seek solace. Maybe finally, if I had to let her go, it needed to be here.

I took hold of the pew in front of me with both hands and lowered myself onto the knee rest, the green leather worn through with the weight of others. I spoke to Yuko's god in the cathedral; I finished the prayer that she could not. I asked that he might set me free. I asked that he might show me how to live again. I asked him to deliver a message. I whispered the words over and over again as outside the neon lights of the city flickered to life. *Peace, Yuko. Peace, Daughter. Peace, my beautiful child. You are the pearl in the shell of my heart. Forgive me. I love you. Goodbye.*

Pilgrimage

*Tera-meguri: Pilgrimages to Buddhist temples made for religious
purposes are called henro or junrei, the most popular of which is
the pilgrimage to the eighty-eight sacred places in Shikoku. These
temples are all associated with Kukai or Kobo-Daishi (774–845),
the founder of the Shingonshu sect of Buddhism. This custom
originating in the medieval times is still maintained today by
devout believers of Kukai. Pilgrims travel from temple to temple,
ringing bells and chanting Buddhistic hymns. The names of
the temples they visit are stamped on their white clothes or on the
notebooks they carry with them. The pilgrimage to the eighty-eight
sacred places is believed to make one happy both in this world
and in the next world.*

I had been back two weeks when Hideo served me some
sukiyaki at dinner and told me he had something special
to show me tomorrow morning. Angela and the children
smiled conspiratorially. Hanako giggled as she picked
up her chopsticks. 'You'll like it. It's a good surprise.' No
teasing or coercion as we shared the beef, tofu and
bamboo shoots would make them reveal the plans. Angela
and Hanako woke me up early. They laid out a crimson
kimono for me, with embroidered white blossom. 'We
thought you might like to wear it,' Angela said. I looked
down at the sashes and cords. 'Don't worry, we'll help.'
They wound the material around my body and led me

to a mirror in the hall. I smiled at the reflection. 'You look very pretty,' Hanako said. Hideo was waiting in the hallway, dressed in a suit and tie. He took me by the arm, led me up the stone steps to a waiting taxi. I recognised none of the streets we passed for a mile or so but I knew we were heading east. Then certain places began to merge with a map of the city I carried in my head: a stone bridge, a row of shops, a confluence of houses on a hill. Their familiarity grew stronger and then we passed a small shrine and all those years of my self-imposed exile fell away. The row of trees we pulled up beside was unmistakable. Hideo paid the driver and jumped out of the car to open my passenger door. I eased my way to a standing position and looked up at the tops of the purple maple and blue beech and peeked through their branches. I clapped my hands together. The house had not changed. How could it still look the same after so many years?

'How did you arrange this?'

'I just came round and asked the owners. The husband is a television producer for Nagasaki Broadcasting Company and will be at work, but his wife is expecting us. She said she had to drop off the children at their grandparents' but she should be back by now.'

We opened the gate and as I stepped down that gravel path the ghosts came out to play. I saw Hideo running back and forth with his kite and next to him Yuko sat on a patch of grass with a sketch pad by her side as a ladybug scuttled over her hand and along her upheld arm. Next came Kenzo digging out weeds and Shige walking up the path to meet us for the first time. I had dreaded returning to my home because of these memories but they did not hurt; they filled me with an extraordinary lightness of spirit that carried me down the path to the god of war straddled over the boar at the door. Hideo knocked and a woman in her late twenties appeared in the doorway. She bowed. 'Mrs Takahashi, what a pleasure. My name is Izumi Fujita. Welcome back.'

I thanked her and we slipped off our shoes and I looked around the hallway. The grandfather clock was gone but the shafts of light bounced off the same corners and hit the same spot by the living area. Their own family shrine stood where ours had, our black furniture replaced with beech wood and rose cotton curtains, the tatami mats refreshed with yellow straw and red silk borders. Despite the differences, the sense of times past flooded the room: the laughter, the tears, those confrontations with Yuko, the matchmaker with her kohl eyebrows, Misaki and I gossiping in the kitchen as we prepared meals. These memories all formed before me in a blizzard of images that left me first joyous, next fearful and finally agonised in a swirling mix of high then low. Izumi excused herself and urged us to look around. I showed Hideo the office where Shige had asked for Yuko's hand in marriage and where we had been sitting when we learned of his death. Upstairs in Yuko's room we found bunk beds surrounded by an assault course of building blocks, stuffed animals and toy cars. I doubted there would be anything left of our existence but I knelt beside the window and ran my hands down the wall to the floor. I smiled at my treasure. Just the faintest image remained beneath the cream paint.

'Hideo, come here.' I touched the outline of a butterfly.

'Yuko drew that when she was a child. She painted them all up the wall. I was so angry with her but then I realised how beautiful they were, a flutter of butterflies flying out the window and away.' Hideo traced the wings with his scarred fingers and grew still for a long moment.

When we had finished exploring, we took tea with Izumi, who was full of questions about the area and the city 'back in my day'. She diplomatically did not mention pikadon and I was grateful for that courtesy. We thanked her profusely as we left and walked back through the garden. I stopped by the chinaberry and turned my face to the hint of sun and its promise of the coming spring. I pointed at the tree. 'Look, do you see those branches? The shape of a dragon's head, there on the right?' He shielded his eyes to look and nodded. 'Yuko would watch those bouncing twigs for hours. She was convinced the dragon was talking to her.' I smiled, awkward with my next disclosure. 'I'm glad you turned up at my doorstep, I am. What a thought that we might never have met.' And then I did something that shocked both of us: I kissed him on the cheek.

He squeezed my shoulder. 'I'm happy you're here too.'

I shook my head in surprised delight. 'It really is good to be home.'

And it was true. I lifted off the shroud I had placed over Nagasaki. This living, breathing, flawed, wonderful city had shaped me in ways that astounded and terrified me, even as my own fire burned down to embers. For so many years I had believed home was the hardest place to be when now I understood, finally, that Nagasaki wasn't just pikadon: it was a ladybug cake made with red candies and chocolate frosting, a sumo wrestler ring made out of children's socks, a child leaning against you while she draws, a young kiss on your old cheek. These were the memories on which to linger.

Hideo looked around the shrubs, yellow in winter. 'It's funny. These past few days, I've been thinking a lot about that question you asked when we first met. I don't know, coming back here, maybe it's triggered a memory, just a faint one. I'm not sure.' He bowed his head and shrugged his shoulders. 'It's probably nothing. I see a snake, bright green, lying coiled on a rock, sunning itself in a garden, much like this one. Why wouldn't I remember that any sooner? You'd remember a snake in a garden, wouldn't you? That's something a child would remember.'

We looked at one another, both seeking confirmation. I stared at this man, a stranger at my door only a few weeks ago. This boy had been raised by a man who had caused me great pain but why let that misery stop me reaching out for this ballast of flesh, bone and blood that stood in front of me? He had risen from the flames and he was extraordinary. He was forgiveness and peace. He was the best of Nagasaki, not how it was but how it is. I imagined the million illuminated pulses of the city: the houses, the restaurants, the bars, the brothels, the pachinko parlours, the hospitals, the temples, the shrines, the churches, the street lights, that anchor us to who we are, what we desire, what we believe, what we love, what our lives will be or will not be. Those roads and buildings hold our past, and our future, loved ones and friends we are yet to meet, apparitions of our dead and those we lose too soon, echoes and whispers and draglines through our personal and joint history. Hideo's life had been changed by another kind of light, so brief but indelible in its power. He had forgiven pikadon, even if it had blinded him to who he might be or would have been. Is the source of us important? He had thought so, and I am glad of the journey he took to find me.

Here was a man to admire, with his heart and his hope and his compassion. No matter the size of the injury, from the aftershocks of loss in this once graveyard city, to the tremors of the lies we tell one another, Hideo had found a way to live alongside all indignities, minor or grave, calculated or thoughtless. He had more than survived, he had thrived. He was our beacon of light. Here, standing under my daughter's talking dragon tree, I allowed myself to believe in this miracle, I allowed myself this gift nurtured by Sato and returned to me by Natsu. Maybe I did not deserve a grandson like him, maybe he deserved a grandmother better than me, but we were the only ones left alive; we were the only ones who could tell the tale of those taken too soon. I held my hand up to the furrows of his cheek and he placed his hand over mine. I smiled and love radiated through my body. I pushed all doubts away. 'Hideo-chan, how clever of you to remember.'

We lowered our foreheads until they touched, just for a moment, the way we had done that last day outside the school. He held me to him in the garden where as a seven-year-old boy he had looked at a praying mantis, or a green snake, it was not important now. His existence was all that mattered to me. I took his hands, rough with scars, and held them in mine, stiff with age, and I said a word that had gone unspoken for so many years, and this word was gentle on my lips and kind on my tongue and true to me.

'Grandson,' I said, smiling.

'Grandmother,' he replied. And even though I could not see it in his face, I knew he was smiling too.

We repeated those words, treasured and for so long lost, and when the tears came so too did the laughter, and in that moment of joy we no longer mourned our dead but celebrated them.

Acknowledgments

This book took a while to arrive. The inspiration began when I worked as a teacher in Japan as a university graduate, the story germinated while completing a writing course at Glasgow University, the first chapters were written in the Middle East and the final ones completed in the North East of England. The only reason I managed to get to 'The End' is thanks to the encouragement from family, friends and colleagues along the way. Please know, every generous word spurred me on.

My huge gratitude for their wise, patient and kind counsel must go to Jocasta Hamilton and the team at Hutchinson, Tara Singh Carlson at Penguin Group USA, and Mark Stanton, my agent at Jenny Brown Associates. I couldn't have asked for better people to help me negotiate the path to publication. I'm also thankful to Jane McCarthy for her compassionate support and guidance through the edits. Thank you to Tim Pedley and Lucy Janes for offering their professional expertise. It is deeply appreciated.

While the story is a work of fiction, the novel's cultural and historical context has been drawn from several sources including the following publications: *Nagasaki: Japan at War: An Oral History*, Haruko Taya Cook & Theodore F. Cook; *The Bells of Nagasaki*, Takashi Nagai; and *Nagasaki Peace Trail: Mutual Understanding for Peace Nagasaki Handbook*.

I owe particular thanks to Bates Hoffer and Nobuyuki Honna, editors of *An English Dictionary of Japanese Culture* (1986), for kindly allowing me to use excerpts from the book.

The book is in part about parenthood, both its joy and pain. I am lucky to have had parents who have taught me about fortitude, love and courage. Thank you to Roberta and William Copleton, and to my brother, Chris, for inspiring me every day. I'd also like to pay tribute to two men I never had a chance to meet, my grandfathers who fought in the Second World War. This book is dedicated to them.

Some unfinished version of this novel would have blinked at me from my computer screen for many years more, I suspect, if it hadn't been for my husband. As he said, 'There's no point writing a book if you don't show it to someone.' Indeed. Neil, I am so happy you were my first reader.

And finally, *A Dictionary of Mutual Understanding* is my profound thanks to the people of Nagasaki, for the kindness and generosity they showed me, for their compassion and dignity in the face of unimaginable tragedy, and for the message of peace they continue to send out to the world. Never again.